ALLSKIN

AND OTHER TALES

BY CONTEMPORARY CZECH WOMEN

Edited by Alexandra Büchler

WOMEN IN TRANSLATION

• SEATTLE •

Publication of this book was made possible in part with financial support from the National Endowment for the Arts. Additional support was provided by Joan Drury and the Ministry of Culture of the Czech Republic.

Cover painting: "Dazzled by Sound" by Klára Bočkayová
Cover and text design by Patrick David Barber

Library of Congress Cataloging-in-Publication Data
Allskin and other tales by contemporary Czech women / edited by Alexandra Büchler.
    p.   cm.
    ISBN 1-879679-11-6 (alk. paper)
    1. Short stories, Czech—Translations into English. 2. Short stories, Czech—Women authors. 3. Czech fiction—20th century—Translations into English.
I. Büchler, Alexandra.
PG5145.E8A44   1998
891.8'6301089287—dc21   97-48891
                                        CIP

First edition, May, 1998
Printed in the United States

Women in Translation
523 North 84th Street
Seattle WA 98103

Acknowledgements

I would like to thank all those who have in some way contributed to the making of this book. Above all, my mother, who first introduced me to the world of storytelling, my friends Esther Kinsky, Sue Brind, Zoë Wicomb, Helen Simpson and Hedvika Fraser for reading some of the stories and offering helpful comments, Mickey Aronoff for her enthusiastic support, Barbara Wilson, Katherine Hanson, and everyone at Women in Translation for bringing the work of international women writers to new readers, and, of course, the authors and translators.

CONTENTS

INTRODUCTION

ALLSKIN AND OTHER TALES is the first anthology of fiction by Czech women to appear in English. Readers familiar with Czech literature in translation will recognize the characteristic features: its inclination toward the fantastic, the absurd, the grotesque and the surreal, its penchant for political allegory and satire, its sense of irony and black humor, its lopsided view of reality. It is a paradox that much of modern Czech fiction owes its richness and stylistic innovation to the fact that from its beginnings it developed under the watchful gaze of generations of censors serving repressive regimes that knew the power of the word in a culture where writers held a privileged position as social and political commentators.

The stories in this anthology claim the same legacy, but the women who tell them often work from different premises, employ different strategies and develop different aspects of the shared literary tradition. They tend to draw on a much broader tradition of storytelling that encompasses myth, legend and fairy tale and on folk culture with its belief in magic and the supernatural. This tradition starts with nation-making legends, recorded in the twelfth century by the chronicler Kosmas and later retold by Alois Jirásek, a nineteenth-century historical novelist. And it is here, at the dawn of Czech mythology, that we encounter some formidable female figures. First and paramount is the legend of Princess Libuše, the "mother of the nation" and founder of the first dynasty of Czech kings, the Přemyslids. There is the legend of the Maidens' War in which Libuše's principal lady-in-waiting, the fearless Vlasta, leads an Amazon-like female army agains men, when the women find their social status diminished after the Princess's death. There is the gruesome legend of the wars between the Czechs and the neighboring Lučan tribe with the heroine a nameless young woman. Abducted during a Lučan foray into Czech territory and forcibly married, she takes revenge by donning men's clothing and attacking her husband in battle on the side of her people.

In these legends, which seem to mark the transition to Christian patriarchy, men ultimately have the upper hand. Libuše, despite being described as a wise and just ruler, is forced to marry and hand over power to her husband. Vlasta and her maiden warriors are defeated and their castle razed to the ground. The young woman who meets her enemy-husband on the battlefield dies by his hand.

For centuries, chastisement and subjugation of women who transgressed against the social code with its strictly defined gender roles has been the subject of folk tales, songs and ballads. As in other primarily Christian cultures, Czech folklore is dominated by cautionary tales about women punished for the sins of sloth, greed and vanity and for the vices of defiance, pride and curiosity—which are miraculously transformed into virtues when attributed to men—as well as by stories of female rivalry. These tales, which endorsed the dogma of women's inherent wickedness and legitimized their submission to men, were largely taken at their face value by the patriotic collectors of folk material, and it was only when examined in the context of twentieth-century consciousness that their script could be radically rewritten and their heroines were allowed to seek power and knowledge.

Czech writers' interest in folk culture dates back to the nineteenth century when the National Revival movement grew out of Romantic preoccupations with history and nationhood. A small but strategically important country in the heart of Europe, Bohemia was a powerful kingdom until the Hapsburgs established rule over its territory in the early seventeenth century that was to last three hundred years. The movement, looking to folk culture for inspiration and uncorrupted national values as much as to erstwhile achievements of high culture, aimed to restore a sense of national identity and return Czech to its earlier use as a language of letters, philosophy and science.

This was also the period when women first entered literature in a significant way as authors. The two most influential nineteenth century women writers whose work achieved the status of classics were Božena Němcová and Karolína Světlá. Both were also passionately interested in folklore. Němcová, a major figure of late Romanticism, best known for her novel celebrating village life and the wisdom of a simple peasant woman, the eponymous *Granny* (*Babička*, 1855, published in English in 1962), collected and retold a number of Czech fairy tales which are still enjoyed today. Světlá, whose work is considered crucial to the development of the modern Czech novel, had extensive knowledge of folk customs and beliefs, which she used to great dramatic effect in her fiction. She was also active in the early women's emancipation movement and created strong, independent female protagonists who nevertheless had to suppress their emotions and desires in favour of moral duty and social conventions. Although Světlá is known mainly for her portrayal of life in provincial Bohemia, her work also marks a general shift of focus from rural environment to the city.

Around the turn of the century, a whole generation of Czech women writers began addressing issues of women's position in society, their emotional life and professional ambitions. They were Teréza Nováková, Růžena Svobodová, Anna Maria Tilschová, Božena Benešová with her novellas of "sentimental education," and Helena Malířová, whose 1908 novel, *Právo na Štěstí*, *The Right to Happiness*, sums up the theme of women's revolt against convention and their quest for emotional fulfilment and social equality.

The fact that, unlike today in the Czech Republic, women's writing of the time was perceived as a distinct entity is evident, for example, from the work of F. X. Šalda, a leading literary and cultural critic, who wrote about a number of women novelists such as

Němcová. In his essay on woman in poetry and literature published in 1908, Šalda warns against the conventional "literature of the girls' boarding school" which "considers all problems of aesthetics, psychology and art through the spectacles of a mature governess," as well as against the "one-sided tendentiousness" of "propagandistic feminist (sic) novel." According to him, a woman writer's primary aim should be to "learn to speak in the mother tongue of her own psyche" and through it "to suggest her desires, paint her dreams, criticize social institutions, voice her demands on men, love and marriage," and, above all, "transform and form man" just as man has over the centuries formed his image of woman. The young Communist journalist Julius Fučík praised Němcová in an enthusiastic essay published just before World War II, in which he discussed her disadvantaged position as a woman writer and insisted on the recognition of the individuality and progressive nature of her work, contrasting it with the oeuvre of another heroine of the National Revival and a paragon of petit bourgeois virtue, Magdalena Dobromila Rettigová, whose main contribution to the movement was her popular Czech cookbook.

In the twenties, during the short period of national independence, debates about women's emancipation were conducted within left-wing circles under the influence of the Russian Revolution. Radical proposals for collective living with communal services were put forward as a way towards liberating women from the burden of house work and childcare. Czech cultural life of the time was at the forefront of European socialist avant-garde. Indeed, nowhere else, with the exception of Russia, was literary activity and avant-garde art so closely related to left-wing politics. Some of the most prominent avant-garde artists, writers and architects who represented a wide spectrum of approaches from proletarian literature to surrealism, futurism and constructivism, had links with progressive cultural circles in Soviet Russia and became founding members of the Czechoslovak Communist Party in 1921. Even though this association lasted until 1929 when a group of seven writers, including two women, left the party in protest against its growing subordination to Moscow's dictate, the ideology behind avant-garde literature continued to be dominated by socialist ideals, including those concerning the position of women in society. This did not mean, however, that women's cultural contribution was always recognized on its own terms. For surrealists and proponents of the Czech "Poetist" movement, woman was primarily a muse or object of desire, a beautiful, decorative feature of the "festive boulevard" celebrated by this new art.

It was in proletarian prose, as it developed into social realism, that women authors played a central role. The leading writers who portrayed class struggle in their work and whose epic novels reflected the historical and social changes in prewar Czechoslovakia were Marie Majerová with her coal mining family saga *Siréna* (*The Siren*, 1935) and novella *Havířská balada* (*The Ballad of a Miner*, 1937, both translated into English in the sixties) and Marie Pujmannová with a trilogy describing the fortunes of two Prague families through the thirties and up to the end of the war. Although Majerová was one of the two Party defectors of 1929 and Pujmannová's family background did not recommend her as a reliable "cadre," they were both adopted by the post-1948 Communist regime and served it enthusiastically to the detriment of the artistic integrity of their later work. By this time, the link between avant-garde art and left-wing politics had broken down. Art, literature and culture in general were seen primarily as ideological tools, and realism was accepted as the only permissible style, capable of fulfilling the role of art as formulated by Marxist-Leninist theory. Following the example of Stalinist Russia, Czech political leaders became hostile to experimentation and ambiguity, in short to anything that deviated from the narrow definitions and ideological certainties imposed by the new order. As a result, a whole generation of artists and writers were driven underground, into the gray zone of "unofficial" culture which maintained continuity with the prewar, mainly surrealist, international avant-garde. The sixties' generation emerged from the shadow of "official literature" during the cultural renaissance of that decade, creating a vibrant environment, where experimentation was once more welcome and literature was passionately debated. This burst of energy, which pervaded the whole sphere of public and political life primed by the liberation process which culminated in the Prague Spring of 1968, was brought to an end by renewed censorship following the Warsaw Pact military intervention in August of the same year.

The seventies became in the political jargon of the time a decade of "normalization and consolidation," a good example of the the way in which language was grotesquely distorted and abused in the name of ideology. History repeated itself with a new wave of purges, particularly severe in the area of culture, education and the media, where those committed to the ideal of "socialism with a human face" were replaced with opportunists free of any ideals whatsoever. A whole group of intellectuals, artists and writers, who had spearheaded the developments of the previous decade, were, yet again, forced underground and into exile, where they performed the role of an absent political opposition.

Interestingly, while the issue of human rights was high on the agenda of those who opposed the post-1968 regime, the question of women's rights was, and still is, practically ignored. It is ironic that the "women's question" was raised far more vigorously almost a hundred years ago, and that in the literary sphere, contemporary critics show little understanding of the specificity of women's writing. This is symptomatic of a wider approach to women's issues in the Czech Republic and other countries of the former Eastern Bloc. In the virtual absence of any debate informed by feminist thinking as it has developed in the Western world in the past three decades, women themselves often concur with the view that cultural and social values are universal, and there is no need for differential analysis. This rejection of feminist theories, which are still misunderstood and misrepresented as a homogeneous, militant, separatist ideology, is in part a legacy of the years when denial of basic human rights united both sexes against a common enemy and expressions of male dominance were easily confused with individual abuses of political power. Socialism, on the other hand, promoted a false equality of sexes, and women were required to carry the double burden of full responsibility for childcare and the running of the household, while also being expected to engage in the building of state economy. To these women, Western feminism appeared to be addressing issues irrelevant to their own lives. Despite the egalitarian ideology of the "socialist" state, attitudes remained considerably sexist and discriminatory, with little recourse to legal remedies. Another reason why the general attitude to feminist ideas has been so overwhelmingly negative is the widespread distrust of any political ideology that is perceived as polarizing. The failure to see that the very rejection of feminism is a product of another, far more pervasive and deep rooted ideology of patriarchal domination, is an issue which is rarely, if ever, debated in a public forum.

As a result, serious systematic study of women's writing as a separate category is a rare exception, and even the expression "women's literature" is a pejorative term applied to romantic novels. An influential publication such as the loftily entitled *Český Parnas: vrcholy literatury 1970-1990* (*The Czech Parnassus: Literary Highlights 1970-1990*), compiled by a collective of academics and published by Galaxie in 1993, features only five women among sixty writers. A similar critical analysis of thirty-nine literary works crucial to the post war development of Czech literature, *Česká literatura 1945-1970*, SNP, 1992, includes only one woman, Věra Linhartová.

Linhartová was one of the women writers who entered the Czech literary scene in the sixties. After 1968, some of them continued writing, although unable to publish, others turned to translation or to innocuous entertainment genres, or withdrew from literary activities altogether. Many went into exile, contributing to that peculiar state of "fragmented cohesion" of contemporary Czech culture. Linhartová, who left Czechoslovakia in 1961 and started writing in French soon after settling in France, is still considered the doyenne of Czech experimental writing and one of the most important writers of the postwar period. Rejecting the notion of narrative causality and objectivity, she makes the very process of writing and the workings of poetic language the focus of her fiction. In her uncompromising dedication to the task of writing as a way of posing essential ontological questions, she is often likened to that great spirit of literary Prague, Franz Kafka. At the same time, her work anticipates postmodernist postulates: "It is true that I use language as my tool, but it is not quite certain whether I speak it, or whether it dictates my speech," she writes in 1961. The short text "A Barbarian Woman in Captivity," with its post-script which places it within the convention of a "found manuscript" by an anonymous, lost—perhaps dead?—author, echoes similar concerns. The female narrator is the perfect postmodern "other," a barbarian to the civilized man she addresses, a passionate spirit to his reticent and almost immaterial persona.

The legacy of literary experimentation and a strong sense of intertextuality are also evident in the work of Daniela Hodrová and Sylvie Richter. Hodrová only started publishing after 1989, and her prose is informed by her theoretical research into the form of the novel and concerned with the processes of defining personal identity as a nexus between events in the life of the narrator, who is sometimes openly identified with the author, and the entire Western cultural heritage mediated through works of art and literature. In the multitude of meanings derived from this search, the self is the ultimate constant and certainty, the measure of all things, "the alpha and omega" of existence.

Richter, who emigrated to Italy in 1972, but continues to write fiction in Czech, is also primarily interested in writing as a product of individual consciousness and intertextual relationships. Like Linhartová, whose work she has written about and translated into Italian, she creates a fluid narrative persona, switching from first to third person in mid-sentence, in what Linhartová describes as "the perpetual to-and-fro between the self and the other . . . toward whom we grope our way, moving in a double spiral around a single axis." Yet, her texts are more personal than Linhartová's—although not necessarily autobiographic—and far more identifiable as the work of a woman. In "Fragments and Likenesses," for example, we glimpse the story of the breakup of a relationship through a set of narrative fragments which in themselves mark the narrator's attempts to piece together her own independent identity.

Richter's publishing history is also characteristic of the difficulties inherent in any attempt to form a historic perspective on contemporary Czech writing. "I only started publishing when it was no longer possible," she says ironically. And indeed, while some of her work dates back to the early seventies, it had to wait for its semi-official publication by one of the exile presses until the mid-eighties with a mainstream reprinting in the early nineties, that is, almost twenty years later. While in the seventies and eighties "samizdat" and exile publishing helped maintain a somewhat fragile continuity, Czech writers often worked in a vacuum, cut-off from a wider readership and without the feedback of a public critical debate.

What happened during that time within the officially designated public space is still awaiting proper assessment. One of the divisions cutting across the literary scene was certainly that between writers who were allowed to publish and those who were banned or refused to collude with the regime. In the mid-eighties, a new liberation process began, this time following the lead of Gorbachev's glasnost. The publication of books like Alexandra Berková's *Knížka s červeným obalem* (*The Book With a Red Cover*) in 1986 was a sign that the official sphere was once again beginning to open up to literary experimentation. Berková's losely connected narratives, which trace the life of a woman from conception to death, form an absurdist mosaic of fairy-tale elements combined with contemporary themes and devices, a technique she takes even further in her following books, *Magorie* (*Loonyland*, 1991), a satirical fairy tale about the state of the country, and *Utrpení oddaného všiváka* (*The Sufferings of the Devoted Lousehead*, 1993), the humorous ramblings of a fallen angel.

When Zuzana Brabcová's *Daleko od stromu* (*Far from the Tree*) was published by the exile imprint Index in the same year as Berková's first book, it was immediately greeted as a generational novel conveying the sense of moral disorientation of young people who grew up in the repressive atmosphere of the seventies, amidst a general disintegration of values. The title of the novel refers to the Czech saying that "an apple never falls far from the tree" (a version of the English "chip off the old block") and points in that sense to the theme of a "generation gap," at the same time acknowledging the symbolic meaning of tree as life itself. Brabcová's generation could not identify with the conformism of the seventies, nor with the ideals of the sixties: "A wretched generation. Autistic. Alcoholic. Riddled with debt. Moodily, unambitiously Eastern. Matter-of-factly, acceleratedly Western. Anchorless, oceanless . . ." For the young narrator, teenage traumas are compounded by this larger, deeper sense of despair, eventually leading to an attempted suicide and subsequent treatment in a psychiatric hospital.

The theme of mental instability, of madness lurking in the folds of everyday life, is startlingly common in the writing of Czech women. Eda Kriesová's work is often set in a psychiatric hospital, as a central metaphor for the absurdity of the outside world. For Jana Červenková's protagonist Irena, the psychiatric clinic is a refuge from a life of emotional and social dysfunction, from a meaningless job, sterile marriage and desperate affairs.

Zdena Salivarová, another writer in exile, also made her debut in the sixties with a collection of three novellas *Pánská jízda* (*Gentlemen's Party*, 1968), which immediately positioned her as a writer concerned with women's emotional world. Sometimes transparent in its intentions, her work is nevertheless an important landmark on the map of Czech fiction, not only because it presents a chilling image of life in the fifties and early sixties, but also because it reacts to representations of women in the work of male writers, notably Milan Kundera, challenging his view of the relationship between the sexes as a game. In her first book, she established a female character prototype to which she would return again and again: a young woman whose desire for genuine human contact and communication is abused and who may lose her illusions as a consequence, but not her faith in the ultimate power of love and emotional honesty.

In 1969 Salivarová and her husband, the novelist Josef Škvorecký, joined the exodus that followed the Warsaw Pact intervention and settled in Toronto, where they established one of the most prominent Czech exile presses, 68 Publishers. Here, she wrote her two novels in which she returned to the theme of a powerless individual in conflict with authority. After a silence of almost twenty years, Salivarová published a largely autobiographical epistolary novel *Hnůj země* (*Manure of the Earth*, 1994), in which she gives a fictionalized account of her life in exile and chronicles the two decades of her publishing activities against the wider background of the Czech immigrant community in Canada.

Salivarová's book came out only two years before another, quite different expatriate novel, Iva Pekárková's *Dej mi ty prachy* (*Gimme the Money*, 1996) appeared in Prague. While Salivarová sees emigration as a prison whose locked gates prevent return home, for Pekárková it opens the doors to freedom, to the magnificent world of endless possibilities. Her heroine, the streetwise cab driver Gin belongs to another generation, and her sexual openness makes her a unique phenomenon in contemporary Czech literature written by women.

Lenka Procházková is another author who writes in opposition to male representations of relationships between the two sexes. Her heroines are in search of a relationship where they could be equal to men in all respects, but their quest mostly ends in disillusion. The story "The Good New Times" is linked to her novel *Smolná kniha* (*The Black Book*, 1989) which is a fictionalized account of her real life relationship with the writer Ludvík Vaculík, who in turn told his version of events in his novel *Jak se dělá chlapec* (*How to Make a Boy*, 1993). While Vaculík, as the tittle suggests, concentrates on the birth of their son, reflecting not only on the nature of modern male-female relationship but also on late fatherhood and on the most important of personal and civic duties, the education of a young child, the focus of Procházková's novel is the bitter experience of an earlier abortion exacerbated by constant police harassment of the couple. Their story unfolds against the background of the bleak reality of eighties' Czechoslovakia, and the bizarre scenes described in Procházková's short story are all symptomatic of that exhausted decade that finally ended with the the collapse of the Communist doctrine.

Tereza Boučková also makes motherhood, biological and adoptive, the focus of her story where the narrator's painful desire to have a child and her unsuccessful attempts to conceive in the post-Chernobyl era mirror the drilling of a well in search for water outside her house. Boučková's prose is sparse and elliptical and in her other novellas this stylistic simplicity combined with fairy-tale tropes— "Once upon a time, there was . . ."—achieves the ironic effect of a fairy tale without a happy end.

Eva Hauser's "Between Us Girls" is a fantasy tale giving the notions of sex, pregancy and motherhood a new sinister meaning. A scientist by training, Hauser uses the genre of science fiction and fantasy to comment on contemporary social mores from a consciously feminist point of view. Her fantasy stories are usually set in pagan times and effectively use devices such as reversal of roles to expose the absurdity of male-female stereotypes. In her science fiction novella *Cvokyně* (*The Madwoman*, 1992) the protagonist, a research scientist, is sucked into a time warp during an experiment and whisked ten years back in her own life. With the benefit of hindsight, she is given the opportunity to reassess her choices in relation to marriage and motherhood. Despite the guise of science fiction, the novella is rooted in the reality of eighties' Prague, satirizing the uncritical acceptance of everything from the ideology of socialist consumerism to gender roles: while the protagonist and her husband have equal status as research fellows, in her "first life," she is the one burdened with house work and child care in addition to her job.

Another writer who feels at home in the world of science fiction and fantasy is Alžběta Šerberová, who originally trained as electrical engineer. Her fiction mostly explores male-female relationships from the point of view of disillusioned women whose seeming independence is really detachment which protects them from emotional hurt. In her fantasy stories, however, she casts an ironic eye at the myth of the male genius: in "$E=mc^2$," female presence wreaks havoc with the budding scientist's concentration; in her longer story "Useless," Šerberová rewrites the script for a number of classic literary heroines, allowing them to escape from plots designed by their male creators.

Elements of fantasy and science fiction have been conspicuously dominant in modern Czech literature, and they have been used in a variety of ways. Narrative fantasy has developed along two lines that ocassionally overlap and intertwine: the mythopoetic fantasy of the folk tale and legend which makes formulaic use of archetypes, and literary fantasy based on the the opposite principle, the free working of individual imagination. The first gives expression to a shared view of the world as a place essentially governed by supernatural powers, aiming to explain it and at the same time to preserve the social status quo. Conversely, literary fantasy goes hand in hand with innovation, and in twentieth century Czech literature it has been associated with a rejection of realistic narrative modes. This tendency was strengthened in opposition to socialist realism adopted by the Communist regime as the only permissible form. The brooding, introverted leanings of the Czech psyche with its black sense of humor were brought to the fore in reaction to the imposed ideology of collectivism and joyful optimism. When the anti-hero of Kundera's *The Joke* writes his ill-judged message "Optimism is the opium of the masses," he is expressing a skepticism central to the distrust of any ideology.

While we find the same skepticism in the work of contemporary women writers, the same absurd humor and inclination towards non-causal, collage-like narrative, their use of the fantastic is different: they are more likely to work with fairy-tale motifs and make references to the legendary pagan past, to superstitions, the occult and witchcraft, in other words, to that part of the cultural heritage traditionally associated with women. Some, like Eda Kriseová, openly validate the irrational, intuitive view of the world against the masculine, scientific quest for explanations, including the male-dominated "science" of psychology that tries to explain away that most inexplicable entity of all, the human soul. Others, like Daniela Fisherová, use fairy-tale figures. In her "Allskin," she tells a modern story of adolescent rebellion, but also explores the archetypal conflict between the individual and society and the complex issue of prescriptive characterizations of women: sanity versus hysteria and madness, order versus chaos, tidiness versus sloth. When Pekárková's heroine Gin touches her African husband's secret amulet—his "male magic"—she makes a transgressive gesture which leads to a total reversal of roles. The title of Procházková's novel *The Black Book*, which is closely related to the story included in this collection, refers to the name given to medieval records of interrogations of witches. Jana Červenková's Cinderella of the science lab, who dreams of running away with the walking trees from her garden, in the end stops looking for her Prince Charming and is transformed in a landscape ruled by the noonday witch. In "Joseph Stalin," Zdena Tomin turns the death of the greatest figure of Communist mythology into a private moment that marks the passing of her narrator's childhood.

What distinguishes the work of many Czech women writers is the effectiveness and originality with which they explore contemporary themes by rewriting archetypal stories of female disobedience and rebellion and experiment with fantasy and fairy-tale motifs in prose which is intensely personal while resonating with the political concerns of a particular time and place. Thus, even in the absence of an overtly feminist debate, Czech women writers have found their own ways of formulating and conveying a view of the world they inhabit by incorporating elements of folk-tale, legend, myth and magic into a highly literary tradition, using what is sometimes seen as a purely feminine ability to reconcile and integrate opposites.

Alexandra Büchler

Allskin Dances on Tables

Daniela Fischerová

T HE RESTLESS SPIRIT of storytelling keeps forever looking back
over the shoulder to see what it can devour, along which snail-
track, still a little moist, we have arrived where we are now. When
I was sixteen, life briefly brought me close to a woman who could
have been my mother-in-law today, had the snail-track taken a different route. I had just run away from home following a great emotional storm and had reached the limits of my own willingness to
survive it: I still remember that almost amused sense of vertigo. A
fellow student offered me temporary asylum. Our relationship was
unimportant. It was one of those vague, brief bonds, which leave
nothing but a shallow imprint, while that which is essential (the segment of memory forever buffeted by tidal waves) is right next to it;
in this case, it was what happened one spring morning when I was
weeding tulip beds with his mother. But more of that later.

I hesitate to mention the causes of the storm so as not to detract
from the focus of the story. Briefly: at home we had just had what is
in the world of espionage called a *dam-burst*, that is, a sudden leak
of information from a highly confidential area. What came out was
that my father had been leading a double life, complete with two different apartments and two different women. He broke down,
sobbed in an undignified manner, saying that he "could not do oth-

erwise; it was stronger than him." My shocked soul had two choices. It could either see him as responsible for his actions and begin to hate him—or believe that he really couldn't do otherwise, that life is always stronger than a human being and all our plans are battles lost in advance. I decided to accept the second version, threw the keys into the letterbox and ran away from home. But the spirit of storytelling is hardly interested in that. What is there to tell of, then? To start with, let us say it is the word "taste."

The mother of my fellow student suggested that I call her by her first name, Milada, but I didn't address her at all, and will always remember her as Mrs. P. She was over fifty and managed a large savings bank. Hers was a position of great responsibility. I once asked her what she did, and she said, "I'm working out the savings plan for the next half-year." I couldn't understand: was it possible to plan an activity as absurdly incidental and arbitrary as banking transactions carried out by thousands of unknown people? She smiled and said that it was possible.

Mr. P. was an absentee husband; the couple had separated a long time ago and Mr. P. had fled who knows where.

The son had been destined to study archaeology, which was exactly what happened, and, as far as I know, today he is an archaeologist. That was also a plan worked out by his mother. It had nothing to do with a romantic interest in the past, but with an interest in the future, based on the annual reports of Charles University. Her plan took into consideration a certain exclusivity (the course accepted students only once in five years), a surprisingly small number of candidates and the great social prestige of the discipline. When the boy was five, instead of going to the zoo, his mother started taking him to archaeological digs around Prague. He would stagger behind the researchers with a little trowel in his hand and an elegant mother in tow. He soon became a sort of team mascot: a charmingly precocious lad who was allowed to watch closely and document the daily findings with his little bakelite camera.

Five years later it didn't escape his mother's attention that there were neglected, empty display cases in the hall of his school (where she chaired the Parents' Association). Through her son she created quite a decent exhibition on the history of Prague, with contributions from the Historical Institute, where she and the boy already knew many scholars by their first names. The mother brought the exhibition to the attention of a television production team. The ensuing program showed two representatives speaking on behalf of the school: the Headmaster and the boy. Is the principle becoming clear? Is there anything I could add to emphasize sufficiently the theme for which the spirit of storytelling has been getting ready all this time and which is already showing through the ballast of facts? And so, to the word "taste" I shall add the word "plan."

At the time I am talking about, the mother concluded that archaeology was synonymous with Egypt (we are standing on the threshold of the sixties and Mrs. P. is a well-informed woman), and that candidates with a knowledge of Arabic were going to be at an advantage. Through her contacts she found an Arab dandy, a pudgy young man from the embassy, to converse with her son for a fee. The room she had allocated to me (called the "small salon") was every other day transformed into a gate of tongues. I refused to learn Arabic, although it had been offered to me, and spent my time hanging around pubs, indulging in feeling of futility.

And it was the volatile scent of futility that temporarily attracted the classroom swot. I exuded the sex-appeal of heresy, and it needs to be said that that was the only kind of sex-appeal I could ever claim to possess. I was a thin, sadly neglected girl. I was Allskin. (We shall get to Allskin in due course!) I was one of those girls who are told, "You could be quite pretty, if you only wanted to be." Allskin didn't want to.

At that time I lived by power of defeatism. I believed that I no longer wanted anything from the world. I was dogged by a murky clearsightedness which suspected a potential *dam-burst* in everything. Our efforts are aimless and our souls have no home. Something far stronger than our will always lurks behind our backs until one day all our plans turn bankrupt. And it is in vain that we try to resist it: deeper than that lies only the abyss of nothingness.

(A picture in the margin: from his childhood, the young man had on his wall an inscription which had been stencilled on a sheet of paper by his mother. It said: *Where there's a will, there's a way!* As an adolescent, in a moment of inspired revolt, he added the drawing of a little figure and the words *"But watch out which way you're pissing against the wind!"* Both contributions to the philosophy of the will had remained there.)

I and the little man pissing against the wind were the exemplary young man's only slip-ups. Our chances were equal: that is, zero.

Mrs. P. had a hobby which consumed a large amount of her time: Dutch tulips. Next to her house she had a garden and, thanks to certain connections abroad, she had a constant supply of prime-quality bulbs. They arrived by express mail in neat plywood boxes and they really were from Holland.

The flower bed was enormous and the planting design was a matter of thoughtful planning. Every year Mrs. P. drew new designs resembling aerial maps. The plants flowered according to plan, creating complex patterns that took into consideration the harmony of colors and the overall impression, whether viewed from the windows of the house or from the street. The results were faultless and she was rightfully proud of them. The hobby expressed her perfectly: it was exclusive, but not provocatively so, laborious and demanding (the tulips required a lot of work), and, above all, tasteful. But now, the time has come to clarify two words: "Allskin" and "taste."

Every day Mrs. P. passes through the "small salon" because that's the only way out of the house, all in beige, calm, on practical low heels. I am lying in bed in a torn T-shirt, dirty socks sticking out from underneath my pillow. I pretend to be asleep and she quietly walks out. That one minute takes away all my will to get up. The sixties are only beginning and the word "taste" has a very special ring to it.

It can be heard everywhere: it is the strict protector of my childhood. One can dress tastefully or tastelessly. People dine and entertain themselves and furnish their apartments tastefully. Even art is primarily a matter of taste. Van Gogh is no longer a lunatic, he is tasteful; his work hangs in offices and dentists' waiting rooms, having been endorsed by the cheery spirit of the time as a suitable accessory. It is a time when my country, having renounced religion, subscribes to a rather hazy moral code. Taste is not simply a personal matter. Taste is a general view of the world, a dogma, and certain prohibited color combinations (for instance, "green and blue, no good for you") carry almost sinful overtones. Taste is as fixed as state borders, as binding as grammar. There is taste and there is tastelessness: mixed cases are rare and decisions are made quickly as to whether a controversial element (at that time, for example, the Beatles) falls into the one or the other category. There are people one can rely on in this respect; and Mrs P. is among the chosen ones.

I find her fascinating and intolerable. I escape from her any way I can. I wander aimlessly through empty Sundays, while she vacuums the crumbs under my bed. Several times we clash in a barren debate, then we keep out of each other's way. When she is not there, I sometimes walk slowly through the apartment with a feeling of envious indignation; everything in it harmonizes like the music of the spheres. I myself have no taste: I am unable to hear those mysterious voices of things calling to one another. What is worse, I deny them. Proclaiming nothingness and chaos, I make stupid comments, bite my nails even at the table and loudly declare that taste is created by the terror of arrogant mediocrity. And beauty? No, I don't believe in beauty either.

And now about the word "Allskin." A long time ago my school organized a children's fashion parade to educate us towards taste. To amuse and enlighten (even humor could be tasteful in a certain tamed form) there was also an example to be avoided. I was chosen for this heretic role; I see myself through the murky layers of time teetering on stilettos on top of tables pushed together to serve as a catwalk. I am wearing blue jeans and a blouse with lace frills down the front. I represent lunacy incarnate; such waywardness is impossible and can only be meant as a cautionary hyperbole. In a few years this combination will become commonplace, but today my classmates happily howl with laughter. There is music. Drunk with success, I hop on the tables to the rhythm of cha-cha-cha like a marten, deliberately pulling a stupid, brazen face to emphasize the danger of my delusion. I am still part of the brotherhood of men. I clearly understand good and evil, the dogma is unambiguous and simple. What an easy magic! I am eleven!

A memory: I am six and the fairy tale about Allskin is being read on the radio. In a bout of strange restlessness I rhythmically bang my ruler on the table, while I stubbornly listen to the voice I am in vain trying to drown out. She had a softer name then: Donkey-Skin. I knew her also under other names: Catskin, Mouse-Coat, Raggle-taggle—but I always think of her as Allskin. Why? It is the ugliest of her names.

In all those stories a young girl, a princess, is frightened by impending courtship and runs away from home. (Sometimes the theme has the added edge of incest; she is courted by her own father.) In a foreign country she covers her beauty with the skin of an animal, smudges ashes over her face and smears her golden hair with tar. She then poses as a dumb kitchen hand by the name of Allskin.

The time of my visit at Mrs. P.'s marks the passing of my worst Allskin phase. To this day I instinctively avert my eyes from my own image at that time: my grief is irritating and dirty. I wear shabby, unpoetic clothes which hang loose on me, without the provocative charm of the hippies who were to enter the world stage a little later. I am not a flower child, I am a slovenly adolescent. I am the image of powerlessness that moves no one, of resignation common sense prefers to avoid, of futility that is truly futile. I have no dirt under my nails only because they are bitten down to the quick.

It must be said that Mrs. P. received me rather kindly. I was a "girl who would grow out of it." She called my parents and told them that I would stay at her place, in all decency, of course, and she didn't accept my meager savings. She made a half-hearted effort at educating me, but she met with such stubborn resistance that she was relieved to be able to give way to her indifference, probably the most genuine feeling she ever had for me. I lived there for nearly three weeks, occasionally indulging in passionless petting sessions with her son, but I think that if somebody asked him today what he did during that memorable spring, he would say: "I was learning Arabic."

A sunny hot morning, late April. The young man is having his lesson and the two of us are together in the garden. I myself lack the stamina required for wandering around town in that bright light. Kneeling on the grass, we are weeding the tulip beds. Concentric rings of warm colors flutter towards the sky. For once, there is no tension between us.

We chat freely, the way women do when they are working in the garden, and Mrs. P. becomes talkative. She tells me about a certain colleague of hers, an elderly lady who has started behaving "strangely." She suddenly does things she has never done before, things no one does. She keeps checking the accounts, not just her own but others' as well, and by doing that she oversteps the limits of her responsibility, slows down work and offends everyone besides. She does that even on her own time; every day she stays behind at work, until dark, into the night, until midnight, and now twenty-four hours a day are not enough to accommodate all those nonsensical tasks. She is terrified that somewhere she may have made a mistake. She takes a taxi to go to the bank from the other end of Prague to re-check accounts she has just sent in. She neglects herself: she no longer has time to change her clothes. Her colleagues complain about her smell. One morning the janitor found her sobbing over a pile of paper covered in scribbles; she was unable to arrive at the correct result all night.

"If she doesn't stop, I'll have to discipline her," says Mrs. P., deftly snipping off some kind of weed. "I don't like to do it, but she makes bad blood at work."

"Discipline? Why? Is it her fault? It must be stronger than her!" I hear myself snap, louder than I had intended. I am surprised to feel my throat constrict: somewhere in that story yawns an abyss. I sense it and the little rake I am holding quivers in my hand. Mrs. P. lifts her eyes and gives me a surprised look, but then she pats the soil with a firm hand.

"Do you think so?" she says calmly. "You see, my girl, I believe she's doing it on purpose. With a little bit of good will she wouldn't behave so foolishly. Every sensible person can see that she is behaving foolishly."

For a while, I remain motionless, only the rake is trembling. I can hardly believe my ears; I'll keep hearing those words for the next thirty years, they will continue to float through the warm morning, sounding so calm in the spring air.

The woman in front of me has seen half a century pass in front of her. She has brought up a son, she is in a position of responsibility. She has an evident ability to live and to survive, she belongs among those who determine taste for the whole world. To her, madness is a silly tantrum, a brazen act of pissing against the wind. With a little bit of good will one can give it up.

I sink my fingers into the soil and close my eyes. My tongue sticks in my mouth like a dry zipper. Hot, dense anger rises in me, floods me like blind foam. That sentence contains everything I am trying to run away from: the godlike arrogance of people who suffer no doubts. The joviality of eye-witnesses to a disaster, the unfeeling righteousness of those who are sure of their accounts, and calm, that smoothly ironed calm! Should I admit that at the very bottom of my protest sits envy? My entire storytelling willpower is nurtured by it—and has been (alas!) for thirty years.

At last I open my eyes and Mrs. P. gives me an encouraging wink. The soft spring air is floating on the wind. And, as it sometimes happens with our inner scale, the convulsive anger subsides, to be replaced by sorrow which penetrates to the marrow of my bone, with nothing in my field of vision but flowers. The morning sun shines through the tulips, light streaming through the living tissue of the petals. It is like an unexpected blow; I have no time to defend myself against their beauty. Tears fill my eyes (for the first time since the *dam-burst*) and I leave yet another house in rash flight.

That is how I ended that peculiar visit, and from there on the life of Mrs. P. and her son continued without my participation.

The times changed a lot. The word "taste" faded and retreated into the twilight of language; the era of its rule has gone. I have to admit that I almost miss it, but the dogma of people with whom I share my life dictates that taste is an imperious scam. The buoys that used to warn swimmers have been smashed against the rocks.

At sixteen I rebelliously voted for chaos. As I grow old, I long to cling to the bedrock of order; I pray for a peaceful rest and make my life as easy as possible. From time to time I see the classroom of my childhood in a dream, but this time I am not the one pacing the catwalk like some monster, I am sitting with the anonymous pack, roaring with laughter until we fall off our chairs in a mad tangle of bodies. We are inside, laughing at those outside without a hint of anger, laughing at insane accountants, at Allskins, at treacherous fathers. Out there is an abyss, I know that, and for almost half a century I have been living competently enough to avoid ending up at the bottom of it.

What took me back to Mrs. P. thirty years later was partly chance, partly the force of gravity of my own footsteps. Mrs. P. had not changed at all. I found her perfectly groomed in a tidy apartment, as if I had left only yesterday. She remembered me and asked me into the salon which was the same as before.

"You look well." She gave me my due, because my Allskin phase had long ended; today, my main aim is to blend in with the background.

"Thank you," I said. "I hear you have a famous son. You must be pleased with his success."

Mrs. P. gave me a direct look. "I have no son," she said firmly. I didn't understand. Only today I saw him on television, chairing some conference. I recognized him more because of the resemblance to his mother than because he himself had stuck in my memory.

"My son ceased to exist for me," she went on without a shudder, "because he himself has disowned me. These days he has a life of his own, where there is no place for me, because he no longer needs me. But I have forgotten him too. He has children—so I'm told—I don't know. He moved out and I don't want to know where he lives. Let's not talk about him any more. I'll make some tea."

I stayed for an hour and we really didn't talk about him. We chatted about trivialities and I was once more fascinated by her steadfastness. Not a hair out of place, not a speck of dust on the table to reveal how terribly she had been betrayed by life. I had to admire her: she had survived the defeat of her own will, her greatest plan had fallen through—but she remained undefeated. She never gave in to the slightest doubt. She was eighty and more unyielding than ever before.

Mrs. P. went to cut the strudel and I absently went to the window. There, I was struck speechless with astonishment.

We were at the height of the spring season and the tulips stood there in all their glory. Among them, right there among the tulip heads, were several collapsing tomato plants in plastic growing-bags. The flower bed used to be planted in concentric circles. Now a thin potato patch crashed into the pattern and underneath blazed a tangle of overgrown, scorched caraway. Beanstalks crept up along rusty pipes. There were no beds or rows, only an embarrassing, offensive chaos of plants choking one another.

At first I thought there must be some mistake; this was totally impossible. There are things that are still not done, even in our peculiar time when no one asks any longer what is permissible. The dogma has fallen, high water has carried away the barriers of taste— yet, it was impossible to imagine the kind of impulse that would allow anybody to plant potatoes among tulips! It had nothing to do with want of space—all around there were grassy lots which would accommodate a whole plantation. It looked monstrous. Only madness could defy all limits. It was a *dam-burst*. A colorful bed of despair stretching from the fence.

Mrs. P. came in with a tray. I hastily turned my eyes away. We started a smooth conversation about nothing.

"By the way, what happened to that lady, you know, the one who kept going over her accounts?" I asked in the hall, one foot outside the door. Mrs. P. frowned.

"Wait a moment." She tried to remember. "Ahh, yes, now I know. She slashed her wrists," she said matter-of-factly. "Why do you ask about her?"

I shrugged my shoulders. She passed me my coat. She didn't invite me to come again and I didn't say I would.

I was on my way out when Mrs. P. suddenly smiled.

"See, my girl, I remember now!"

Her face grew younger with a happy memory.

"Do you know that she came here once? She fell in love with my tulips. Kept looking at them, couldn't get enough. A strange woman, but she did have taste."

Translated by Alexandra Büchler

Far from the Tree

excerpt from a novel

ZUZANA BRABCOVÁ

"An apple falls not far from the tree."

—An old Czech proverb

SOON AFTER CONCEPTION, amidst the waters of the womb, I experienced something which might without hyperbole be called an anticipation of the world. And indeed: shortly before birth I knew for sure what light and darkness were like, a nuclear warhead, or the post-war population statistics. And maybe on account of that, the babble of the weird sisters in our Prague flat, just after mother brought me from the maternity hospital, was simply neither here nor there. Even without their unscientific prognoses it was more than evident that insofar as I had arisen from the waters, into the waters I would return, inside this strange prison-barred shell into which I was planted,

teacher,

like a pearl

by the others.

I wanted to do only two things, Josef: to give birth to a son and to write a book. The first I shall never manage now, and so I have to attempt the other, with the blade of a knife at my throat.

Our home. Our anthem. My hermetically sealed home with its dummy heaven, my anthem, during which even the dead have to stand at attention. Our generation, autistic, alcoholic, riddled with debts, moodily unambitiously Eastern, matter-of-factly acceleratedly Western, our generation that is anchorless, being without sea. For Bohemia (my country) was last flooded by the sea in the Paleozoic age.

The sea. When I look out of the window, I can see the water slowly rising, swallowing up the dryness of the crumbling plaster on the wall opposite, firmly encompassing the tree trunks bent by the flood, working—yes, this water works—systematically, savagely and purposefully, endowed with a will.

Rolling on the surface is a scrap of newspaper, a cigarette packet, a ping-pong paddle and the swollen corpse of a sparrow. I turn away. The walls of the room exude damp. I climb off the chair. I'm cold, Josef, infinitely, wetly cold. I wrap myself in a blanket and close my eyes, so as to concentrate better on my writing

with a blade of water at my throat and with time,

beating inaudibly now,

on its last legs.

"Prehistory ended the moment Man invented writing," said Slavík, the teacher, impressively, and just as he began to take his violin out of its case to celebrate this inestimable victory of the spirit with a composition by Suk, Řeháček started to undo his flies.

"You're an idiot . . ." I whispered into the first bars of Suk's "Song of Love," but Řeháček pretended not to hear.

Řeháček, my desk mate, was again about to demonstrate the abysses which divide people, their unbridgeable otherness, something he did more or less constantly during history classes, which bored him terribly. And I at that time—irony of fate—was just beginning to sense with beating heart the shared something which does not divide, but unites us all with a metaphysical, timeless bond. I was twelve. At that time the factories were starting to churn out barbed wire, at that time foreign forces squatted in barracks, at that time even the dead had to rise for the national anthem. Řeháček was right; only I was blind to it at the time, because every time, instead of Řeháček's truth beneath the bench, I watched the tragic figure of my weepy crazed teacher Mr. Slavík, whose violin cut an ever deeper groove in his throat with every passing day, like the inexorable blade of a singing knife.

"Řeháček, what was it that began then," I whispered into my hand, "when people started to write?"

The teacher sawed away in front of the blackboard, furrowing his brow with concentration, while the bow in his fingers teetered over the strings.

"I can't hear you, he's making such a racket."

I didn't repeat my question. Řeháček wouldn't have answered it anyway; his lack of interest in everything which had nothing to do with sex or mathematics was quite remarkable. I loved him. I loved him, because he was freckled and ginger, because he was fun and immoral, because he let me copy all his maths exercises, and because he adored American skyscrapers, which inspired me with fear. And his album full of photographs of those fantastic buildings, which rudely penetrate the heavens, which are monstrous, intoxicating and beautiful like the whole of their century, this colorful album is all I have left of Řeháček now.

The teacher finished playing and didn't even notice that a paper swallow was circling over his head.

I open my eyes with astonishment. Hold on, Josef—something's not right here: why did this ginger boy elbow his way in here right at the very start? Starting a book with your first childish love is worse than banal. And I've no time for banality at present . . . That murky water ahead of me is sure to have flooded the ground floor of this building by now . . . .

I can still hear the crash of doors, the cracking motion of cupboards, the stamp of heavy studded boots, vague yellings, and damp confusion—that's the others trying to move their offices from the ground floor up to the higher stories, attempting to save their card-files and telephones and revolvers and their porter and their detainees from the water, that undisciplined element which put a spoke in their wheel, which wasn't part of the plan, and which cannot now be frightened off.

So the malevolent water drives them on from floor to floor; in an obstinate attempt to preserve their order and regime and working duties they flee before it ever higher with their arsenal, but their order is getting damp, their regime is staring them in the face like a drowned man, and their revolvers, all the revolvers of all the others, wherever they are in the world, are gripped by the mother of rust and the father of decay.

Of course, we shall perish with them, but what of that? Out of the sea we came in the form of a little trilobite and into the sea we shall go again, in the guise of culture and wearing the mask of civilization. But, before this happens, I am here as part of their arsenal, I in a cell, in me a book, and in this book the inexplicable existence of Řeháček.

"We'll help you. Pavel Řeháček . . . ."

"Yes, now I remember. After I got back from the summer holidays . . . that was in nineteen seventy-two . . . ."

"Those summer holidays were also memorable for something else, both for you and your parents, or am I mistaken?"

"You're not mistaken. Grandpa Václav died, they found him in the loft, covered with a map of the Krkonoše Mountains."

"And at the end of July you went to Křečhoř for the funeral. But let's get back to Řeháček for a moment. After you got back to school at the end of the holidays the place beside you was empty."

"Can I come and sit next to you?" Katka asked during break.

She leant gently on the corner of my desk, tossed her long mane of hair back mechanically and gave a smile. She's beautiful, I think to myself. She's beautiful, she looks fifteen, she uses make-up, she has the best essays in the class and also the loveliest legs. Stupid, stupid, stupid hussy.

"Řeháček'll turn up, you know. He always disappears the first day after the holidays."

I try to return the same dazzling smile, but I feel only too well how my face changes it into a parodic grimace.

"What do you mean, silly, don't you know? The family went to Vienna in July and they didn't come back . . . ."

The bell rings. She gets up and goes off with a shrug of the shoulders to her seat. I turn after her uncomprehendingly, with a small, soft eraser in my hand. The old-hag fates turned down the sound, just like Dad sometimes does, when he's writing his Sunday sermon during the TV news. The bell stops. Everyone around me opens their mouths vacantly, laugh soundlessly, I can't even hear chairs falling, or torn pages of textbooks, I can't hear anything at all. Only the clammy white eraser in my fist starts to produce a kind of tiny wailing sound.

Slavík the teacher comes into the classroom. With a sweep of the hand he asks us to sit, launching immediately with a distant gaze into a long speech about beautiful Bohemia, my own Bohemian land, this paradise of earth, where the hills consort with the sky and the soul soars with desire—once again he'll use those sentences with the savor of starch, those branching sentences full of participial phrases, the same word order in his heart as he had last year, the year before and as far back as the memory reaches, only the voice a little more quavery. But I have the sound turned down. And instead of him a deathly silence, a silence without the schoolmaster's trumpeted patriotism, without his violin, without the scraping of chalk on the board—silence with a screen full of two-dimensional faces which surround me, which imprison me, which stifle me. They can't even let you cry in peace, I rage. What are you gaping at, I whisper, you stupid hussies with beautiful legs, leave me alone, you stupid, stupid, stupid hussies. Don't break the circle in which I totter, don't break my silence, my deathly silence without Řeháček.

"And what about you, Věra, where were you in the holidays?" the teacher's voice draws me out of my sweet pain.

I say nothing. Quickly I wipe the tears with the back of my hand. Finally I manage to say, "We were at Grandpa's funeral. My grandfather's still dead, you see."

"Is that what you answered?"

"Yes."

"And what did the teacher say?"

"He nodded sympathetically and stroked me on the head. He was embarrassed. Actually he was always embarrassed. And also, it might interest you to know, he was a Party member."

"Always?"

"Always. Can't you see him? Over there, in the whirlpools by the wall. Watch closely how he struggles with the water, how he clutches hold of the lifebelt of his violin, how bravely he does battle and will go on doing battle in his blue shirt right to the very end. I'm sorry for him. And yet, at the time, when he frowned and refused to explain Řeháček's disappearance to me after class, I so much wanted to take revenge! But why on him? You say it was none of his fault. Only I, with my childishly infallible obstinacy, sensed his far-reaching guilt . . . My intuition hypnotized me even then; from then on I hated Slavík with that deep and icily pure hatred which only a child in this world can feel."

"Can you be more precise about what you mean by his far-reaching guilt?"

"He was one of those who prepared my future. And that future deprived me of Řeháček; that's all."

"Isn't that a bit simplified?"

"Do you know how I used to get to sleep for a long time after that? Instead of counting an endless line of sheep crossing a plank bridge, I would whisper into my pillow, till I fell asleep: Řeháček in Vienna, Vienna in Austria, Austria in Europe, Europe on planet earth, planet earth in the galaxy, galaxy in the universe, universe in the universe, universe in the universe, universe in the universe . . . Perhaps it was thanks to this fable that the idea of the infinite didn't seem so unimaginable . . . Ginger-head was the first warning. Others followed. And yet, now at this moment—I only have to get up on a chair and look down—the sight of my miserably brave teacher decidedly fails to give me any satisfaction. Once, teacher, you said, 'Bohemia was flooded by the sea in the Paleozoic age,' and in your eyes there glittered two sparks of archetypal horror. You couldn't have known that only a few years later that sea would return and roughly, barbarously, without any respect for your mixed-up Czechness and your leather-bound copy of Palacký's *History*, engulf you and your country once more and leave it to rot at the bottom. That's the closing curtain, the last full stop on the end of your half-century without God, my dear drowning teacher, vainly clutching your violin, yourself already in a glistening white case of sea-salt."

"But we haven't got much time left either. Cut your story shorter, please."

Kampa Park is all made of glass, and as I run, it collapses beneath my feet with a deafening crunch. Women with strollers, the next generation in the strollers, pensioners with old graying terriers, athletes in running shoes, the Abbé Dobrovský's statue—all turn curiously to look at me with their two-dimensional faces.

"What's going on? You look in a flurry." Dad asks absent-mindedly, without lifting his head from his damned files. Dad is a well-disciplined Protestant pastor, and well-disciplined Protestant pastors are not favorably disposed to being in a flurry. Dad is the image of equanimity, calm and dignity. Dad is infected with the miracle of sanctity like other people with the flu. Above all this, Dad is my mirror.

"Where's Vienna?"

"You ought to know that by now. It's in Austria."

Dad is Dad.

"I have to go there right now."

He looked up at me finally, in surprise. The mirror. I prefer to lower my gaze.

"What's got into you?"

"Řeháček's in Vienna and he's left his skyscrapers behind with me. I've got to return them."

Dad sat me on his lap, removed his glasses and took a deep breath. It was clear what I was in for: these were the gestures which regularly introduced those patient explanations which my respected father inflicted on me from time to time in the fatally mistaken belief that the most instructive way to speak to a child was as you would to an adult.

I fidgeted restlessly. Father's knees were hopelessly pointed and uncomfortable. Doctor Black, our century-old tomcat, settled himself much more comfortably on the closet and peered at us, biding his time.

Dad talked and talked, and meanwhile Kampa Park turned dark and the strollers disappeared, as did the pensioners with their terriers and the athletes in their sports shoes; Dad didn't even allow himself to be disturbed by a six-pointed warning star which fell through the open window on to the carpet, and which Doctor Black sniffed at inquiringly; nor did he allow himself to be disturbed by Mom either, who appeared in the doorway and disappeared again by magic; and then it was night, and day came, and the hour hand on the dial rushed on, and Dad closed his eyes in order to concentrate better, and as he went on explaining in his indefatigable voice, his hair turned white, and I began gradually to grow old on his lap, and so time flew on to meet its end, and stars were born and perished, and Doctor Black became only the spectral shade of some age-old creature, and I understood finally with horror that Dad existed neither in time nor in space, in other words that I'd never escape from his celestially level-headed voice anywhere, whose sound not even the weird sisters could turn down, and which would even plunge after me into the depths of the murderous ocean.

I wasn't the slightest bit interested in an outline of all the important political events and situations over the last ten years. I wasn't interested in revival processes, incursions of foreign armies, falls of governments, divisions between East and West. I wasn't interested in any divisions.

"Řeháček's Dad was a chimney-sweep. And chimneys are the same the world over, aren't they? So why couldn't he go on sweeping them in Prague?"

Daddy gave up. Doctor Black gave a mysterious, animal smile and mewed: "Tell her she'll understand it when she's a bit older."

Unobtrusively, I pick up that burning-hot, six-pointed star from the carpet, hide it under my pajamas, clean my teeth, and before I fall asleep, lulled to sleep for the first time with my sorrowful little rhyme, I look through Řeháček's album piously one last time. But before I bend down for that star, Dad puts his glasses on again and declares with renewed hope: "Věra, these are things you'll understand when you're a bit older."

The others now ask me a tiny, thinly suspicious, totally inessential question ("Just one little question by the way. Of course you don't have to answer it if you don't want to . . . ."): Just what are your relations like with your father?

Father of my father, Grandpa Václav, I can see both of you clearly. Somebody has mockingly swapped your posthumous roles: for you, eternally paradisiac, in meditative consultation with God over the map of the world, with a halo over your lifelong oh-so-doggedly Communist head, you gaze solicitously down there where your life-long Christian son, who will never rise again from the dead, decays in the spiritless material of earth. But that's something I know only now, once I was happy and it was hard for me to . . . .

And what of me? To whom shall I be attached, when the surface closes over me?

This question is, of course, not an answer. So, then: friendly re-lations, atmosphere of cordiality. My relations with my father, fer-vent, eruptive, in an atmosphere charged with the ominous swirl of ashes and seed. But that is now. Once.

I am happy and it's hard for me to arrange my face so as not to show it. From time to time I check myself in the rear mirror, to see if I'm looking tragic enough, singing inwardly to myself: Mom, this black suits us so well! Why don't we wear it all the time? You know very well I like this color best: I love night, Doctor Black, black comedy, black humor and all the black blues of Uncle Tom.

Only you're so far away in your mourning, which I don't under-stand, and your silence, which irritates me, in the adult space pro-hibited to me unless I'm summoned. I believe in color. In this somewhat grotesque blues amidst the hot-summer goose-gaggling Bo-hemian countryside—that as well. But in you? And your mourning?

Dad: when you enrolled at the university in Prague, Grandpa Vá-clav locked the gate and refused to open it to you for seven years. Patiently you knocked, certain that one day it would be opened to you, as it is written. For seven long years you lived in front of your father's door, awaiting that moment when you would hear the key turn in there, on the other side, day and night you, who are my father, prayed on the Communist threshold, hidden from the truth by your paranoiac hope and the shadow of Christ's crucified body—and sure enough: after seven years he opened up to you, exhausted by the corrosive tears of Grandma, blinded by the crazed colors of his maps and perhaps also somewhat persuaded by the Russian-toned surname of your wife, my mother. She smiled at him so broadly, that his aging heart thumped with unconscious memory. For in my mother's smile there lay and lie to this day the Russian steppes. But do you see it, Dad? I'm not sure. I even sometimes get the feeling you didn't ever realize what it was that softened Grandpa Václav's hostility. After all, it was neither the sheep-like patience of your faith nor your philosophical outlook: it was just a single expansive, thousand-year-old smile of a woman, out of whom I was born.

But now, in the back seat of the car, I'm not thinking of smiles which instead of faith move mountains. Entirely captivated by the black of Mom's clothes, Dad's suit and my own dress, with the still living flowers beside me, I follow Dad's pale hands on the steering wheel.

I turn round. A figure by the roadside shakes his clenched fist at us. No, you have to understand. It's not fitting to take hitchhikers when we're on our way to a funeral.

"Aye, aye, it's over for him now."

Grandpa, what's over for you now: death or life?

The inscription above the cemetery gate reads: WE WERE LIKE YOU, YOU WILL BE LIKE US. I don't understand and I want to ask: "Mommy . . ." I tug at my mother's sleeve, but she frowns and ignores me.

Dad supports Grandma in an understanding gesture: she is also painfully aware of the absence of a priest, and the four unseemly bricklayers with their unseemly nose-blowings huffing and puffing under the coffin, and that terrible word Honor on the ribbons of the wreaths, so unsuitable for this moment that Dad closes his eyes so as not to see it. Perhaps I'm doing him wrong. It's quite possible that he's crying.

People from the village coming along with us between the graves peep back curiously at Dad. "So that's put an end to that hatred." "Nonsense . . . they were reconciled for a wee bit by the end." "Reconciled? Don't be a fool. Every time he came out from Prague to see him they argued till the crack of dawn. So the Horáks said and they should know—their house is right opposite."

Whispering, the rustling of lindens, strange knocking sounds over the cemetery wall—I'm not hearing. I'm terribly hot, my tummy hurts and my black dress sticks to my body. Behind me a creeping crowd of alien, village and therefore incomprehensible people, around me stone angels with broken-off wings and bulging eyes and in front of me, in front of me is a mysterious box, inside the box Grandpa Václav and inside Grandpa a quieted heart, a silenced dream, a blinded map of the world with five orange-colored oceans.

Now I know. Those strange knocking sounds over the wall . . . On the way to the cemetery, through the missing planks in the surrounding fence I could see a soccer field encircled by a race-track. Probably there are tennis courts next to the cemetery. I liked that idea, and for a moment it allowed me to forget the sun, the pain and the death. But only for a moment. In the silence I follow the course of the ball, its flight above the level of the wall, this way and that, this way and that. But in the regularity there's a pendulum, and inside the pendulum time, and inside time again that incomprehensible magic formula: WE WERE LIKE YOU, YOU WILL BE LIKE US. Mom's hand is moist. The movement of the ball gets faster, while everyone around has stiffened in fixed poses: Dad, Grandma, the angels, the villagers, the trees and those four men beneath the burden of the coffin. My head is spinning in a circle, this way and that, this way and that, and my happiness is gone, parked on the back seat of the car in front of Grandpa's house, in front of his heavy, so unwillingly opening gates.

Suddenly the ball changed its course, it flew over the wall, bounced off a marble dove (here lies the Böhm family) and landed at my feet. I'm afraid to bend down. No, not because of that. Nobody's looking. All of them, moving now again like puppets on transparent strings, are shifting towards the grave. I'm afraid, because it was the hags, the fates themselves who lobbed it there right at my feet, just next-door to death, this spherical Angst. I don't want it. Mommy, your smile, the steppes—hold on to me! But something forces me to my knees, go on then, pick it up, and I fall, I roll, felled, amongst the urns and the watering-cans, and I still just glimpse Grandpa vanishing in the hole in the ground, father of my father, and behind me I hear also the words: "Just imagine, with the shortage of preserving jars this year, people were pinching them at night from the tombs, I saw old Knitl coming back from the cemetery myself, his bag jingling with them . . . ." And then there was only darkness and in the darkness my pale hands, which have to pick up whatever the others have foisted upon me.

That was the first time I "fainted." I have to put the word into inverted commas, because this state of mine has nothing to do with loss of consciousness . . . Quite the reverse: at such moments, it's as if my consciousness, my real "self"—or rather, a multitude of some mysterious "selves" within me—detached itself from all that is superfluous and encumbering in matter and in the senses which intermediate matter, and found itself in a state of being as pure as water. Like water . . . Yes. I am, I exist transparently in the kindly ocean of my mother's body, I have neither legs arms senses heart nor mind, nothing that a person needs in the world, because the world is not, there is no earth's axis nor atomic nucleus, there are no violin-playing patriots falls of governments changes of regimes preserving jars nor even grandfathers vanishing in the warmly obliging earth, there is nothing, only mother and the sea, only the sea-mother.

When, with these and other meandering words I tried to describe my state to the others—and they demanded this of me frequently—their faces always darkened and their pencils started flying mercilessly over the paper. With great displeasure they followed my mystical submarine account, because for mysticism they had only an ironic shrug of the shoulders, and as for water, of that they were— if it did not flow in an orderly fashion through pipes—instinctively, and therefore enormously, afraid.

I admit that at certain moments this "escape" beneath the surface (that's a somewhat more accurate description) was something I tried to induce artificially: in math classes at school, during one of Dad's ever more epic bouts of explanation, in awkward situations and at times when someone's service lobbed me another spherical Angst . . . But I never succeeded. For the water, like every punishment and every pleasure, comes supremely unannounced.

Water. Rolling on the surface is a scrap of newspaper, a cigarette packet, a ping-pong paddle, a salted teacher, and here, in the middle of the cell, me, me on my knees, weirdly mumbling some kind of words in the rhythm of the psalms.

Translated by James Naughton

The Woman from
the Region of Tyre

Tereza Boučková

MY HANDS WERE dripping with blood. I tried to hold in the blood which had begun to flow from my womb with sudden violence. Whole clots were falling from inside me, and I so much wanted to close myself up. Blessed Virgin Mary, who bore in your womb the Creator of the Universe . . . .

I was not allowed to switch on the light and I could not see what was falling through my impotent fingers into the bowl which the nurse had brought me, even unto our mothers bless the hope of their lives . . . I held my breath and pressed my legs together tightly and when morning came even my cheeks were smeared with blood.

"We're going through to the ultrasound, please sit here," said the nurse, pushing a wheelchair up to my bed. On the way I kept my hand on my slightly bulging tummy, preserve in their wombs the fruit of their expectation, Holy Virgin, Holy Virgin! and the doctor scanned over it a few times and said, "The uterus is empty."

Amen.

"Not a drop, right, and then all of a sudden one dig and it starts gushing out, frothing out all over the place," and as if to demonstrate he opened a bottle of beer and poured it out into his glass.

"When it starts gushing I'm not letting anybody down there, right, nobody!" After his fifth beer our neighbor was so resolute that there was no choice but to accept it. He leant his pickaxe up against the chair and added: "It'll take at least two barrels of beer."

It was meant to be finished in a fortnight. A month went by and, with increasingly forced admiration, we listened to what it would be like when the water started to gush out, and when, after an entire day of drinking beer, coffee and vodka, our neighbor decided to get moving, we almost felt guilty. He just started up the air-compressor and disappeared sacrificially down the ten-meter hole.

"Tough one," he informed us shortly afterwards, when he had resurfaced, switched off the air-compressor and poured himself vodka.

"To do this job you need the Fire," he said, then poured several shots of Fire into himself, started up the compressor and slowly disappeared down the hole.

Shortly afterwards he resurfaced, switched off the compressor, poured himself another vodka and said, "Tough nut to crack, this one."

And so the best explosives man in Czechoslovakia came to us, Milan Pupíček himself. He had explosives crammed into the back-pocket of his trousers and detonators in his shirt-pocket. Behind his back our neighbor gesticulated wildly that we should bring some Fire quickly, and so we had to buy three bottles of It. During the afternoon they finished off two of them. In the evening the explosives expert staggered over to the well and, disappearing into its depths, cried out wheezily, "Like I said, if I can't blow this thing out, nobody can!"

Another month of emptying bottles. Our neighbor's friends started coming over and our home turned into a drinking den at our expense. Autumn had begun. The hole was seventeen meters deep and the estimate had been for twenty. Must just grin and bear it. Our neighbor wanted more vodka, more money. "It's up to you," he said, "but you know I'm not slogging away in the winter, so think it over." He could afford to take liberties. He knew we were in a hurry, that we would badly need the well. Perhaps by springtime—my hands had not yet dripped with blood and the little bean in my abdomen was rhythmically beating with the rhythm of its little heart . . . .

When, once again, they sprawled on the veranda and opened the beers I dared to ask whether they were going to start working.

"You're not telling me what to do and what not to do. I don't take that from anyone!" My neighbor blew up with me.

I couldn't bear it and I started shouting.

I blasted him with everything that had been building up in me for months, I shouted, and within a week, Blessed Virgin, within a week, there was no more need to hurry with the well.

I could not tear my eyes away from the place where her coat was lifted slightly by a bulge of hope.

"So how's it going? Everything all right?" she asked generously, and all I could do was shake my head and rush towards the door.

"Why me, why does it have to be me?" I cried out in an attack of hysterics from the miscarriage and they could not get me to be quiet . . . .

Vincenc, Dominik, Anežka, Žofie . . . .

With the momentum of a mind that did not want to accept the truth of the body, I was choosing names for my long-desired, dead baby.

"Doctor, I can't bear it any longer, it hurts so much . . . Please . . ." Instead of doing anything he called over from the telephone, "What exactly have you had to eat?" and I started screaming at him that I could not move my arms—and my arms really were hanging like rags from my shoulders. I could hear her in the distance as she cut through the rest of my nightgown, which was only hanging around my neck in any case.

"Well, now that's all over?" said a short-cropped blonde head to me when I stopped screaming. It was as if a snake had passed through my body and set its teeth into my belly. Despite the nurse's harsh scolding I could not stop the moaning that gave some relief from the pain biting with cruel unpredictability into my innards.

And then a doctor came to have a look at me, and removed from my ruptured oviduct a second child my body had somehow not wanted to give birth to.

I did not even have the strength left for tears.

It is done.

Trolleys with women on them. They cannot wait to get it over with. The doctors work as if on a conveyor belt. This afternoon several dozen of the species Homo sapiens will end their lives in the bucket under the table. The women sleep for a bit then, and the very same day they powder their noses and go home, or to the cinema, it's no big deal.

The corridor is locked even during the day, smokers bolt themselves in the toilets, the single shower is unheated, in the room there are selections of clipped-out uteruses, clipped-out ovaries, and what shall we have for dinner?

They could mix those embryos into our pasta, so that this high-principled and humane free-of-charge medical intervention could pay its way.

Tomorrow my friend the nurse will teach me to inject vitamins into my own bottom. I must get myself together as quickly as possible, I must be in good working order. I must have a child.

We hung over the upper segment of the cylinder and shone a torch into the bottom of the well.

"Michal could dig down below," said Simona, demonstrating the digging by pantomime, "and I would stay up here and haul it up with some kind of pulley," and in mime fashion she climbed hand over hand up an imaginary rope. "You can't leave it in this state anyway."

Our village friends' resolution to help us was touching. They themselves had a house which they had never finished working on, piles of animals, a big garden . . . It was clear to all of us that we would not actually achieve anything. We did not have the tools, the winch or even the pulley, in fact, we had no idea how to sink a well and—apart from anything else—none of us had the courage to go down there ourselves.

We sat on the cylindrical tubing and looked down the dark hole. It was as hopeless as the view down the elevator shaft of a six-story house. It was more hopeless than that.

Jarka sat smoking on the rim of the sink.

"Five years ago you could have a smoke here without any problems and now you've got to watch out. It gets worse and worse. They clamped down on the cure program. They've banned smoking and now we can't even make coffee here . . . ."

An element hissed in her mug. It was ten o'clock, time for lights-out. Jarka was putting nail-polish on. Afterwards, as she expertly shook off her hands for the varnish to dry well, she told me how she and Marcela had picked up two Yugoslavs from West Germany who had a Mercedes and who were taking them to Tuzex tomorrow to buy them whatever they wanted. It was absolutely clear that this would not be for free. As she was leaving the next morning a program about AIDS was on the radio. They were warning girls who had relations with foreigners at their leisure that they should not behave in such a way, that such behavior was very dangerous.

"Aren't you scared?" I asked.

"It'd be best if there was no fucking at all."

That evening I found her squatting behind the gates of our bathhouse weeping. I tried to pull her up.

"Filthy bastard!" she jabbered half-drunkenly and pushed me away.

"What happened?"

I squatted down next to her. I felt sorry for her.

"He did it to me."

"What did he do?"

"Absolutely everything. And he only gave me chewing gum in return, the sod!"

It was May, the month of love. With the sudden sound of an anthem, some pioneers from somewhere or other marched up to decorate the head of Lenin, dominating the main colonnade, with red tulips. The very same evening I moved a few of them a couple of meters on, to where there is a statue of little Francis, whose job it is to fulfil the great desire of infertile women.

With the tulips I decorated his little willy.

It was nothing but "Sorry" and "Excuse me" and when I invited them in for lunch they did not want to bother us. Except that they were completely soaked to the skin, and so they let themselves be persuaded, and thanked me effusively for a total failure of a meal.

Then one of them challenged my husband to a game of chess, the other sat down at the piano, and light music poured agreeably through the house. The only things that betrayed the fact that the two of them were not here on a cultural exchange were the dirty wet workclothes hanging above the stove. It rained all day. The sky loomed relentlessly and it did not look as if it would get any better.

Both men struggled into their outer layers, which had had absolutely no chance to dry in such a short break, and they totally ignored our pleas for them not to go back out into such foul weather.

When the rain became torrential and I ran out to fetch our new well-sinkers back into the warm, the growling of the pneumatic drill echoed from the well and by the winch at the top a muddy figure was singing, "It's raining, it's pouring."

I could not go past the toilet without vomiting into it. With a little imagination I found pigmented marks on the central line of my abdomen! My breasts enlarged, but I searched in vain for stretch-marks on them. The heartburn and increased salivation were nothing special. My bladder did not hold so much water since an enlarged uterus was pressing on it. The arches of my feet had been dropped since I was born, but my nervous irritability had noticeably increased. With the help of the gynecological textbook I had been studying for several years, I calculated the date of birth, and name upon name crowded into my head.

After fourteen days of pickled gherkins for breakfast, sardines and lemon juice for lunch and horseradish sauce in alternation with wholegrain mustard for dinner, blood appeared on the sheets and in forlorn hope, I let them take me to the hospital to save the child I was not expecting.

I had stretchmarks on the brain.

In two weekends they did as much work as our neighbor did in six weeks. And on top of that they were always in a good mood. They dug down several meters past the level designated by a qualified hydrologist, so that the supply of water would be as great as possible. They even dug out more than we had ordered. It all went incredibly smoothly. The well was ready. Ready and dry.

Except that, contrary to the physical laws of socialist realism, they not only continued working, but even brought a new water diviner along with them, so that we could find out that we had dug in the wrong place. Although his divining rod grazed his belly, it nevertheless spun. A good three meters from the well. There a second magic stick described eighteen circles, which meant that the chaps in the well would, if they had mercy on us, build a wooden platform four meters above the bottom, and dig a hole to one side.

Then over coffee the water diviner told us how many springs he had found before, and how water had spurted from each of them five meters into the air, but that we must have some kind of little cave here, into which the spring was discharging, because when the tectonic plates collided and crumpled occasionally something didn't quite fit and blah blah blah. The compressor droned day and night. My husband went down into the well along with the well-sinkers to help press on the pneumatic drill, which was eating into the designated place with utter distaste.

With great self-denial they dug out a three-meter tunnel. No cave. But the water diviner had not been mistaken. There really had been water here. In the so-called Silurian Period, four hundred and forty million years ago.

A trilobite detached itself from the walls of the tunnel.

Three days before ovulation crush thirteen granules of something miraculous, mix with the yolk of one egg and one teaspoon of honey, take on an empty stomach and leave several hours to digest. Do not do heavy work. Every evening do Mrs Mojžíšová's exercises. Behave with continence before ovulation. Believe. Strengthen buttock musculature. Do not ski. Relax. Measure basal temperature first thing in the morning. Believe. Drink Mrs Kamenická's hormonal tea. Be cheerful of spirit. Utilize days of fertility. Believe. Do not smoke. Do laundry on washboard. Do not wear narrow trousers. Go to the mountains — one infertile body-builder conceived there. Believe. Do not worry. Do not be nervous. Eat oatflakes. Believe. Do not skate. After intercourse do shoulderstand. After intercourse do headstand. Believe. Move bed away from center of magnetic flux. Believe. Do not build snowmen. Believe. Do not think. Believe. Believe. Believe.

I cooked him a good dinner. He did not praise it. I put on seductive music. He did not notice it. I began coiling my way towards him. He went on studying his handbook, *Motorcycle Maintenance and Repair.* I was faithfully observing the doctor's instructions and persistently chased my husband away on days of recommended abstention, which formed an oppressive majority over days of supposed fertility. We had a falling out. Our household was not quiet, our household was mute, deaf and tense like the calm before the storm. In this fertile atmosphere I worked out by the Knaus-Ogin Method that today was the optimal day for conception, be cheerful of spirit, believe. I sat on my husband's lap and tenderly removed his handbook.

"Today we must make children," I whispered into his ear. He pushed me away saying, "I'm not a breeding rabbit!"

We hung over the uppermost segment of the cylinder and shone a torch into the bottom of the well. It did not glisten. We sat down and looked resignedly down the dark hole. It was as hopeless as the view down the elevator shaft of a nine-story house. It was more hopeless than that.

Our well-sinkers loaded up the compressor, the pneumatic drill, the winch and all the hoes and shovels and things and drove off. They promised us that they would be back in the winter, they said that they would get through to that water . . . We didn't believe them.

I set out for the doctor's because, once again, we'd had no results. He examined me and said he could see no reason why I should not conceive.

"Do you do it right?" he asked, and his eyes twinkled craftily. "Describe what you do."

I looked at him and the ritual of our lovemaking flashed through my mind. Well, first of all I put on my armor, my long, pot-bellied nightie and at least two pairs of socks, the inner ones thin, the outer ones thick. I grease my lips with lip balm and powder my face with Acnepure. I stuff cotton wool into my ears. And in this seductive and desirable state I skip lightly into bed and do Mrs Mojžíšová's exercises. I throw the window wide open and dive under several blankets. If my husband somehow manages to dig his way through to me and tries to kiss me, I cry out, "Help, I'm suffocating," and immediately squirt drops into my nose.

"We do it just like everybody else," I said.

I put them in the only other room our little house had to offer, and night after night I could not sleep. I kept going to see if they were breathing, if they needed anything. They breathed. They ate up all their dinner. They pooped until our house smelt like a pigsty. They grew. Hundreds of flies moved into our house and it was impossible to flush them out. We would have to make a special home for them. My husband took a holiday from work. He read all the technical literature. He sketched several outline plans and finally set out for the top of the garden with a wheelbarrow full of boards, nails, screws and tools. He spent the whole of the afternoon there without the sound of a single sawcut, a single bang, in fact any noise at all. This was repeated day after day. While my husband stood under the walnut tree thinking, I carried them out one by one every morning and back again in the evening, until it stopped being any fun and I let them sleep rough. They were big and fat by now, and nothing could happen to them. Something did happen, though, to the neighbor's onions, where I found them in the morning, bloated and contented. That was it! We sharpened the knives. We had blood everywhere and the stench of scalded feathers. We felt sick. We swore that we would never again eat meat, never again.

The next day we had duck liver and onions for lunch. One infertile body-builder had conceived after eating duck liver.

What is the questionnaire like? Is it very detailed? How many generations back do we have to confess for? Who will make all the decisions about whether we are suitable? Street Vigilance Committee Party? Government? State?

It was against the interests of the state that I should study, hold a passport, work as anything other than a cleaner, that I should live here at all . . . It was also against the state's interests for my mom to see her children, who had gone to live abroad because the state's interests had not allowed them to study or work according to their abilities. It was against the state's interest for my mother to know her children's children who had been born abroad without permission or compensation.

Why should it be in the interests of the state that we adopt a child when we can't have our own? Why can't we have our own? Who is the state anyway?

It has been scientifically proven that a person's conduct and behavior is ninety percent determined by their genetic make-up and that only ten percent can be influenced by upbringing. Just consider the fact that mothers no longer abandon their children because they are poor or seriously ill, but rather because they are narrow-minded, selfish, cynical. They drink, smoke, shoot up, prostitute themselves, and they don't give a damn. Their children are already mentally deficient as a result of the conditions of their pregnancy. Add to that the gift of their genes. These children are aggressive, stupid, demented even. You tell yourself that you are saving a child by giving it love and a family, that you are making a good person out of it, but you are really only wrecking your own life.

I have loads of childless friends and they are happy. You should learn to live without children. You should learn to live without children. You should learn to live without children. You should learn to live without children.

"Press the green button, unwind the cable and then wind it back again, until it's tight." I pressed the button, unwound the cable, and when I tried to wind it back it got caught between the drum and casing of the winch. Using a screwdriver, pliers, a hammer and a mallet I managed finally to get it free. Then, when the drill came up, I couldn't get it out. To get the explosives in as deep as possible it had a terribly long drill-bit, which kept jamming between the concrete segments. I worked it up and down and it always lodged in the same place. I needed to detach it from the chain tying it to the cable so that I could manipulate it more easily. But then I would have to pull it up without the aid of the winch, using my own strength. And it was so terribly heavy! One moment of hesitation and the person standing twenty-two meters below it would cease to be. I swore as strongly as I knew how, and I was crazy with fear because in the end I did have to detach that chain. When the drill finally thudded to my feet a wave of heat poured over me, despite the rain and the cold. We hid behind a tree and touched the wires together. The detonation deepened the well by about a meter. Our well-sinkers had come back to us as one man. And the other man was me.

On the jubilee day of the twenty-fifth meter we brought the third in our series of water diviners to visit. It should be said that those before him, who had come after the inception of our water operation, shared the opinion that where we were digging there was no water. Of course the place where there actually was water was different each time. Once it was in the potato patch, once a little way from the birch tree, west of the vegetable cold frame . . . .

This time it was not far from the plum tree. And as always there was supposed to be a very rich spring there, and as always this particular water diviner had never been wrong, and as always they would send for him when they bored and did not strike water and he would be guaranteed to find it and everything would turn out fine and the water would spurt five meters into the air and blah.

"So where will it be?" the well-sinker asked us like a taxi driver. Downward!

I left him with new faith, a box of hormones for my husband and two packets of contraceptives for me. When I discontinued the pill, my ovulation should be stronger, giving me a greater chance of pregnancy.

"I don't want to give you false hopes, but I think that this should work," said the new doctor who agreed to see me thanks to sympathetic friends. And so we each ate our pills and were both nauseous.

When that long-awaited moment was due, we went on a mission of insemination to the mountains, be cheerful of spirit, believe. The very next day my whole organism broke down and I started to menstruate.

I should learn to live without children.

Why didn't we abandon that tank? Why did we go on using that water for more than six months?

Those were beautiful days. From morning to evening we sun-bathed on the terrace. For a long time before, and a while afterwards, it did not rain. We had no water. Our rainwater tank, which we used for everything except drinking, was completely empty. The earth was scorched, the flowers withered, the vegetable beds cracked.

Finally the first rain came. We connected all the gutters up to the tank and caught every last drop of water, and then washed and bathed in it, rinsed our food in it, watered the garden. And we really made that dose from the first days last. Perhaps if there had been no accident at Chernobyl I would now have a one-year old boy who would already be saying "Mama" and making his first little steps. Why did it have to happen just before I became pregnant? Why did we not yet have a well? Why did we not abandon the tank? Why did we use that contaminated water for more than six months? Why did nobody inform us of what should be done in the event of such a catastrophe?

It is my baby's first birthday. In memoriam.

The last blast came at one in the morning. Our well-sinker then poured spirit into a bottle, lit it and poured it as deep as possible into the entrails of the earth, so that the poisonous gases from the blast would disperse as well as possible.

He was on his feet again at six. At seven they were both by the well. He and my husband, who had learnt to drill and hammer down there, thirty meters below the surface of the earth.

The work went on all day, with a pause for breath only at meals. In the afternoon, after the next blast, the well-sinker let himself down and immediately called back up to us that we should wind him back up again quickly. We pulled him out green and listless. He could hardly hold onto to the cable. It was lucky he hadn't fainted down there. What would we have done? How would we have pulled him out of that meter-wide tunnel? Brr, better not to think about it! Not to think at all.

When after three days of heavy work he was leaving for home, we wanted to pay him. He wouldn't even hear of it. As he was going out, we slipped the money into the pocket of his anorak. He put it on the veranda table. We ran after him to the car, chucked it in through the window and ran off home. He brought it back.

We begged him to take the money. We couldn't accept such a sacrifice!

After long haggling he kept half of it. The second half, he said, was for my husband. That evening we felt strange. Almost as if we'd hit water.

"If there are any problems, say you're from the TV station and you're here to film," Mrs Zajoncová instructed me, as we marched down the corridor of the institute in big rubber slippers. Behind the first set of doors whose glass I peeped through there were two rows of metal cots with children in them like convicts behind bars. The next door led to a playroom. There were toys there, cheery pictures, colored curtains, and it looked like any other children's room, except that here one baby was standing in a play pen, another was crawling across the floor, another was lying on its back examining a thoroughly disinfected plastic duck, and nearby sat a nurse who had not one but two children in her arms. Then a door onto the balcony, where children go for outings to metal cots with even higher bars. Behind the last set of doors that this deceit allowed me to look through, a tiny human bundle was sleeping in a cot, just as unwanted and unloved and innocent as the rest of them in this sterile home for sucklings. As I looked he started moving and purring so sweetly and helplessly that my heart was wrenched. We submitted an application for adoption.

"She's out whoring with soldiers, you don't have to tell me!" Even his face was transformed. For his whole life love and goodness had shone from it, but now it was distorted with a pathological anger.

"They've stolen everything from me. I haven't got any money, those soldiers, boys . . ." and again, for the hundredth time, he ran out of the house and chased off in whatever direction sprang to his mind, across flowerbeds and the rockery, he tried to push down the fence, shove away the tree; everything that stood in his way had somehow to be conquered. When he had managed to find the gate and escape to the street he galloped off somewhere, anywhere. From his whole life a variety of strong moments had tangled themselves up together and made themselves into the phantasm which chased him now from place to place, day and night, without rest, without sleep, and he was so tired that I could hardly drag him home, but as soon as I got him into an armchair he stood up and chased off out again. There was no one to entertain or restrain him, and he fought with me, shouting "Oh-oh! Help!" and at same time he was falling with weakness and exhaustion.

Mum, who looked after Grandpa completely without any help, was very tired and needed a rest. She brought him to me for three days, even though I was alone here too. We both hoped that Grandpa would calm down, that he would remember how he had built this place, how he and Grandma had lived here together. But the reverse was true. Grandpa raved all the more. He thought Mum was his wife, and that she had left him . . . .

"She's out whoring, the sly bitch," he swore, he who had never uttered a vulgar word in his life, and all night he would get up and totter around the room, chased by a nonsensical idea. At the same time, he didn't know how to do anything. He didn't know how to eat, what to do when he needed to go to the toilet, and instead of going to the bathroom he climbed into the cupboard . . . When I was dressing him in the morning I thought to myself, well here's your baby, then, your long-desired child, there, one little shoe . . . and the other one . . . and now let's go for a wee-wee, there we are, that's right.

We didn't sleep the next night either. I borrowed some sleeping pills from the neighbors and in the afternoon, when his raving was reaching its peak, I gave him one of them. It didn't work. I gave him a second, a third, then a fourth, but Grandpa was so deranged that the pills had no effect whatsoever. I was in despair, and I felt like giving him the whole lot, going and getting another tube for myself and finishing with it. When suddenly Grandpa toppled over. I knew that I had killed him.

"Grandpa, breathe! Please, breathe!" I shouted into his ear and dragged his limp body onto the bed. "Grandpa, please!"

When Mum came in the morning we were sitting in the armchairs like two corpses. Grandpa was still completely out of it, and I was exhausted and empty.

"Just imagine, we've got a new little boy in the family," she said, and smiled happily. "He was born last night, they say he's very beautiful and Kát'a's ever so happy . . . ."

I could feel my mouth distort and my face twist up. I tried to contain it, but it was no good. My face curled up into a grimace of weeping.

"Don't you ever come round here again!" I bid farewell to the fourth and last of our water diviners. He had advised us to fill in our thirty-four-meter deep well and dig a new one.

"There'll never be water here," he said, as he walked round and round and his rod didn't even twitch in his hands.

Surely we can't fill in a work that has cost us so much time, so much nervous toil . . . ? And why should this diviner be right? The walls of the well were damp, the stones were sodden with water like mushrooms . . . There must be a spring there!

I went and tore off a stick, grasped it like the water diviner did and started to circle the area around the well. And the stick moved in my palms! As if some invisible force was turning around its axes.

I called my husband and he laughed at me. So I took him by one hand, into the other I put one end of the fork, and thus our circumference was closed, and the miraculous occurrence was repeated! And we rejoiced and everything started all over again.

Drill, blast, disperse, extract, drill, blast . . . I confirmed all the springs flowing through our garden!

In the end even the path to the chickens went along a spring. The stick danced around unerringly on the veranda, in the kitchen, on the roof of the garage, even in our so-called dry closet. It twisted wherever I set my feet. Perhaps I had water in the belly.

To hear his first cry, to feel those hungry lips on your body, to kiss his little hands, to press him to your heart.

On the fifth day of the cycle swallow the first gravosan tablet and repeat for the following four days. Utilize days of fertility, be cheerful of spirit, do not believe. According to all irrational laws of intentionality, this time it should work, because I have put in the application, my pregnancy-related stress had gone out of my mind, I am relaxed, I am not thinking about anything, I am looking forward to the child entrusted to me, I have stopped dreaming of my own, I am relaxed, I feel a new life beginning in my body, I am relaxed, I hear his first cry, I feel, I feel that I will soon go mad.

It was as hopeless as the view down the elevator shaft of a sixteen-story house. It was more hopeless than that. Although the walls were utterly wet, not a single drop detached itself from them to fall together with another and a third and a thousandth and fill the hard-conquered space, which we had so stubbornly and nonsensically named a well.

We hung over the uppermost segment of the cylinder and shone a torch into the bottom of the well. It did not glisten.

The ground was as hard as concrete. The sun was beating down. Flies festooned my head and there was no way of chasing them away. Dig a little hole, put a spruce tree in it, cover with soil and press down hard. Keep the distance between them. Mrs. Šebková, pensioner and lifelong forest worker, made diligent and faithful progress, and it did not seem that she was tiring at all. My head started to ache. My legs sweated in rubber boots, and blisters rose on my feet. The hoe pressed into my sore palms and my heroic dream of renewing the forest began to crumble in harmony with my whole body. Flies flew into my eyes and my ears and my nose, the trays of seedlings showed no sign of diminishing and we still had four hours left of roasting and frying in our own juices.

When I reached home at noon, I just managed to get my shoes off, thudded into bed, and didn't wake until my husband came home from work. He sat next to me at the foot of the bed and said, "Tomorrow we'll go and have a look at the little boy. He's half Gypsy and no one wants him."

We tossed around all night, each of us alone with our fears and our heads full of depressing ideas. In the morning we rose heavy-limbed and weak with sore throats that had suddenly taken hold of us both.

Then to sew button-eyes onto the head of the clown I had made the evening before for the little boy. After all, on the first visit you have to bring a gift.

"Quick!" my husband urged me, so that we wouldn't miss the bus whose stop was quite far away. As he locked the door I ran to the well, shifted the wire mess that covered the dangerous abyss, and from the neighboring pile of stones I picked the largest that came to hand.

If signs from God really exist, there must be water there now, I thought to myself when I had tipped as far as I could over the cylinder so that the stone would fall down the middle and not shatter on the walls before it reached the bottom. I threw it. But my husband seized my hand and didn't let go until we were getting onto the bus.

We sat in the corridor on the ground floor and waited until the consultant called for us. At this point my mother turned to me seriously and said that she had spoken to Mrs Zajoncová, who had spoken to the nursing doctor who did not agree with them offering the little boy to us.

"Apparently he's much more backward than the other children in the institute and there is a great probability that he will not develop at all. You must have the courage to say no."

You'll only ruin your life, a voice cried out in me, you should learn to live without children! Forget all those futile attempts to conceive, my head was splitting, those doleful looks at the bellies of pregnant women . . . These children are mentally retarded, you'll ruin your life . . . such a tiny bundle of humanity . . . they're aggressive, dim or even demented, I've got plenty of childless friends . . . unwanted unloved innocent . . . and they're happy . . . just then he moved and purred . . . learn to live without children . . . so sweet and powerless . . . you'll ruin your life . . . I've got plenty . . .

"Please come in," said the consultant.

We walked up to the door of the visiting room.

"We inform all friends that our dearly beloved . . . passed away . . . .

He expired in the prison of the Ministry of Justice at the age of thirty-five.

We bid farewell to him . . . mother, brother, grandmother."

Thus ended the life of a man who wanted to live.

Here, now, and according to his own truth.

And I ask, how does a mother feel who lost her son this way?

And I ask, what did I do to stop it happening?

I have been wearing down my soul and my body with the feeling that there was nothing worse than what was happening to me now.

I managed to convince myself that a child is equal to happiness.

But a child is responsibility. Responsibility for the whole world. Our son is about to have his first birthday.

Translated by David Chirico

Note: In the last passage reference is made to Pavel Wonka, a political prisoner who died in custody as a result of police brutality.

Théta

excerpts from a novel

Daniela Hodrová

F ATHER BECAME ILL IN January, 1984. He was always feeling extremely tired. At the beginning of that summer he went for the
first time into the hospital on Kubelík Street, the Žižkov hospital of
dubious repute. The window of his room, which he shared with six
other patients, opened onto a courtyard closed off by a block of
apartment buildings. One hot afternoon, Karel Milota and I went
searching for the courtyard so that we could at least look up at his
window on the top floor. We walked into buildings and carriageways
filled with unfamiliar smells, stole along well-worn steps toward
doors leading to the courtyard. All the doors were locked, until finally one let us through, but in the courtyard we came up against a
barrier of fences and walls which blocked the view of the hospital
window. At that point we were still unaware of my father's diagnosis. The courtyard with garbage cans and a rack for beating rugs, similar to the courtyard of my childhood, reeked of ashes and rotting
vegetables.

All August they gave father treatments of 40 Gy doses of cobalt
radiation at the Vinohrady hospital, pavilion B. By then father was
back at home. Those fifteen out of eighteen prescribed trips across
the city that he had to endure, despite the fact that barely any hope
remained, were agony for him. I used to take him there either with

my brother or with Eva Tomášková. Father waited for the arrival of the car very impatiently, he was afraid of missing his radiation appointment at 4 p.m. Once, when I couldn't go with him and my brother was late, he stopped a stranger in the street and drove off to pavilion B with him. I always used to wait for father in a narrow hallway crowded with the sick, or rather the condemned. At that hour, around four o'clock, they used to bring a beautiful girl with a shaved head down the hall in a wheelchair; she would fix her slightly slanted oriental eyes on me every time. I knew that the radiation wasn't causing my father any pain, yet still I suffered while the ominous sound of the cobalt bomb went on inside. I imagined how, precisely in the places where they had outlined two purple squares, the cobalt rays were penetrating my father's emaciated chest, attacking the diseased tissue. Father would emerge every time a shade paler, more exhausted, nearer to death.

By the end of September I was allowed to wash the marks away. That was the second time he had to go back to Kubelík Street; after the radiation therapy he stopped eating and grew so weak that he could barely walk, the only thing he liked was milk which he never used to touch before. After sixteen days he left the hospital at his own request; I supported him, practically carried him, he didn't want to wait for the ambulance, we weren't far from home. It was only when we had gone as far as Škroup Square that I noticed I was still wearing the hospital slippers over my shoes.

After that, everything careened unstoppably toward the end. Father started talking about someone who was supposed to come: When will that man come? And then, in the late morning of October 30th, two paramedics grasped him under his arms, "flew" him into the elevator (he was in his pajamas, not even with my help did he have the strength left to dress himself), and brought him back to Kubelík Street for the third time. He didn't want to go to the "croak house," as the locals nicknamed that hospital, he longed to go to the Vinohrady hospital where the head physician, Dr.

Petříková, had been kind to him, but he resided in the wrong district. At that time I wrote to the director of the theater, asking for his help; he never answered. I asked Dr. Indruch if they could at least put father in a smaller room, shared by only two patients. I think he scarcely believed me when I explained that my father was an actor (evidently he had never heard of an actor by that name); to him father was simply a patient with a lung tumor, *moriturus* or rather *moribundus*. He granted my request. Father was put in a small, narrow room with an old gypsy. The gypsy would sing softly to himself all day long: *Nane man, nane man* . . . His singing had an undefined, monotonous melody to it /*ni rat davesoso chi baro pharipen*/, he never stopped, not even on Wednesdays and Sundays when his sizeable family would gather around his bed /*andre mro jiloro*/, underage children waiting outside /*Nane man, nane man*/. They urged him to drink, he refused; they watched him in silence for a while /*ni rat davesoso*/ as he sang /*chi baro pharipen*/, then they all left /*andre mro* . . . That's when Romany became the language of the dead for me, unintelligible as the language of incantations. My father's suffering went on to the sound of the gypsy's singing, perhaps it was a chant for the dying, a lament for the dead.

At that point I went to see my father every day, always around half past four. Sometimes I managed to slip unnoticed past the front desk, where an old woman in a white coat sat. Knitting. Usually, though, I didn't get past the Kubelík Street entrance without lengthy explanations, pleas, a bribe. Once I had to escape from the old woman, I could hear her shouting after me even as I ran up the stairs. On November 15th I went to the hospital at the usual time /Arachne weaving her silk in the darkness/ I was rushing /anxiously silken threads . . . / because I was bringing my father three scrambled eggs, they weren't refrigerated eggs, the Black hen had laid them in the yard in Rosice; I held on to the yellow enameled cup with its lid as if it were a holy relic. I ran through Milešovská Street /weaving in the darkness—*nane man, nane man*/, crossed Ondříček

Street /anxiously the threads—*ni rat davesoso*/, ran through Fibich Street (the streets in this quarter are named after musicians), past the deserted park with tree stumps (there used to be a Jewish cemetery here, all that remains is its oldest section and the plague hospital, which is now the seat of the ŠTUKO plasterers co-operative). That fall our dog Rozina still used to run around there, but soon after father's death they dug a huge pit on the site of the park from which, eventually, shot up the deathly white stem of the television tower (Karel Milota called it the stinkhorn mushroom—*Phallus impudicus*). I passed the telephone exchange /she was knitting silk—*chi baro pharipen*/, inside which little red lights were flashing, and turned into Kubelík Street. At the front desk I hurriedly put on the dark blue cloth slippers. Arachne didn't try to stop me this time, to my amazement she didn't even look up from her knitting. I am racing up to the fifth floor, entering room number 6 (was it really number 6?).

He was lying there. His body was wrapped in a sheet with a blue stripe along the edge, only his white feet were protruding, a tag dangling from his left ankle, ZDENEK HODR, 11/15, 4 p.m. The room was unusually silent, the gypsy wasn't singing. Drifting in through the open window from a window in the opposite house came some isolated phrases from a film that was showing on television. What was distinctly audible in particular was the voice of the announcer reading off names, the names of those who approved of the attempt made on the life the *Reichsprotector*, Reinhard Heydrich. I turned back the corner of the sheet. I stroked my father's cheek, his hands, I touched that place, where they had drawn the mark of death on his chest. In the house across the street they were cooking dinner, the smell wafted into the room. Mr Smolík, who plays the professor in the film, was telling his students: I also approve of the attempt on Heydrich's life. His voice sounded quite close, although in reality we were separated by the breadth of Ševčík Street and the gulf of time. I sat by my father with the eggs, now cold, in my lap (later that night grandmother ate them and became immortal). The gypsy's dark oriental eyes were fixed on me: Don't worry, lady, he didn't die, death just went into him. He asked me to leave him my father's cup as a keepsake—*kuchi*, he called it—and took it into his hands with unusual tenderness. It was a cup with a blue onion motif on it, with a barely perceptible chip along the rim. The next day, when I brought father his suit to the hospital, I gave it to Arachne who, I realized, was not only the gatekeeper, but also the one who dressed the dead before they were put into coffins /Cocoon watching over its existence, lets the weaver's threads pass through/ and a nurse handed me the cup wrapped in coarse tissue paper: he must have taken it from your father . . . .

I think that soon death went into the gypsy on Kubelík Street too, he was apparently suffering from the same illness as my father. Later I saw both of them in a dream (or did I read that in Eliot's *Wasteland?*). They were walking upwards, occasionally letting out a short sigh, each one with his eyes fixed on the ground before him.

A novel about the search for one's father. Telemachus is searching the world for Ulysses. In an adventure novel the hero is searching for his unknown or disappeared father. In an initiation novel the novice is searching for divine initiation. Paternoster . . . the elevator in the radio station building on Vinohrady Avenue, formerly Stalin Avenue. In my childhood, this building, to me, was the labyrinth. The monster's name was Paternoster. Eternally ascending and descending. Today, it represents to me time, the cycle of disappearances and reappearances, of death and rebirth. Those who want to get off the monster or to get on its back must do so precisely at the moment when the floor of the doorless cabin is level with the corridor. Decapitations and quarterings are being carried out continuously here, severed heads, trunks and legs keep growing back on the victims' bodies. The spectator stands witness to countless executions, a public anatomy lesson taking place before his astonished eyes (Dr. Jesenius's renowned anatomy lesson is mentioned in my *Chrysalises*), bodies parading by in an endless and continually repetitive sequence, being disassembled and then reassembled again into wholes, although this time slightly different ones. The passengers are not aware of their transformations, these are apparent only to the spectator.

And who am I as I write this novel? Who do I want to be? The one descending into her past or the one standing aside, watching that other being descend? It's a difficult decision, therefore I keep shifting my position. Down there or up (for what is down is also up)—within a novel anyway—I am reassembling my *membra disjecta* into a fragile, ephemeral whole (one such whole bears the name of Eliška Lamb). I am Eliška Lamb, but at the same time I am the one observing her. Every time Eliška jumps onto the platform of the elevator cabin she agonizes over picking the moment when the platform is level with the corridor, then tries to take as big a step as possible. The more often she gets on, the more dextrous she becomes, her step growing increasingly confident, and then, as she is ascending or descending, she gradually forgets the anxiety she felt when getting on. Much more difficult, it seems, is getting off the elevator. I must take a somewhat bigger step each time lest I remain hovering in the world of the novel. The novel would then carry me along regardless of my will. I want to see my actual self getting on or rather jumping on to the paternoster of the novel, riding up or down on the monster's back, jumping off into reality, from a greater height each time. But how long can I keep lengthening my step, really a leap, it is becoming increasingly precarious. I am afraid that I will forever be reeling about within the sphere of a foreign, fictitious existence, that somewhere halfway along the path I am setting out on I will get stuck—a trunk without a head or a trunk without legs, or a severed head—an irrevocably incomplete being.

My writing desk is in the place where father's couch used to be, his deathbed; we cut it up and splintered the wood, perhaps thinking that we could annul father's death this way. I call the couch his deathbed, although my father actually died in the hospital on Kubelík Street, but it was on that couch that he endured his months of suffering. On this death desk I am writing a novel about a suffering city and about Eliška Lamb, who is searching for her dead father. Eliška's descent to her father will simultaneously be a descent into herself, into her childhood and into her own non-existence. I lay my burning cheek against the desk's cool surface. I begin to descend.

All at once I feel the air stir against my face. I raise my head and see that the curtains on the windows are billowing like sails. I approach a window. The square has turned into a stage—into the theater of the world. Some people are disappearing into a dark passageway (I can only sense it, the church blocks my view), and others are emerging from it. Each one is carrying some kind of burden. And when I look through my opera-glasses, I see that some have heads of birds, others of ground squirrels, one looks like a ram, another like a dog, or perhaps more like a wolf. One woman is hiding a swan's neck in her upturned collar, another, with her bloated stomach, resembles a cocoon waiting for the hour of its metamorphosis. And suddenly in the midst of that crowd, shuffling in and out, up and down, I spot a child wearing a dark gray knitted peaked cap. The child is threading its way through the crowd, maybe it's lost. Moving close to the child is . . . I recognize her by her cap which is similar to the child's, differing only in color—it's bright scarlet. It is precisely by this close fitting cap (a cowl?) and also by the long velvet cape that I recognize her, because Death got her face from a picture that used to hang in the tavern in Modřany, and it looks just like all other faces in that town, except perhaps a shade paler. A gust of wind blows open the cape of the one who is moving unnoticed through the crowd, and I see: she is not leading the child, although she stays close to it—woe! she is warming her bony fingers in a Persian lamb muff.

Eliška Lamb, of course, did not know it yet, but for many years afterwards she was convinced that precisely at the moment that she lost her Persian lamb muff somewhere along the cemetery wall, her mother, somewhere in the mountains, died. In reality it happened three years later, when her mother, leaving for the mountains again, took the muff along. By now it is hard for Eliška to remember what her mother looked like, she only knows her from some dozen wedding photographs taken by Drbohlav, the theater photographer, in which her father is wearing a dark pinstripe suit and her mother a wide-brimmed hat decorated with bird-of-paradise feathers, as was fashionable in those days, just after the war. In the photograph of mother standing with father inside the church and then sitting with him in the carriage that drove them from St. Ludmila's Church to Peace Square and from there to the house across from the Olšany cemetery, mother looks like a movie star.

And then she knows her likeness from two other photographs: one is of the whole family, Eliška is a newborn, wrapped in swaddling clothes (note, the first cocoon!), and the other is of mother sitting with Eliška and her stepbrother. Her stepbrother is in pajamas, he had a bad ear infection, and Eliška is wearing a dark dress with a lace collar and a butterfly in her hair, which is actually a giant bow. There is, however, yet another photograph from the time of her brother's illness. In it, she and her brother are already alone. Each time she looks at that other photograph, it seems to her that that is when her mother left for the Tatra Mountains, during the interval between the taking of the two photographs, even though it had to have been a few days, or perhaps even a few weeks, later. Evidently this is a repetition of what she already experienced once before with the photographs from which the muff vanished (or was she not the one who experienced it?). Mother departed from the photograph into the Tatra Mountains, and in those days Eliška believed that if she put on the dress with the lace collar and her brother put on his pajamas, mother would return to the photograph and to their home. And she thought that that's when she would even find the lost muff.

I am writing this about Eliška Lamb's mother, for my mother, in fact, died much later, when I was twenty-eight. Also, she didn't die of tuberculosis, which she had contracted during the war and then treated for several years still after the war (when I was a child, the word pneumothorax had a magical power), but of the disease that afflicted Nora Kožíšková; and Helena Syslová. I used to go to see her in the St Francis hospital, pulling on plastic slippers and ascending the stairs rumored to have been constructed from the wood of the executioner's scaffold used after the battle of White Mountain. The death that I am writing about now is not hers, but the death of Mrs. Lamb, Eliška Lamb's mother.

Eliška Lamb doesn't know exactly when her mother died. She only remembers the moment when her mother left for the mountains. She left behind a half-empty armoire in her bedroom. Eliška used to shut herself up in that armoire every day. She would sit there, her knees pulled up to her chin, inhaling the scent of her mother's clothes, of silk and dusting powder. The top of her head brushed lightly against the dresses hanging above her, the clothes were coming alive, rubbing against each other and against her burning cheeks. Several empty hangers, set swaying by the motion, rattled mysteriously. Sometimes Eliška would wrap her head into one of the dresses and, holding her breath just like when you go for a chest X-ray on Jesenius Street (Inhale, hold your breath, exhale!), she would wait for the giddy moment of metamorphosis.

One day, from within the armoire, Eliška heard the word caverna. Her father said it. Grandmother cried out: Oh no! That night they told the children that mother still had to stay in the mountains for a while, the mountain air was good for her. After that, no one at home ever spoke of mother again, and Eliška never asked, she came to terms with the fact that her mother was in the mountains, living in a cave (for caverna, as great-uncle Leopold Petroušek explained to her, means cave in Latin), with stalactites hanging all around her.

Some time later Eliška again enters the armoire, curls up with her knees pulled up to her chin so that, without even realizing it, she assumes the fetal position. To no avail does she move her head, raise her arms, to revive mother's orphaned dresses so that she could bury her burning face in them. The empty hangers rattle mysteriously above her head like the heaps of shells in the house of Diviš Paskal's great-grandmother, the mother-of-pearl queen. A trace of the scent still lingers here, the scent of silk and dusting powder, but even that gradually disappears. In the corner of the armoire Eliška discovers mother's crumpled silk scarf. Carefully she spreads it out on the floor, what if the scarf contains a message? And truly—behold a circle in the center of the scarf, within the circle glides a sailboat, three white lilies float above it, and beneath the circle are the mysterious words EXPOSITION PARIS 1937.

Eliška Lamb arrives in Paris on August 20, 1968. When she wakes up the next day for the first time in the city which she has dreamed of over her mother's scarf since her childhood, she learns the fate of her native city. She only half understands the accounts told in a foreign language, in her mind her city has become a heap of ruins. She doesn't even know if her house is still standing, or if her dear ones are alive. And on precisely that day in Paris, although it only seems possible in a novel, she meets, after many years, her first love. It is strange that Eliška Lamb, as a grown up, never ran into Pavel Fink in the suffering city, and that she saw him of all places in Paris, not far from the Nôtre Dame Cathedral, and of all days on August 21st.

When Pavel Fink steps into the narrow room with a window to the courtyard in the cheap little hotel in rue Racine where Eliška is staying, he is not wearing his childhood sweater with reindeer on it, which she saw him in on the merry-go-round. He is holding Ála Antošová (or is it Fink by now?) by the hand. In his other hand he carries a small brown hardtop suitcase. Eliška knows the suitcase from the time they were leaving from Balbín Street in an old blue bus, heading for Midas's summer camp.

That night she slept on the floor and left them the bed. Through half-closed eyes she watched as Ála climbed naked into bed beside Pavel Fink, she saw Pavel Fink stroking Ála's growing stomach, putting his ear to it, maybe within he would hear the voice of the one who was conceived in the suffering city and would be born abroad. In the middle of the night, when Ála and Pavel thought she was asleep, they turned on the light, opened up the suitcase on the bed, and slowly and lovingly looked over all the things they had bought. Eliška Lamb could still visualize that nocturnal scene long afterwards, in a train full of sleeping Czechs returning to their homeland (Pavel Fink and Ála were not among them) when, huddled under a coat, she shut her eyes. Underneath, in bold newspaper print, the caption read: PRAGUE: 21 AOÛT 1968.

I am shedding my skin. It is causing me unspeakable agony. My cuticle is already cracked in two places anyway, there where, some time ago, Truth grazed my throat and the talon of Reality gouged my forehead. I am not Eliška Lamb, I am Daniela Hodrová. Are you content, winged gentlemen? Are you resting firmly on your plinths atop the roof of the Vinohrady Theater, or are you getting ready again to take flight, to which your metal wings make you so ill-suited?

Eliška Lamb doesn't exist. It was I who saw Mr. Chaun with his Creature, it is I who am descending into a tropical landscape where a dying poet in a wheelchair—my father Zdeněk—is composing his last poem; it was I who rushed down the corridor to Studio 6, who, dressed in Joan of Arc's costume, danced with Comrade Midas, I who heard the young man singing "Where is my home" as I was returning from Kubelík Street. It's just that now, having shed Eliška Lamb's cuticle (in several places tattered shreds are still hanging from me), a strange feeling overcomes me: what if Eliška Lamb goes on living, independently of my will? What if all fictitious characters from novels continue to dwell somewhere, just like the dead, enveloping our world in an increasingly airtight sheath formed even of all our feelings and memories (Břetislav Kafka, in his *Experimental Psychology*, calls this sheath a *protonation*)? And how then, having discarded all the larvae, taken off the countless waistcoats like a circus clown, am I to express the difference in the vantage point from which I view my past as a performance, seated in the wings from where I can follow more closely not only the play but also the entrances and exits of the actors? They are waiting behind me for their scenes, for their cues; I can feel their hot breath on my neck, hear what they're whispering, and when I turn around I see that some of them are standing about with their hands up, because, as my father once explained to me, it will make their arms look whiter. By now I know the performance of *The Night of the Iguana* almost by heart, but each time it unfolds in a slightly different way. I also know in advance how it will end, yet I continue to harbor a glimmer of hope that, one day, I will be able to enter it and change its course.

And which point of view is actually more truthful, closer to reality? The point of view of the spectator looking out from the darkness of the auditorium across the footlights and believing temporarily that real life is taking place up on the stage before his eyes? This illusion is at its most perfect if one adheres to the rule of the three unities—of time, place and action (which, however, I keep breaking), and this holds especially true when the place happens to be the stage itself, as is the case in Pirandello's *Six Characters in Search of an Author* or in Bartoš's *Stage Revolt*. Or is the more truthful point of view the skewed one of an actor's child, peering over a fireman's helmet, the view, obscured every now and then by dark-colored shawls, in which repartee from the play-as-reality mingle with those of the actors in the wings, backstage, coming from their lives? From out there the spectator perceives only the text of the play, only the actors' bodies and voices which, for him, fuse with the characters; here, backstage, the actors' voices mingle with the insistent whisper of Mr. Hovorka, the stage manager, calling actors from their dressing rooms to the stage, and with the whisper of Mrs. Nedvědová, the prompter, reciting the lines of all the characters, word by word, in a monotonous voice, so that the actors' repartee actually comes off as a resounding echo of her disinterested drone. Where are you, gentlemen of stone, to answer this question for me?

I know how my descent is going to end one day. I will slide down the ramp toward the auditorium which, however, will no longer be of this world. For the past is akin to a utricle of a carnivorous plant, to a pitfall, to a gravitational trap. Mr. Turk, who is an entomologist, but also knows about carnivorous plants because they actually belong to a related field, would say that it could be one of the genera *Nepenthes* or *Sarracenia*, a kind of pitcher plant. The trap-like organs of a pitcher plant consist of three zones. The task of the first, outermost one is to lure and direct the victim to the neck of the utricle and for that purpose it is equipped with nectar-producing glands and with spines pointing in toward the trap. The second zone leads the victim further into the trap. On the way down, the nectar-producing glands become smaller, scarcer, and gradually disappear. The surface of this zone allows for movement in the downward direction only. The more frantically the descending victim attempts to escape as it realizes what danger lies ahead, the faster it gets to the bottom. Deep within, at the very bottom, where the greatest metamorphosis takes place, the cavity is as smooth as a womb. *Regressus ad uterum*. Return into the devouring and life-giving womb where the past merges with the future.

I will be swallowed up by the carnivorous past which has burgeoned in the tropical landscape on the stage of the Vinohrady Theater. There it waits for me with its gravitational trap. The plants entwining my bare calves are not carnivorous. For the moment I am still within the first zone. I am tasting the nectar of the past. Nepenthes—"grief-banishing"—was the supposed name of the as yet unidentified drug the ancient Greeks used to mix with wine into a potion to induce forgetting. Forgetting? But what I long for is a potion to induce remembering! Am I then actually moving in the right direction? By now, however, I have already reached the edge of the second zone, its surface allows for downward movement only. I am descending . . . .

I am entering the Olšany house of my childhood. I call it that because it stands across from the Olšany cemetery. We lived in that house until I was thirteen years old. I often dream about returning there. Surprisingly, the house in George of Poděbrady Square, where I have been living for more than twice as long, hardly ever comes into my dreams. Over the many years since we moved I have actually entered the Olšany house only a few times; once also, early in our relationship, in the company of Karel Milota. It is a ceremonial journey for me, which is why I make it only rarely. Each time I embark upon it in reality, in a dream, or in a novel, I get closer to the mystery of the place and to the meaning of my existence.

Behind the heavy front door there are seven steps of grayish marble, the same marble which lines the walls of the hall up to the height of a man's shoulders. The marble is already badly cracked (its cracks have begun to form dendrite crystallizations), and even the steps are chipped here and there. As a child I used to walk down taking two, three steps at a time, I could actually jump down from the very top; it was a dangerous leap, a slightly weaker push-off meant I could have landed on one of the lower steps. On the other hand, had I pushed off too hard, my head could have ended up in the glass of the front door.

Now, however, I ascend the stairs very carefully so as not to miss a single one, as if my ascension of the seven steps were a kind of a ritual formula whose words must be uttered in a given sequence, none of them allowed to be left out. At the top of the stairs I stop. Two wings of a swinging glass door block the way like a gate through which it is impossible to glimpse the interior of the house; beyond them there is darkness, their glass reflects a slightly smaller and somewhat slanted front door. I remember that this reflection always fascinated me. It seemed that, through the door wings, I was not about to enter the interior of the house but, instead, to re-enter the smaller, slanted front door and pass again into the space below the seven steps which would be proportionately diminished. It would be very difficult to ascend those miniature steps, each little step just barely able to accommodate the toes of my foot; yet even then, then in particular, I could not afford to miss a single step. And after that I would reach another double swinging door, also small, reflecting an even smaller front door. And I couldn't enter it at all, not even if I stooped all the way down, not even if I crawled. Let alone then try, without changing into a marionette, to ascend the tiny steps, so tiny that one's fingers at the most could walk up them.

Once, when I was not quite seven years old, the image took me so strongly that I grew dizzy and had to lean against the wall. By chance Peter Celestial happened to be walking by (in fact, he had probably been lurking behind the door, because had he just come out of his apartment, I would have noticed him). As the boy with the seraphic name (his name is not invented, the superintendent's son was really named that) flung open the double doors, I felt an excruciating pain: the middle finger of my right hand was caught in the hinges. Within three days I had a case of blood poisoning, only then did I confess what had happened; my finger was operated on by Dr. Tošovský. In those days I was convinced that the boy with the seraphic name had done it on purpose so that he could make me sit on their vinyl-covered kitchen sofa and blow at my bluish, flattened finger.

Every time I passed through the swinging doors as a child, I would throw the whole weight of my body against them, and when they would swing open I would charge through so that the heavy wings wouldn't hurl me back down the stairs or crush me between them. Even though I always ran through fast, I always managed to inhale the smell of cabbage emanating from the superintendent's apartment. Behind me, I would always hear three booming, progressively fading reverberations of the still swinging doors. I never looked back, as though such a look might enable the doors to reel me in, to crush me in the narrow crack between the wings and then spit me out again, flattened like the finger, into the space before them, before the perpetually smaller and smaller, eternally repeated reflection of the other door. And at that moment the wings of the swinging door would be so heavy that, however much I tried, I couldn't get them to open again.

This time I didn't run through the door, after all, I have been grown up for a long time, I'm practically on the threshold of old age, I know that one adequate push is sufficient and then I can fearlessly (truly fearlessly?) pass through. I passed through unhurriedly. And having passed through, I even broke the ancient taboo and looked back; and I actually saw, for the very first time, the door wings swinging three times to the booming, reverberating sound which resounded as it always had. And then I froze. At that moment my (her) eyes spotted the name on the door of the super's apartment: JAROSLAV BRIAR. It throws me since it had always been HELENA CELESTIAL. Of course there's nothing strange about this, I haven't walked into the wrong house, only in the course of the three decades that we have no longer lived here, the people and their names have changed.

I continue (she continues) along my (her) way. I am (she is) always curiously excited upon penetrating into the interior of a house. I worry (she worries) that I (she) could disappear into the house like into a black hole. Even today the unusual spaciousness of the house surprises me (her). In this case, oddly enough, the rule that a space, perceived by a child as enormous, shrinks in the eyes of an adult, does not apply. On the contrary: never before has the house seemed so large to me (her). It appears to me (her) to be a bizarrely grandiose and almost monstrous project by an unknown architect in which the staircase forms a U-shaped frame within the vast, empty space of the house. There is nothing in the middle, the gaping empty space exists perhaps for the sole purpose of introducing the notion of an abyss, a void with a grayish marble bottom, into the tenants' lives.

Every time I (she) walked or ran up the staircase (CHILDREN UNDER 14 YEARS OF AGE MAY USE THE ELEVATOR ONLY WHEN ACCOMPANIED BY AN ADULT), I (she) had to fight a cowardly impulse to walk closely along the wall, keeping as far away as possible from the abyss in the middle, frightening and enticing at the same time. Coming down was even more dangerous. On one side breathed the abyss, on the other the wall was coming alive with strange pictures: images of phantasmagorical animals and contours of alpine landscapes began to surface on it. And then, between the fifth and the sixth floors, there appeared one day the sharp profile of an old man with a prominent nose, the crown of his head looked as if it had been cut off. Now I am (she is) approaching the spot. Just now I am (she is) passing a picture of a tropical landscape with palms that I have (she has) never noticed before. He is still there: beneath several coats of paint the profile of the old man with the crown of his head cut off is discernible. Doesn't this portrait look like a death-mask? Only today do I (does she) recognize the features of the papal envoy, his profile had been stamped here many years before father was cast in that episodic role. And the same is true of the tropical landscape which I begin (she begins) to recognize now as that of Costa Verde. And if I (she) were able to read the fresco of the future, I (she) would also discover, amid the clusters of seemingly haphazard stains and cracks, all my (her) various likenesses from birth to death and, simultaneously, all the landscapes of my (her) life.

She is standing in front of their Olšany apartment. The name on the door reads DAVIDOVIČ. She presses her body against the door. She tries to breathe as quietly as possible, even tries to hold her breath so that the one pressing her body and face against the door from within can't hear her. The being inside is also breathing very quietly so that the one on the threshold can't hear her. In spite of that, each can hear the other clearly (or have their breaths become one?). She is contemplating the name Davidovič. She is sure that last time it still read ANASTÁZIE MARTÍNKOVÁ. They had exchanged apartments with the Martíneks at the time. Alice Davidovič was her classmate but she lived near the gate of the Jewish cemetery, she might even have been the rabbi's daughter. Later on . . . They both hold their breaths. The one inside is wearing a knitted peaked cap, she will shortly go for a walk along the cemetery wall with her father and brother. She will be hiding her hands in a Persian-lamb muff. Who actually . . . ?

Had she been thinking up to now that the only thing that has happened, is happening and will happen in this novel is the death of her father, she realized the moment she stepped through the swinging doors of the Olšany house and, unwittingly, into the next novel, that her father's death is only one of the countless events in this narrative and, if she wants to reach the bottom of the abyss where the Irradiated One is waiting, she must proceed through all the other events which at first seemed totally unrelated to her father's death. Suddenly she realized that just as her every movement encompasses all her previous movements and also all the ones she is yet to make, so is her life unfolding amidst a throng of existences, of other characters' lives which continue but, at the same time, at any given moment, are repeating all their phases. She can capture only mere fragments of those lives and only insofar as they live within her. In the multitude of existences she carries inside her, it is very difficult not to lose one's own likeness, to remain oneself. And the identity of an object becomes equally problematic, that of her muff, for example. Her muff? That muff, whose origin lies somewhere in the dark ages of a novel, does not hold a spell merely over her childhood but also over the lives of many other people, be they real or fictitious, possibly over those of the whole world which coils up and spirals back onto itself, as Teilhard de Chardin said (and

Michel Foucault repeated after him), for even the most insignificant and most ordinary object (although such a muff is hardly an ordinary object) contains within itself all other objects and human lives, and even the historical events of the world with their endless chain of causes and effects. Finding the lost muff would then mean . . . .

The letter ϑ (théta), which appeared to me in the likeness of a beetle drowned in the toilet bowl of the Ural hotel, had not always been a proofreaders' mark. Originally, as Eva Stehlíková explained to me, it conveyed a different meaning, naturally one closely related to the modern one. Medieval scribes used to write this letter next to the names of deceased monks: ϑ meant *thanatos*—death, dead. I suppose that had Umberto Eco, author of *The Name of the Rose*, known this detail, he would certainly not have failed to use it in his novel.

I am beginning to discern a possible interpretation of the Rosice "lamb" text which, as long as I didn't know the meaning of the letter ϑ (am I going to pay for my curiosity with my life as did the monks in Eco's novel?), seemed indecipherable: a blind knight or a letter. The letter is neither α nor ω, the letters of Christ the Lamb in The Revelation of Saint John (I am the Alpha and the Omega, the beginning and the end, the first and the last), but ϑ—the knight Thanatos. In this novel ϑ means descent to the dead one, to the dead of this city. Besides this meaning there is, however, an additional meaning, only seemingly contradictory: ϑ, if I am not mistaken, signifies a strange undulation which binds an organism to its life.

I am struggling through the manuscript. It is growing into a primeval forest around me, I am becoming lost in it, myriad tendrils of sentences coil about my arms and legs. A beast darts among the trees. Brightly colored tropical birds are screeching in the treetops, here and there a wood nymph or a wild man hides among the luxuriant tangle of acanthus branches, further away grotesque creatures wearing pointed fool's caps are scampering about. Have I landed on a page of a medieval manuscript? Or is this the landscape of Costa Verde? That's what it is, the text has turned into a wild landscape through which I am descending to the sea. When I bend over the manuscript, I can smell its scent.

Eliška Lamb, the one whom I have made into my cocoon and in whom I am anxiously awaiting my last metamorphosis, has known how to write the letter ϑ for a long time. Her hand slips but rarely on the paper and at that moment a letter from the alphabet of an unknown language comes into being. The strange letter forces its way onto the paper like a coded message from a world of which Eliška has but a vague notion, that world terrifies and entices her at the same time. The wild letter, a mutation of the letter ϑ, begins to disappear only after several applications of the white correction fluid with which Eliška always carefully conceals the constantly resurfacing unknown character, perhaps for fear lest it bring forth some unexpected, horrifying meaning (can there be any meaning, however, more horrifying than the original one?), which could no longer be covered up.

Wearied by prolonged reading, Eliška Lamb suddenly lets her hand slip again, another monstrous mutation of the letter ϑ comes into the world. Engrossed in her reading, she doesn't notice it this time, doesn't immediately cover it with the white correction fluid (WHITE FLUID . . . *cosí sbagliare non é piú un problema!*) the way one covers the body and face of a dead person with a shroud or a sheet, her eyes are eagerly hurrying along the lines of the novel. And that's when it happens. The strange letter, more like an alpha than a théta, stirs. It is crawling along the margin of the text. Eliška Lamb stares at the phenomenon in astonishment. No, this is not a *Blatta orientalis*, the cockroach which appeared to her in the Ural hotel, this is a scarab, an Egyptian hieroglyph meaning "to be" (CHPR— *cheprer*), and it has come alive. And Eliška, following with horror the pilgrimage of the To Be beetle along the top of her writing desk, suddenly understands: under particular circumstances, a strange, practically inimitable squiggle on paper, touched for an instant by a ray of sun, becomes a living creature. Which interwoven strokes, which phantasmagorical scrolls on the manuscript page, and which circumstances could bring her to life, help her fight her way out of the cocoon of a fictitious character into her existence? For that's what seems to be the issue, now she knows it, not to be a mere cocoon, an invented character someone else is writing about. But in what manner, through which gate could Eliška pass from the world of the novel into reality? And wouldn't she then, much more than in the scene in the church of the Virgin Mary of the Snows, be running the risk of being whited out, deleted (to remove her from the face of the earth like a typo would be no problem for the author!) simply because in a margin of the manuscript, beside her name, will be written ϑ, a letter that kills?

Eliška Lamb lays her head down on the writing desk, upon a stack of papers. And just as her forehead touches the papers—the proofs of Elsa Morante's novel *Aracoeli* are suddenly no longer lying on the desk; instead, her head is resting on a manuscript called *Théta*—it happens. Somewhere, close to where it says "lays her head down on the writing desk" (the desk has undergone a metamorphosis too, it's no longer the battered office desk on the sixth floor of Odeon Publishers but a table with lion claws standing in a house in George of Poděbrady Square), my pen slips, and just then a host of the afternoon sun's rays hits the paper . . . She grabs her pen, begins to write: I am Eliška Lamb, the beginning and . . . .

I am descending. A steep winding path leads me down. There, in the shade behind the myrtle bush, I sense the entrance to the cave. Within is the one who hid Dionysus (or Gabčík?) from the bull, she who rode the dolphin naked, she who, when Peleus captured her, changed successively into fire, water, a lion, a serpent and a cuttlefish. In order to make her sons immortal like herself, she burned their mortal parts; having no time left to burn the ankle bone of the last one, she disguised him as a girl. She lead the Argonauts safely through the Wandering Rocks. Thetis?—Marie Lamb.

Translated by Tatiana Firkusny and Véronique Firkusny-Callegari

The Funeral

Alexandra Berková

> The cemeteries are full of those without whom
> the world could not exist!
> —*Heinrich Böll*

THAT'S ODD, SAID the man in astonishment, a fellow's hardly got properly started—and already it's time to finish, because he's dead . . . .

—so he said, and his soul left the body—it hung about for a bit, ready to return, just in case—suppose for instance they removed that lump which was clogging up his heart—

—but it took quite a while before they found him, and then there was a big fuss and hubbub; they hauled him off the ground into an armchair, then back out of the armchair on to the ground, surprised, uncomprehending, jostling around and saying: but how come? how come he's dead? when only a moment ago he was alive?

—and they slapped him about the cheeks and called him by name—then they shrugged their shoulders, covered him with a large poster and went their ways, clearing their throats awkwardly—

—and his soul was overcome with a great sorrow, because it had nowhere to live, nothing to do here anymore, and so it sent a last message of greeting to all who knew it, and went to join its ancestors.

But the funeral was something no-one could remember having experienced for a very long time!

From the loudspeakers on the square the widow's sobbing resounded from the crack of dawn, inside the gates of the house of mourning allegorical floats were assembled, behind them a throng of curious onlookers. It was not long before the widow came into view: her coat turned inside out and with the buttons at the back to demonstrate non-acceptance of the dead man's death, solemnly she passed by them and went to stand at the head of the cortege. Music sounded: the procession moved off.

In front, just after the widow, there stepped the highest-up representatives of the community: the most attractive, the wisest, the most delicately well-fed, the best lamenting—

—following these, other relatively high-up representatives: the more delicate, the better, the more wisely well-fed, the more attractively lamenting—

and finally the other high-up representatives: attractive, delicate, well-fed, and wisely lamenting —

—they walked at a solemn pace, as befits dignitaries, now and again someone nodded his head, coughed, blew his nose, sank at the knees . . . .

—and now here come the guilds!

cloakroom attendants, arsonists, freemasons, coffin-manufacturers, sponsors and censors,

Nobel-prizewinners,

envoys, outlaws, conscripts and cousins,

former monarchs, future rag-and-bone men, men for a rainy day—

—all here to pay their respects to the widow's grief . . . .

Meanwhile aged Great-Aunt in the house of mourning saw out the last remaining guest and shut the front door. Many a chore awaited her yet: washing and putting away the crockery, the furniture, the corpse of the late lamented: also, the clothes and coffin had to be returned to the rental shop by the close of the day. Aged ancient Great-Aunt tied on her apron, and started slowly to undress the deceased, singing to him all the while her ancient same old song:

"You were born into anxiety behind a screen and you died into anxiety behind a screen, oh my sweet boy, pity you didn't say the word, I would've come to hold your hand at least—what's to become of me here all alone, aged Great-Aunt, with my skin like an old prune . . .

all my own I've put in the ground already, five sets of mourning garb I've torn to shreds, I've buried my mum, my dad, sis, brother, all my aunts and all my uncles, nephews and nieces—what's to become of me here all alone, aged Great-Aunt, with my skin like an old prune . . . ."

At this point a stranger came up to her, he doffed his yellow helmet, and he said: this is a kind of dumb thing to be wearing on my head, but they told me to wear it, so I does. I knew him, you know. She still thinks about him, all the time she does. Years and years it is, since all of it happened.

Well, well, said ancient Great-Aunt.

I can it see like it was today: the silence. And how he rose to his feet and said the word: I. You wouldn't understand that, you wouldn't.

Ah mmh—said Great-Aunt.

A woman never understands a thing like that, said the man.

Meanwhile beneath the windows the allegorical floats pass, tableaux vivants, living images of glorious moments in a person's life:

—on the first a woman raises up high a plaster babe-in-arms, she marks it with a number and carries it off behind the screen, returning a moment later to raise up high the plaster babe-in-arms, mark it with a number and carry it off behind the screen, and so on ad infinitum—and all around the first things of Man are depicted: the first wee-wee in the potty—the first class at school—the first wet dream—the first marriage; the first kiss, slap, tooth, and smile—all reproduced in rich-colored plaster—in the center of the cart an upright young sapling in blue, a man's vertical take-off in the color of hope—

—on the second are depicted horizontal things, broad and basic: a bed, a pastry, a desk, a map, an escalope and some letter-writing paper, a gramophone, a plate and a bath—all that belongs in a ripe, full-blooded and widely spreading life—and the tree in the middle is stout-trunked and bushy, in the red color of meat—

—on the third the last things of Man pass by: medicinal pills and reading spectacles, medals, slippers and rusks, diplomas, teeth and collected writings, cold tisane, boxes of photographs and new spring shoes—all in the color of the ashes to which all things on earth return—and a naked tree in their midst—

Meanwhile Great-Aunt carefully brushed and folded the garments of the deceased and laid them in the coffin. Then she wrapped the body in an old tablecloth and threw it over her shoulder. That integument of yours is heavy, my boy, you mustn't eat so much in the future, she said, leaving the house. She had to take a roundabout route, following the back paths, to avoid disrupting the festivities.

Now dashing down the high street come the motley clowns and conjurers, with much blaring of party whistles, rattles and hooters, tutu dancers popping off garish firecrackers, everything flashes and glitters, the whole place is full of singing, hue and cry and clamor: here some singer declaims his song beating its rhythm on a metal barrel, here another shrieks and accompanies himself on a washboard; here a pair pretend to wrestle, another to be in love, this man tears out his hair and roars of his solitude, another cries out: mommy!!—

—but now there come cackling masks bearing great mirrors, in which the people on the pavement see themselves as equally attractive, wise and well-to-do as those at the head of the procession . . .

—and all rejoice and greet the conjurers with great acclamation, a couple of bold spirits even try to grab a bit of the action—a colored bow, a sleeve, or at least the little finger of their object of adoration—

—and all are happy, they wave and laud the travelling minstrels with their fond illusion of having helped people to live so merrily and well—

—and one woman said to another: look at the beauty of it all! you know, happiness is something I just adore!—and my little brat, however much I take him and thrash him, he just won't be happy, not never . . . !!!

The old woman with her bundle walked slowly on. The man in the helmet joined her after a while and walked along beside her.

Well, well, said Great-Aunt, there you are, you see. Loads of folks are passing on, and here I am, still around in spite of it all. I simply wake up in the morning every time over and over.

I was fond of the chap as well, the silly fool, said the man. She thinks I wasn't, but oh yes I was.

They say I was spotted the other day in town shopping at the Co-op. Lord, says I, maybe that could finally be the sign; before she died, you see, my poor mother started to split in two like that as well, said Great-Aunt.

The things that happen, said the man.

Slowly the sky is overcast with gray-black clouds, but above the horizon a low evening sun still glows. On the eastern side it works marvels: against the dark purple backcloth of the cloud last year's dried-up grass shines yellow, upon it gleam whitely the pinkish-tinged crowns of the bare birches. The refuse dump on the side opposite blazes with colored wrappings and fragments of broken pots and tin cans.

It's going to thunder, said Great-Aunt, lowering her bundle and sitting down on it. Bad things come out of the earth at this time, come and sit yourself down here on something soft, she said, making room next to her for the man. She took out a bottle: there's nothing wrong with me, I just gets a bit run-down now and again. Many's the time I just have to take a wee dram first thing in the morning.

A pale girl in a house with gargoyles gazed out of the window until the noble procession had disappeared round the corner, then she looked at the roof of the house opposite: the brick chimney glowed red-orange against an ink-blue sky. The stucco of the house shone yellow and the window panes had a metallic hard mirror-like sheen. It's going to thunder.

The girl returned to the manual of her scholarly catechism:

"Everything is relative. Everything is thus a matter of relation. The only valid relation is that of love. It follows validly that God is love."

The girl put her fists over her ears, fixed her gaze on the sunlit roof opposite, and began to recite:

"Love is a centrifugal force, relaxing, creative; it brings forth good. The absence of love is Angst. Angst is a centripetal force, tensing, deadening, egocentric; it brings forth evil."

This is what is keeping her away from the festivities.

"Without God, that is to say without a relation or love we fall into an existential inferno."

Because she has to take this exam tomorrow.

"Breathing in—and breathing out; the time of accumulation of stone and the time of dispersal of stone: oscillation is the basic motion of the universe."

But she wants to go to the celebration.

"In other words E=mc^2."

She has to go.

Great-Aunt and the man drank and stood up. The gray quilt of clouds above them was rent and on the horizon it fell in tatters to the ground.

It's raining over Bytiny, said Great-Aunt, taking her bundle up on her shoulders. The man walked on beside her.

Things are complicated so often in this life, he said, only you wouldn't ever grasp how that is. A woman doesn't grasp things the way a fellow does. Women have it simpler. Take for instance the time he got up and said that word into the silence: I. You wouldn't understand that. She doesn't understand that either.

Great-Aunt straightened her back and looked up: lovely white fluffy clouds were suddenly rolling about in a blue sky like nobody's business. Great-Aunt breathed in: mmmmh-don't-you-feel-it? It's spring. If things go well, summer will follow.

The man went on: take for instance the subject of death. You're not afraid of it. I am. I've always been. Not that I'm a coward or something—it's not that I—what I mean to say is—if you think that *I* would ever—

Course not, of course I don't, said Great-Aunt.

There you are! said the man. It's not that I'm afraid—but I fear it, if you follow me, if you know what I mean.

I do, said Great-Aunt.

Because: we die—and then what then, eh? Nobody knows. Only, that sort of thing don't interest a woman, questions like that, women don't care about that. That's just the way you are, you see. Sort of simple and straightforward. Looking after people, and that sort of thing.

Um ah well—said Great-Aunt, shifting the bundle over to her other shoulder.

But a bloke—a BLOKE, you follow?—he's in the world for a totally different reason! A BLOKE, he's—he oughta—he has to—know what I mean?

Yes, yes, said Great-Aunt.

Has to PROVE something!—DO something!!—simply in a nutshell—leave some kind of TRACE—or IMPACT!—after himself—something GREAT!!—you know what I mean . . . .

I do, said Great-Aunt.

Anyway a woman can never understand that kind of thing . . . in a nutshell, there's got to be something—SOMETHING!!

—only you see I've got terribly little time in which to do it, there's the rub. A person can die any moment—and what if I don't manage to achieve it?—what then?—eh?

—well then there would be absolutely nothing to remain after me—

—and that would be really terrible—

—I mean—I find it absolutely unimaginable—

—the man walked on for a moment without saying a word.

And yet a man can die any moment! any moment!

Any moment something could fall on my head!

That why I'm wearing this dumb thing. They told me to wear it, so I does.

I'd be glad to help you any way I could, mister, but I don't know how, said Great-Aunt, putting her bundle on the ground, rolling it to the brink of the refuse dump and pushing it over. Well, now, my lad, she said, this is the most I can do for you—tidy up your mortal integument. The wind'll scatter it with earth and birch trees will grow, she said, shoving on top some broken glasses, cans and grit.

If only you could see yourself now, Franta, you with all your fine talk—there you are in that sack and I'm still here.

Back at the cemetery the festivities were still in full swing: the chair-lady of the Union of Abandoned Women welcomed a new member, a chorus of girls from the Marian Sisterhood sang, while the main speech was delivered by an arch-enemy of the deceased: he valued greatly the great value accorded to his publication *The Cycle of Time in Nature*; he raised the subject of the depth of his grief; then in con-clusion he nicely recalled some moments which never were, and an-nounced the climax of the entire celebration: the Great Widow's Dance.

The multitude fell silent: the widow slowly came forward and traced out a circle—the space in which she would tell her story—then she closed her eyes, raised her arms—and gently lowered them again shyly—yes: she is a little girl again now, quite naive: she twitches the corners of her skirt, skipping with little tiny steps through the dew-dropped meadow—sniffing at the flowers—she is delicate and fragile and oh so utterly, utterly happy!

—but now—look—some unknown rough person descends upon the fragile maidenly dream!—is this not some enemy?—will he not harm her?

—she ought to run away, but she is bound inside by silver threads—ah, what is budding there in that tender heart?—

—a sweet jelly-like feeling at the knees—and HE is so powerful—so strong—

—he'll stop at nothing!—but—ah!—at nothing!—oh, my God!

"The first scene of the maiden's seduction concludes *giocoso in-nocente* (playfully, innocently), and after a brief pause it is followed by the next section, the two halves of which—*allegro appassionato* (vivaciously, passionately) and *andante affannato* (slowly, anx-iously)—convincingly illustrate the deep inner life of the misun-derstood wife and her solitude at the side of her selfish husband, totally bound up in his work, failing to grasp the deep inner life of his misunderstood wife. The final *allegro sdegnoso* (briskly, defiantly) culminates in a thrilling *presto furioso* (swiftly, furiously) over the death of the husband."

The commentator cleared his throat under his breath, adjusted his tie and went off to find some entertainment.

Meanwhile Great-Aunt and the man walked slowly back. The man said: in the second class of primary they taught us that time was a property of matter. Which means in fact that as we shed matter from ourselves, we lose our own time in the process. You've no idea how much of life is lost to us this way! Just take the hair for instance! Now I for example have kept all my teeth stored away. I did have my finger and toe nails as well, but she went and threw them out. But I still have my child's plate with a tin mug—and the mess-tin from my military service—and the plaster as well from the time I broke this here finger—also I always have my photograph taken once a quarter—in order to keep track—but do you know—it's as if somehow or other—this simply doesn't work?—Most likely there's something I've forgotten—only what?—what do you reckon?

I dunno, said Great-Aunt, I reckon nature is supposed to take its course . . . .

The widow finished her dance with a terrific climax: applause. It was a convincing performance. The beaming widow received her con-dolences.

—all so sudden, wasn't it?

—and who's going to get the house?

—and still he said: you'd just leave me here to kick the bucket, wouldn't you!

—as the singer says: if love's sincere, a person's sex don't matter!

—and wow, the appetite of the man!

—a scythe wouldn't suffice . . . .

—ah how flime ties . . . .

—you get those funny sort of days, don't you—you wake up first thing in the morning—and there you are, fed up already . . . .

—anyone making for Erewhon?

—I know the feeling, my dear! the tears I've wept! those nights!—I was saying to him only the other day: here am I, frantic with fear, you beast, just in case God forbid anything should happen to you—and you turn up two days later calm as anything, nothing the matter with you, except you're pissed and you stink to high heaven!

—But here the gong sounded, a signal that the official part of the ceremony was over, and the memorial fairground could start. The windows of the booths flew open with a clatter and there came again a racket of hooters, rattles, whistling and shouting and the voices of the hucksters:

Roll up, roll up, roll up!

The future has been and gone, cast aside all decorum and roll up for your taste of happiness! Here we have to offer you a spray of Number Five perspiration, a holographic Santa, self-polishing thigh-boots, self-suffocating braces, brawn in a powder mix and perfect reproduction fire, indistinguishable from the real thing! Roll up, roll up, roll up!

Meanwhile the pale girl gazed at the opalizing soaps and phosphorescing creams, the invisible make-ups, lotion that makes hair go bleached as if in the sun, an ointment that makes the skin sunburnt, she bought a spray with the fragrance of celery leaf, saying to herself: what am I doing here? why am I here? what do I want here?—and when she looked about, behind her was standing that boy—the one she sees from time to time—and he said: here I am. Did you call?

You were the one that called, said the girl.

Come with me, said the boy, giving her his hand—

—and they bought a little poster with the catechist's photograph, one of a host of others all around, and together they recited the words:

"Croak it, Big-Mouth, croak it!
croak it, Big-Mouth, croak it!
beat 'im! thump 'im! wallop 'im! eat 'im!
smash 'im! waste 'im! throttle 'im! kill 'im!
Croak it, Big-Mouth, croak it! croak it, Big-Mouth, croak it!"

—and Professor Big-Mouth Sitting Bull belched after supper and said, I'm off to lie down, I'm not feeling too well, have to get some sleep before I can face those brats again, those young scallywags, that mob that refuses to know that God is love . . . .

When the tired widow returned home, she found Great-Aunt sitting by the front door on the coffin.

How's things, Auntie, she said.

And Great-Aunt smiled oddly, and said: now I've tidied up the house for you already, but I don't seem to have the key on me, must have swallowed it by accident, silly old me—do you feel that wind too?

And Great-Aunt by the booth said to the pale girl holding the manual: I liked these two best out of the sprays: the scent of a babe-in-arms and the scent of sun-dried washing—

And Great-Aunt on the field path said to the man in the helmet, well now don't you worry your head too much about that, there are much more complicated things in the world, pitchforks for instance—

And Great-Aunt on the coffin smiled and said apologetically to the widow, today I'm a bit frazzled—

And Great-Aunt on the field path said to the man, where are you off down to, my dear?

—and she rose up in the air like a puff of white dandelion—

—and the man in the helmet sat down in the grass with his bottle—

—and after one swig he grasped the meaning of Zen—

—and after another he started to speak the language of the animals—

—and after another he reached *satori*—

—and after another he laid a golden egg—

and after another he fell asleep, and by morning there was nothing much to him . . . .

And the girl and the boy went off somewhere together—there they embraced, they stroked and cuddled each other, tasting and finding each other most delightful—

—and they called each other sweetheart—

—and the spring mayflies whirled about them—and one old mayfly said to a young mayfly: I'm much too—much too old—the good will to live is draining from me—but you still have many seconds of life before you—dance, boy, while there's yet time, in the dance of love the meaning of all things lies, when the last of us falls, then comes the end, and winter and darkness—

—and the mayfly who does not dance, dies, without understanding a thing. . . .

Translated by James Naughton

What Nothing Looks Like

excerpts from a novel

Jana Červenková

When Filip was six, he once asked us:
"What does Nothing look like?"
My husband Bedřich laughed confidently and said:
"You'll soon find out."

ONE DAY I OPENED the office door and found a large sheet of paper on the desk: *Dear Cleaner, please return the half-empty bottle of rum we left behind yesterday.*

With my wet rubber glove I fished for the nearest pencil. Hand trembling with indignation, I wrote underneath that there was no bottle of rum and they can do the cleaning themselves.

I vaguely remember that, even stylistically, it was the worst piece of writing I'd ever produced. I imagined the note's addressee whose rum had been consumed by an exuberant colleague. Now he's absolutely sure that only a dipso with this kind of primitive, drunken handwriting could have done it.

Luckily, I had only two days to go till the end of my notice, before I started working in the Research Institute.

Sometimes, one shouldn't be too hard. Take the case of Irena Hojerová, an example of a persistent effort to be an intellectual. Throughout history, there have always been people who had to try hard to be this or that.

And what does the word intellectual mean? For some it's a pejorative term, a term of abuse, for others a word for something so elevated that they would never use it to describe themselves, certainly not aloud. For Irena Hojerová, it is an outlook, a world view we choose to adopt, and this particular world view tells her that things can be puzzled out by using your head.

Life has always confirmed this view for her: Irena Hojerová managed to think up a good half of what her simple mother never needed her head for. It may have taken Irena a wee bit longer, but imagine the joy of discovery! That's why she has never been ashamed to call herself an intellectual.

The nine-year-old Emmanuel Kant apparently once came up with a naïve philosophical game: he spun round as fast as he could to find out whether the world was the same when you weren't looking at it. I found myself playing this game for years, and at a much older age. At nineteen, I went out with men I wasn't remotely interested in. All afternoon I would listen to a balding thirty-year old telling me about his promotion to foreman and what a difference it made to his wages. I would then try to imagine myself as somebody completely different, maybe a young shop assistant from the corner delicatessen, who, as I was convinced, would have been duly impressed. I helped myself with my parents' "sensible" grown-up talk: And how much are you going to bring home now? Of course, I wasn't in the least interested. And when I stood him up the next time we had a date, he may have thought that he wasn't a good enough catch.

On the whole I would always seek out situations I had not been destined for, ones I had been meant to miss. Obsessed with being where I was not, where I would never be. Wanting to be someone I was not. To take a walk along the bottom, knowing all the time that the person walking there was somebody else. Because I didn't belong there, I could come up to the surface whenever I wanted to.

The nine-year-old Kant was a scholar. He wanted to examine his world and find the truth in it. I wanted to enter it. Knowing from the beginning that it simply must be different behind my back. At times I even tried to persuade it to be that way. So that I could intervene in it.

Only in confrontation with an alien world did my own make sense. Possibly it was being filled with proof rather than knowledge. The nine-year-old Kant was far more honest in his dealing with truth.

Punishment took a long time to come, but in the end it did.

The world was at last found to be different behind my back. Far more real than I would have ever thought. I am still where I am not and who I am not. But this time, the alien world is for real, it's mine and I'm afraid it's the only one I have.

Don't be mistaken: Irena Hojerová is not a persecuted victim of the totalitarian regime. She doesn't have to work as a cleaner, she never got into trouble. When others were getting themselves into trouble, she was at home washing nappies. She never got mixed up in anything, no one simply ever thought that she was worth it.

After my antics with unsuitable boys, I chose a man I could look up to.

I knew we were going to build the Tower of Babel together because we would understand each other without a word.

"I always thought you were the sort of liberated artist who wouldn't tie herself down or be told what to do, and who would make love with anyone she felt like ..." I was told many years ago, when I was already married, by a colleague of mine as he walked me home, with no result, like so many times before.

"Is that what you call an artist? You have a funny definition of art," I cut him down to size. After all, I do make love with whomever I want to. I was terribly proud of my own freedom which I had never before perceived as such.

He shrank next to me, treading lightly as if feeling the pavement with bare feet. And I went on enthusiastically, telling him how I loved all men—all of them in a single one . . . .

I don't remember what he said. And only now has it sadly dawned on me that at that moment, I was thinking mainly about myself. Dozens of men passed us in the street, all handsome, and I belonged to all of them.

What I do remember is that Bedřich, my husband, was much more taken by the idea than I was.

The plaster falls like muscles off a leper's body, revealing the bone. Mice scuttle up and down the invisible paths along the walls of our house. When I was a child, they had a whole fairy-tale city in their underground burrows. This is the third time I am setting up a trap, knowing they are going to avoid it. I no longer hold it against them. There's a new civilization for you, more viable than ours, which is going to devour us one day, and create its own culture. Behind the peeling wallpaper gloats a gray void.

Summer rains ease out the weeds in the garden, leak through the ceiling of our house and into the wardrobe. Everything smells of mold. It is also part of the new, more vital civilization. In the garden, the bindweed entwines its long tentacles around piles of bricks, they have been living in a perfect symbiosis for who knows how many years, the bricks now belong to it.

The chickweed has crept further up from the foot of the mountain of sand, the top of which is all covered with thistles, dozens of thistle plants growing through. The stacked-up steel beams slowly disappear among nettles. Our hopes and dreams of many years have now become the bottom layer of a future archaeological dig, giving in to that new, vital civilization.

I am standing in the middle of this crop trying hard to find reasons why I should weed the pile of sand. Every year I find fewer and fewer. And so I prefer to take the two plastic bags I had brought from work because they might come in handy when we start renovating and spread them on top of the damp wardrobe. I remove the sodden, molding coats and hang them around the garden like scarecrows.

"Theater performance in nine letters . . . is it a happening?" Bedřich asks himself.

I'd love to be a bindweed. To have support. To embrace and entwine upwards. Grow little white bell-shaped blossoms. I put on a dress with a breath of cinnamon.

"Don't go to work, stay here with me," says my husband desperately like a five-year-old, because he has understood the scent of cinnamon and the ringing of the garden bindweed's white bells.

What would I do here? Rot and fall apart like everything else? Like you? What have you ever done to stop it? Pickle yourself in alcohol, that's what.

A bereaved couple at their own funeral. No, thank you.

Everybody is on vacation and the Research Institute is empty. Yawning in the tired summer day with its breath of stuffy laboratories, yawning with its few windows the cleaner opens every day for the wet floors in the corridors to dry.

She goes about her mopping slowly and thoroughly, it is the only work that still makes some sense. And if one of the scientists wanders in, he greets her, saying, "Why don't you take a break? There's nobody here."

In the locker downstairs in the basement, her dress breathes out the scent of cinnamon. She doesn't confess to anyone that she too is on holiday.

"What do you do these days?" acquaintances ask.

"Cleaning."

"What a life! Nobody pesters you about anything, everyone is polite. I'd like to chuck it in where I am, perhaps there is another vacancy?"

"There is, do you want me to arrange it for you?"

"Well, not just now," they all decline my offer of an easy, independent job, "what I mean is, when I'm really fed up here . . . But you *don't have to* work as a cleaner, you haven't lost a job anywhere," her acquaintances recall.

"It's more convenient," I tell everyone, and they catch on: in the past ten years I have lent my name to four best-selling crime novels. The Cliffhanger imprint only publishes best-sellers. And so it follows that it's enough for me to mop a few staircases, a splash here, a splash there, two hours and two hundred crowns in cash.

Now of course Irena Hojerová is not banned as a writer. That's why she can lend her name to her former school-mate Otto for his crime novels published by the best-selling imprint Cliffhanger. Irena is not their author. Which means she doesn't get huge royalties. Just a bad name: Otto's novels are getting worse and worse, but Irena thinks she has to take it on the chin because Otto is a dissident, while nothing untoward is happening to her.

A real man would go and work on a construction site, if he had to feed a family," my outraged mother said at the time. "These days we have no unemployment, it used to be much worse when you really couldn't find any work."

For my mother, the only difference between blue and white-collar work was that intellectuals didn't have to work hard and dirty their hands. My parents worked hard all their lives.

I resented Mother's self-confident, decisive tone of voice. How dare she so energetically send a PhD to go and work on a construction site?

How should a woman married to a fallen hero behave? With that thought fresh in my mind I told Bedřich I couldn't care less how much money he was going to bring home, all I wanted was for him to find a satisfying job. I wanted him to know I was on his side.

I certainly didn't have to worry about sinking to the level of a grasping woman. But then I didn't know that Bedřich was going to find satisfaction in solving crossword puzzles. As if his life depended on unravelling their messages which were always the same: *Long Live the Great October Revolution. Sport Makes Good Health.*

If at least he did some sport.

A tired summer was followed by an even more tired autumn. The garden was full of trees. Even those that should have been cut down a long time ago. Their branches engaged in a battle. Underneath, sand and bricks, and nowhere to hang the washing. With a basket-ful of wet laundry I scramble through a gap in the fence left by the neighbors. They let me use their garden.

"Auntie, when the lawn is wet, you're not allowed to walk on it. Daddy said so," scolds the little one next door.

Trees covered with apples. I am outnumbered and I know I am going to succumb. I'd like to feel hostile towards them, I'm sure it would give me some relief. But I feel like a supporting branch in-stead. The apples are not ripe yet, but they have already begun to fall. Every day a red carpet under the Red Delicious. A yellow one under the Gold Ontario. I talk to the apple-laden trees, trying to convince them, explain to them that they are not dependent on man, that they had been here first. That the meaning of their lives is to maintain their kind and they would be better off without our civilization . . . .

I find consolation only in the synthetic fragrance of my apple shampoo. Its indifference tells me that human beings do not have roots and duties. That human beings cannot grow heavy and then shed fruit. That all they can do is give off light fragrance and allow themselves to be carried by the wind.

I have never associated the arrival of death with falling asleep, but with morning awakening.

It was four o'clock at dawn, the hour of executions, and the sky had yet to decide whether it would leave the darkness on or make light. I woke up with a feeling of terror, my heart clamped in a stranger's fist, and I knew that this was my end. A person who becomes helpless and useless, who only spreads Nothing around like a plague, should die.

And yet I trembled with fear, shaking violently, teeth chattering. Then I felt that, after all, I and my life had never agreed on such an end. That this would be a far too embarrassing denouement for me to allow as the author of my own story.

"There's really nothing wrong with you, it's just nerves," the cleaner was told by the Research Institute's doctor. "But if you don't change your current lifestyle, you're risking messing up everything inside . . . Do you live with your husband as man and wife? . . . You see, I'm not asking whether you are married," the doctor explained to the cleaner.

"No," she said with an indifferent expression on her face. Nothing sometimes takes on the shape of an empty mold. A violin case, a matchbox.

I no longer dream and that's why I have to make my dreams up. Like this one about our apple trees who heard my desperate pleading. At last I managed to make it clear to them that they were not dependent on people. And so one night they left the garden holding each other by the hand. I watched them from behind the curtain with a bated breath. The Cox's Renette opened up the hole in the fence and the Gold Ontario held up the rusty wire-mesh until the last tree was out. I shivered a little when Mother's apple tree stepped over the low wall, coyly holding up its fruit-laden branches.

They walked away, down the dark street, clambering on their crooked roots like a flock of clumsy penguins. Like toddlers setting out on their first journey out into the world.

What was I afraid of when the trees were leaving? What was the deserted garden like, bristling with rusting beams?

"Why don't you find yourself a boyfriend?" asked the Research Institute's doctor. "There's no reason whatsoever for a woman like you not to have one."

The cleaner shrugged her shoulders.

"Shall I prescribe one for you?" he joked, but prescribed her some sleeping pills instead, then dismissed her from his surgery because he didn't think she was entitled to any more problems.

"This is going to be goulash for drunks, isn't it? I'll be the first one in the queue then, because today I am a drunk. Any objections?" She had none. She liked the man. He wedged himself next to her between two tables, as if he had no intention of leaving before the end of the birthday party. He was Associate Professor Václav Jech.

The frozen goulash, hard as concrete, resisted the wooden spoon and the electric cooker alike.

"So what do you do when you're not being a drunk?"

"When I'm not a drunk I'm a pathologist. These are my two variants. Not that they ever overlap, God, no! But there's not a third one."

"Your wife must be pleased with you."

"Yep. She managed to divorce me only last month. That's a good reason to be pleased, isn't it?"

"It certainly is."

"Now her only problem is how to get me out of our place. That's going to be a bit more difficult. With my build, if nothing else, it's going to take a couple of strong movers."

The frosty crust on top of the goulash began to show the first signs of tectonic activity.

"Fifty is a dreadful birthday. Mine is coming up in six months, The birthday boy and I used to be at university together. That's why I got so drunk today."

"What do you mean dreadful? You can do your work and what's more, no fool dares to interfere."

"So that's how it is. You think there are not that many fools around."

"All right. But at least they're educated . . . It doesn't happen to you that somebody would mistake medicine for ideology."

"Eight years ago I successfully defended my post-doctoral dissertation and passed the required exams, but until this day they have refused to award me Associate Professorship, the reason being that I'm not a Party member." It sounded like a triumphant threat.

"Do you know how many people are much worse off?"

"That may be true, but you must understand that it doesn't make me feel any better."

"If nothing else, no one forces you to falsify the results of your research," the cleaner persists in her optimism. Even the frozen goulash had softened to the extent that she could now plunge the wooden spoon in it.

"And what does it really mean to you, the fact that you're not officially an Associate Professor? Do you get paid less?"

"I think not. But if I were Associate Professor, I could probably secure a position I'll never get this way. To hell with it. It's almost a question of social standing. They've given it to so many imbeciles . . . ."

"In your field academic titles still carry some prestige. In mine, I'd be embarrassed to have one."

"What are you . . . ." He stopped short. "Why are you . . . here, for godsake . . . ."

Even the goulash came to a simmer.

"Don't worry, I'm not banned or anything, I can publish my things. But they get rejected. Not positive enough, they say. Apparently there's always a bright side to life and the writer's task is to discover it . . . Cretins."

"Of course there should be a bright side to life, especially to life. At least that's what we want, don't we? But where to find it?" He gave the cleaner an understanding, kind look of a man whose knowledge is being used by society without acknowledgement, and whose ex-wife is throwing him out of the marital home.

"I think you've never been to a pathology department."

"No. I'm far too much alive for that," I joked.

"Now you're talking about the autopsy room. Lay people often make that mistake. It could be an interesting experience for you. I could take you there, show you around . . . Anyway, don't you want to leave your job?" Václav Jech asks the cleaner. "I need a hand in the laboratory. There's a woman who comes in from the department, a stupid cow who can't be trusted, but I have to be grateful to have her. I can't let her file samples because I would never find them again. She rinses the beakers with water, leaves a bit of material inside, and it doesn't occur to her that she might cause damage to another patient . . . ."

"The pathologist is the first one to examine material taken out during an operation and find out what's going on. It is only on the basis of his diagnosis that the surgeon decides how to treat the patient. All those golden hands depend on us. I'm not saying that because I am a pathologist myself," Associate Professor Jech gave the cleaner a lecture when she finally sought out his laboratory at the surgical clinic. This time he was sober. "But unfortunately people bring all those bribes, all the envelopes and bottles elsewhere," he laughs. "We are the noble knights of medicine! And how often do you think those golden hands pass a bottle my way?"

Being sober, he no longer calls her by her first name. But in the end a glass of vodka is found anyway.

"And they don't even know what to do with the stuff. I know one who exchanges the spirits for sugar and coffee with a deli manager, so that he doesn't turn into an alcoholic . . . And yet, all pathologists drink themselves to death. I could tell you names . . . Take the one who was here before me. They all drink themselves to death."

He spoke harshly, at that moment he seemed to her like a kamikaze, sitting in a hermetically sealed cockpit without landing wheels.

"Have you ever seen a histological specimen?"

A numbered slide with a thin layer of human tissue sealed in paraffin. It is tinged with blue and purple. Under the microscope it creates a map of fantastic, faraway lands beyond a thousand mountains. But maybe they are not so remote. There is something intimate in them, we resemble geological layers, the creased surface of the Earth. Maybe we even have something of its luscious vegetation and frosty flowers on the window panes. Our layers vaguely resemble the layers of a tree trunk, but they don't have the same peacefulness, the simple harmony of wood . . . .

Suddenly, it is as if these exciting landscapes started to corrode the grey Nothing and lure the cleaner away on journeys that had not been possible until then. Beyond the barriers of our touches is a wide free world, which still has a meaning and a natural order. It could perhaps give meaning to everything else.

The only discipline worth studying is medicine because it saves human lives, a high-school classmate told me many years ago. I opposed him then because I also always knew what I wanted: for me, it was more important to know what people do with all those saved lives in the end.

"This is beautiful," the cleaner sighed over the microscope.

"Isn't it?" Associate Professor Jech agreed.

"What is it?"

"Sarcoma," he said, "The patient's a goner."

But by then she was also a goner, she might like to save people's lives, but at that moment she didn't know what to do with her own. She was not going to go back to the gray corridors and computers at the Research Institute.

"My God, how wonderful," Associate Professor Jech rejoiced one late afternoon in the middle of an empty laboratory, and the metal filing cabinet with patients' records also cried with joy, that cold, heavy safe of truth strictly kept away from the patients.

Another bottle was found. They discussed the laboratory staff and gossiped about the female lab workers. I prefer not to see them. And they discussed his domestic troubles: my ex is obviously counting on marrying again, and then she'll bring her new husband into our flat and throw me out on my ear. And do you know what a friend of mine told me? (By that time they were calling each other by their first names again.) I mustn't think it's a joke, lots of men would be grateful for as much as a room in a single men's hostel.

And his daughter defected to Vienna, after it had cost him an arm and a leg to get her accepted at the Science Faculty. And in the end, when he spoke to her on the phone, she said: why do you care about not having me there? I always meant nothing to you anyway— Nothing? Is it nothing to look after them, find them a university place, then a job? And the problems I had with the Professor because of her, as if it was my fault. In this country, we are all always treated as if we were under age, as if we had no rights . . . .

They also discussed the problems with Comrade Chief Physician, who won't be called anything else but Comrade Chief Physician, or sometimes Professor, but that also counts as a unindictable term of abuse. It's not that he can't perform an operation, but at least five people who should be in a more senior position have stayed behind for reasons known to everybody. Watch out for him!

Now I was already his little Irena. And so I told Václav that I wasn't going to let some lab technicians drive me out, I have a friend who is a lawyer and can help him with his flat, and Comrade Professor Chief Physician is hardly so powerful to be able to sack a cleaner. There may be ten others waiting to do his job but who would he find to do mine?

"At last I'm going to have an ally here," Václav Jech sighed happily, because we both knew that this would become my most important mission.

This place was going to be my building site. I was going to leave my house to the mice, the mold, television broadcasts and newspaper headlines. Because that's where life was, here in this laboratory, giving me one more chance, and this time I was going to take it up.

And what else did Václav Jech tell the cleaner? . . . What? . . . She doesn't remember. All she knows is that at the end of the day, when they'd finished the last bottle, the Earth dropped off. Galileo Galilei finally found a stable point in space and fired the globe out of an enormous cannon into the universe. It cruised through the galaxies, shattering planets into thousands of meteorites, travelling along its new, infallible trajectory. No, not the Earth. It was that foolish woman. Driven by the omnipresent Nothing which had been pumped up full of air over the years.

He succumbed to her force of gravity, turning into hundreds of thousands of meteorites, freed meteorites, which had never wanted to keep together, all they wanted to do was to keep falling on her surface. I tell you, madam cleaner, blow me down with a feather, no woman has done this to me for years and years . . . Tears rolled down her cheeks.

The apple tree they had cut down and poured cement over grew through the foundations, rising above the frozen wall and blossoming in the middle of January. Glorious and invincible. It no longer begged. It was fragrant, generous and majestic. From a distance she could hear a sparrow's twittering:

"Jesus, how did I get mixed up in this . . . ."

And the apple tree, confident in its glory, its supernatural power, indulgently surveyed her surroundings.

"You're not listening to me," a frightened Václav Jech shook her. "We can be together just from time to time, do you understand . . . My life is very complicated . . . There are other women, you see, and my relationship with them is also . . . professional . . . But I wasn't so bad, was I? I'm no longer a great performer, but I'm not that bad either, am I?"

And the cleaner nods as if in a dream:

"No you weren't so bad."

"You have somebody else, don't you? I'm sure you have somebody else, you just had to have it today, didn't you? You can't do it with me all the time, I'm sure you have—"

Why is he mouthing such stupid insignificant things when there is an apple tree blossoming in the middle of the house, in the middle of January?"

"Why do you run away from me?" says Bedřich reproachfully every time I am about to leave for work.

"Because staying here would drive me mad," I try to gloss over the fact that somebody has to mop the floor and wipe the glass and sort out the specimens in the pathology lab, and that I am paid to do it.

"How come? What's the problem?" he is surprised every time.

Nothing. I have a husband who showers me with tokens of his affection. He really watches over me all day long.

It starts with morning coffee and reading aloud from the newspaper. Then he goes to have a look at the thermometer and discusses what I am going to wear that day. If he expresses his opinion and doesn't immediately receive a positive response, he gives me a worried glance, trying to find out whether he may have unwittingly committed some offense.

I have to force myself to use a kind tone of voice. If nothing else, I have to accept all those sweets and flowers politely, although I know that they are bribes for the plaster falling onto the cooker, for the door between the kitchen and the toilet, that has been hanging on its hinges without a door frame for years, with a two-centimeter gap which startles our visitors over and over again.

But to him, politeness is not enough, because he is doing all this out of love. His love is big as castles, or at least as big as our whole renovated house, complete with a garden planted with rhododendrons and roses. I don't want a man who brings me roses. I want one who would slap me across the face. So that I could pack up and leave. But only the apple trees can go, I can't. I hate love.

Every Tuesday can be written off. It's a day in excess, a deformed blob stuck on to the rest of the normal days that follow each other. Like a tumor on the natural organism of the week.

The atmosphere in the lab is uneasy. Václav Jech, my Assistant Professor, is wearing a crisp white coat and from early afternoon, there is a bottle being chilled in the fridge which he always brings himself. The cleaner knows that this time she won't be getting the glasses ready. And she has to vacuum and dust. And empty the waste bin once more before she goes.

The Associate Professor is going to remind her, already before lunch time, with secret but eloquent gestures that today she has to leave half an hour earlier, and is everything going to be ready before then? He is going to pace the laboratory, all excited, the cleaner's hands are going to shake and the glass beakers are going to smash in the sink.

Because every Tuesday the Lady comes. Straight from a royal salon and a royal dream. Radiance and scent.

"This woman has done more for me than anyone else in my life," confides Václav. "She's the only one I can be sure of."

Idiot, you idiot, cries the cleaner somewhere inside and her tears are unreal glass drops. They crash into each other, tingling, piercing each other with their sharp points. Yet, it is dry outside the window.

Whether or not she had said to herself that she was going to love the pathology lab and Associate Professor Václav Jech with it, she is forbidden to do so every Tuesday. On Tuesdays she ceases to be the mistress here, maybe she's not here at all, maybe she is just suffered like the smell of formaldehyde. The main thing is to air the room. Václav Jech must feel like a great sinner in front of the Lady, since he is so adamant that the two must never meet.

The next day the cleaner carries out the empty bottle. Secretly, avoiding the lab technicians—it's the divorcée in particular she likes to help him deceive. And she empties the ashtray with the virginally white cigarette ends and the cigarette ends covered in red kisses. She does all that with a resigned, nostalgic calm, the same way people dispose of the Christmas tree or of withered wreaths from a fresh grave. And in comes the Associate Professor and tells her worriedly: "She keeps asking about you. What kind of person you are. I think she suspects something."

The cleaner gives him an uncomprehending look from underneath her apron.

"Yes, Professor . . . Of course, Professor. Yes, yes . . . Definitely . . . ." hollers Václav Jech into the receiver in a tone so servile that I am not sure whether he's imitating some brown-nosing yes-man.

But the conversation goes on for too long and contains too many scientific terms, those shamanic incantations which always tell the cleaner: there's your broom and floor rag and mind your own business.

She doesn't. She can't leave now, can she? She bombards his back with silent signals, to remind him that he who has a cleaner is strong and afraid of nothing. And that she would do anything for him, kill, lie, steal, commit adultery, bear false witness.

But the inaudible signals bounce off his back, disintegrating into silence punctuated by the words yes, Professor, and the cleaner feels as if she is spying through a keyhole.

When he finished, he turned round and started. He had forgotten all about her during the conversation. And what else could he do now but open a bottle of vodka, pour two glasses and say: "I am a man who prefers to fight rather than plead. But this guy is a real swine." And he knew that by saying that he had not mended anything. That was when he realized the extent of his own shame. And the cleaner, as the bad-weather girl she is, could see that this was her moment. That now she was his best and most indispensable friend.

"They have never sent me anywhere, it's always the Party members who travel abroad. And who defect, of course. One of them took with him the research results of an entire team and sold them in Switzerland, they hadn't been published anywhere, you see. But next time, they send another Party member . . . I've always said to myself that I mustn't be a whore, for a few privileges . . . .

Then, out of the blue, he cut his monologue in the middle and looked at me as if he were going to cross-examine me. I could see that today's bottle of vodka was not enough to wash away his anger and humiliation. That things were getting dangerous around here, because nobody in their right mind would get drunk with an uncomfortable witness just like that. Everyone else but me would have already scuttled into safety, but I let him pour another glass for me, I am drawn into that world where I don't belong and where I experience incredible adventures.

"Somebody has been informing them about what happens in this lab," he fixes me with a penetrating gaze.

"Who?"

"That's what I don't know for sure. But I'm on the trail. And I'm going to be very careful from now on."

I say nothing, embarrassed by the miserable paper threats issued by a man whom I wanted to admire come hell or high water. Because his over-confident, loud prophesies mean nothing else but: Don't you dare tell anybody about this! Woe to you if anyone finds out that the fearless fighter crumbles at the mere thought that he might fall into disfavor with his master.

After a year of our intimate friendship I still can't be sure whether he is really interested in science or in the thousand crowns he makes in overtime to save up for a new flat. We haven't come any closer to each other, despite having drunk gallons of vodka together, chatted for hours and hours and even experienced a little bit of passion.

I watch the darkness under the open third-floor window. It's like an ocean. One could swim in it, dive to the bottom to retrieve an amphora full of gold, a singing conch or at least a simple shell. What is the miracle you are waiting for? The apple tree in the middle of the house is not going to blossom, don't you remember, they've cut it down and burnt it. And the magical landscapes of human tissue the Associate Professor enters every day through the gate of his microscope will never be yours. You are equally unbearable to him as Bedřich is to you, haven't you had enough? There's nowhere to escape with crumbling dilapidated walls everywhere and sarcoma lurking under the skin . . . .

This is where Irena Hojerová ends.

Not by a banal act of throwing herself out of the third-floor window, because then they would fill the amphora with ashes instead of gold, and every day Bedřich would place a fresh bouquet of flowers next to it. Another activity to prevent him from rebuilding the house. But then, he would no longer have to. And what about Václav Jech? What would he do?

Why think about it at all since Irena Hojerová vanished quite differently. She turned into Agatha. True, the name is slightly . . . how shall I put it? But she's the one to blame, she's chosen it herself. She had no option, after all: there was already another Irena at the psychiatric clinic. True, she could have gone for another name, but she was caught just as she was wondering yet again whether she should in the end write a detective novel. (The culprit would be the gardener.) One could say that it was a moment of carelessness; almost everyone was conceived in moments like that, so why not Agatha?

A new name is like a dress bought in a hurry. I suspect it makes my waist look shapeless, and I don't know if my bra strap is showing in the scooped neck. I'm afraid to look at myself in the mirror. Afraid to stretch because the seams may give. Agatha. What a stupid idea!

"We have visiting doctors and therapists, but it's really the group that heals, the therapists just direct it," explains my new fellow patient while she's helping me with the suitcase.

"How can one lunatic cure another?"

"Everyone can help someone else. Each of us lacks something and has what others don't. A patient should confide in others as much as possible, and in turn they say how he or she appears to them . . . ." She strives to give the impression that she had come up with all those words she's parroting after somebody: "The ideal result of therapy would be for all of us to come out of here completely changed. It's really like the American concept of brain-washing, we wash each other's brains . . . Here is the post office, by the way, and over there is the supermarket where those on duty do the shopping."

On the way to the chateau housing the clinic the meadows were fragrant with freshly cut grass. Hay harvest time. Suddenly I was soaked in that swooning fragrance. I can't go on, I can't listen to this, I can't go and voluntarily have my brain washed. Scrubbed, rinsed, wrung and hung to dry. Even the meadow would run away to escape the hay harvest if it could and had a place to go to. Now I was the meadow, breathing out the last report of my own existence.

"A person should remain herself," I reply—replies the false Agatha. "What you think and what you do is something you have arrived at in some way, not something you can shed so easily . . . ."

It's not just a new story Agatha has stepped into here. It is a whole new genre. A short story. She has been transported into a world of condensed, made-up, soluble problems. The silver-gray floor has given way under her, she doesn't have to mop it any longer or wash the glass beakers and defend herself from the aggressive Václav Jech. She doesn't have to go back to her run-down house, sweep the falling plaster, defend herself from the non-aggressive Bedřich. Who could wish for more?

The characters from Agatha's novel, whom she used to shepherd together in vain, now surround her, sit down next to her and offer her their life stories. At last she can hide among them, be one of them. She can even make them up, make up new, better lives for them. Agatha can wade through all those soluble problems, splash around in them, swim, dive. It may even be beautiful to drown in soluble problems. They envelop her like the swarm envelops the queen bee.

How many times does Agatha want to start again? What is she throwing herself into, with her house and Bedřich waiting at home, and Václav in the lab: doesn't she remember them?

Ask too many questions and you'll find out too much. Only Agatha has stacked up all those questions, but so far she has received just one paltry, uncertain answer. She no longer wants to save human lives. Is that too little, or too much? What do people do with all those lives in the end? Bedřich has to pull himself out of his hole, and so does Václav Jech. But most of all Agatha. And if they don't? Well, that's their prerogative.

How many departures does she owe her life? She has to pay up her debts one day.

The path in front of the chateau is covered with crushed white marble and the roses are sighing all around. But that won't stop her, it's possible to take a deep breath and quickly slip through their festive gateway. One can survive those few moments of ridicule, she certainly can.

Agatha (or is she again Irena Hojerová?) is setting out on a journey at high noon, her hands free. Voices follow her from the loggia of the chateau. Are they voices or tympanums . . . kettledrums . . . cymbals? A mad percussionist plays the hot summer sky and the tops of linden trees carried by hundreds of bee wings dance ceremonial dances. To the sound of red-hot cymbals and tympanums stretched out to bursting point, the midday witch roams through the landscape heading for the land of eternal noon. The scorched grass falls at her feet. The stables and cowsheds are padlocked, the viper curled up on the rocks flees, and the sun trembles in orgiastic ecstasy.

Agatha too, or maybe Irena Hojerová (it's time to return to oneself) heads in the direction of noon along the southern path. Isn't it her turn now? She flees like a meadow fleeing the hay harvest. The burning ridges breathe her in and out through their powerful nostrils and at every step there is more of their breath and less of Irena, but no one comes to meet her on the white southern path, only the forlorn tingling of a silver triangle carries through the hot air. Ting . . . ting . . . ting . . .

Translated by Alexandra Büchler

Between Us Girls

Eva Hauser

M Y MOTHER WAS always completely impossible when she tried to talk to me in confidence—woman to woman, as they say. I couldn't stand it.

That evening I had come back from a date with Jirka and I was feeling rather in two minds, because on the one hand, it was extremely irritating that I was nineteen and still a virgin, but on the other, those dates with him left me feeling utterly drained. Jirka would always set off silently, walking at an unbearable pace, and wouldn't slow down until we reached some distant corner of a park, or the wasteland beyond city limits where neglected patches of grass nestled in between enclosed lots. And then he would start to undress me, regardless of whether it was cold or hot, regardless of whether it was light or dark, regardless of whether there were people around or not. It bothered me terribly; before, I had never realized that I needed privacy for sex, and half-light, but now it was quite clear to me.

I began to consider the possibility that I might solve the problem by taking him home. On Friday evenings, my mother was almost always away—ever since I was a girl I had been used to having Friday evenings to myself. She returned long after midnight. But a strange thing happened; somehow, quite selfishly, I found I didn't want to sacrifice that time to Jirka. Or was it that I didn't want to let an intruder, a stranger, into our flat?

I wasn't sure, and I needed to think it through. I wanted to creep off to my room to consider it, but my mother wouldn't let me.

When I took some Emmental out of the fridge in the kitchen and started to nibble it bit by bit (in the evening, I don't eat anything except a little cheese, even when I'm hungry, and even though Jirka keeps on telling me I should put on weight—perhaps just for that reason I want to slim down and make him mad), my mother came out of the living room and, despite the fact that she knows I can't stand it, she sat down next to me. She pushed the magazines I had been trying to read while I was eating to the other end of the table, and cleared her throat. She was in a proper tizzy, and was almost unable to speak—she was always like that when she wanted to have a heart-to-heart.

"Ah, erm . . . you know, Monika, we have to talk about something . . . ."

I stared at her reproachfully, without a word, and chewed my cheese. Why couldn't she leave me in peace, when I came home tired after a hectic day?

"I can't let it wait any longer. You're a grown woman now, and I see you're going out on dates with boys . . . ."

"Mom, for God's sake, I've already read a whole library about sexual behavior and contraception and sexually transmitted diseases. At school we constantly have some kind of compulsory sex education classes. I can't even imagine a more boring topic! So don't bloody start, I'm not a little girl!"

My mother flushed crimson and winced. She put on an important expression, which means that she frowned sternly, puckered her mouth, and started to take an incredibly long time to choose her words. She also started to sweat.

"You know that I myself never . . . never had . . . anything to do with a man . . . Well, in short, I think that you and I are different from other women. It's a very peculiar thing, and I've never spoken with you about it openly, because . . . ." She threw her arms up helplessly, choked nervously, and then burst out: "Because you wouldn't believe it." She fell silent and looked at me almost pleadingly. She was waiting to see if I would buy it and whether I would hear her out.

I felt my blood pressure rising in response. What, for heaven's sake, was this supposed to mean? Did my mother have some kind of bizarre fixation? It was true that she had always avoided men for as long as I could remember, but . . . What could she have in mind? Was she perhaps a lesbian? Or was she terribly afraid of something?

"You told me that my father died before I was born," I reminded her.

"Well," my mother's crimson blush changed into a scatter of red blotches, spread unevenly over her ashen features, and she lowered her voice to the limit of audibility. "It wasn't that he died, exactly, it's more that . . . he was absorbed!"

"What?" I almost screamed. I was starting to feel genuinely afraid—for her, perhaps for the whole of my world, my home—but at that moment, I wasn't quite able to think it through to all the possible consequences.

"You know, I didn't believe my mother either, I was horrified when she started to hint that something was amiss. I thought then that she'd completely flipped her lid . . . but it was true. Did you know that, under certain circumstances, the embryos of certain animals—mice, for example—can be absorbed back into the womb? Perhaps when the female meets a more desirable male?"

No, I didn't know that. I shivered just to think of it. But in the final analysis, it was only something that happened to mice. And besides, an adult human male was not just a ball of cells like the embryo of a mouse.

I shook my head and shrugged my shoulders, both at once, unable to utter a word.

My mother continued brokenly, "My whole life . . . I've had the feeling that that man is somehow still alive in me. Step by step, I've discovered that other girls don't have the same masculine dreams I do. Do you think you also have something of that in you . . . something of father?"

She was so tense, she had stopped breathing. Perhaps she hoped I wouldn't know what she was talking about. I, however, knew at once, and all too well. My mother was not talking now about her partner, the man who had been my father, but about the man who fathered her. Often, it happened to me that memories or visions— or I don't know what they could actually be—surfaced in my mind, in which I had a man's body, in which I had been transmuted into a male form and sometimes even experienced sex as a man. It was a perfectly normal part of my world, but all the same, it seemed to me that other girls didn't know anything like it, and that in contrast they were aroused by things which had no effect on me. In these memories, I had a man's body, I felt my hard, muscular chest, my soft belly—which, however, had a quite different shape from my real belly—and my long, hairy legs, which wanted to take long, decisive steps. Most peculiar, and most disturbing of all, though, was understandably the notion that I had a penis; here was concentrated an intensity of sexual arousal, such as otherwise I did not know.

Yet, while it was a fact that other girls didn't talk about these things, did that have to mean that they didn't experience them? There are so many things, after all, one simply doesn't talk about! It occurred to me, suddenly, that my mother was probably a psychopath. It was hard to come to terms with this discovery so quickly, and to react in an appropriate manner. Flustered and uncertain, I smiled at her.

In that moment, it was as if an additional weight had settled down on her. Now she knew that we were both the same, that I knew what she had been talking about. She could go on: "It happens immediately, the first time you have intercourse with a man. It doesn't matter what kind of contraception you use, you will start developing an embryo. And he will start to be absorbed. You will ruin him. If you really love him, if you are dependent on him and you don't want to lose him, it will be . . . terrible for you."

I was all agog. "But, Mum, what if he uses a condom? Think about it, it just can't work like that! What if he used, let's say, a vibrator, or some other sex toy? Do you want to tell me that, even under these circumstances, I would become pregnant and he would be . . . absorbed?"

My mother shrugged her shoulders and chuckled softly. "You have a scientific mind. I never tried it. Perhaps it would never even occur to me to try such things. But I beg you—promise me that you'll be careful."

"Hmmm," I put on a neutral face. I had decided I would have to keep a close eye on my mother and keep tabs on all the manifestations of her progressive psychological disorder. So many years of solitude . . . At the same time, though, I began to be gnawed by an imperceptible doubt: what if my mother was right? I had quite a mind to try it out.

"I have an empty flat, my parents are at their cottage," Jirka announced.

With these words he freed me from having to make the difficult decision between taking him home, continuing to suffer through those dreadful scenes in public, and giving up on her plan completely—which, however, would have been extremely boring.

So we were going to have privacy. I hoped that I would finally get rid of my detested virginity, which, when I compared myself to the other girls, was starting to turn me into a psychic cripple.

Not long afterwards we were walking down a street full of exhaust fumes on the way to his house. Of course I was a little agitated— what if my mother was right? But I didn't believe it. I kept repeating to myself that, from a scientific point of view, it was nonsense. Maybe I'd better not tell him that I'd been to the family planning clinic for some pills, I thought. That way he would have to take care of contraception as well, and then perhaps it really would be impossible for anything to happen!

And on top of that I calmed myself with the cynical reflection that, even if my mother happened to be right, it would be quite a nice way to get rid of Jirka. Because my feelings towards him were getting to be truly ambivalent. His body was quite pleasant to the touch, but when I had to talk to him, he bored me, and when I imagined I would have to live with him for a longer period of time . . . No way!

The decor of his flat was loud and somewhat tasteless, lots of horridly garish draperies and a sideboard stuffed with cut glass and the like. He offered me a glass of beer and undressed me. Probably he was in a hurry; who knows when his parents were supposed to get back? He laid me flat on the couch and put a large towel under me. Hey, what if I start bleeding, I wondered? Somehow I wasn't afraid of anything and felt only an enormous curiosity. He turned on the radio to a station which was playing some down-at-heel pop music. He lay down next to me and started to run his hand over my body. "Are you looking forward to it?" he asked. I laughed, I don't even know why, probably nerves. A nonsensical question. How could I be looking forward to something I didn't know? It seemed to me that my response had disappointed him, but fortunately he didn't make a fuss about it. Gradually, I began to attune myself to the pleasant feelings which were being brought on by his foreplay, and later the sex act itself seemed like something long since (even if hazily) known. It was, however, completely different from those masculine memories which sometimes surfaced in my mind—it was much less intense, just a gentle stroking or tickling, not genuine passion, the potent whirlwind of feeling that sometimes seized my body during those masculine fantasies.

The music on the radio changed to a spirited marching band and suddenly the whole situation began to seem ridiculous. Understandably, though, what pleased me most was that I had this experience behind me and that it had been neither repugnant, nor so marvellous that I would somehow be beside myself from it—it had simply been pleasant, and I felt well enough satisfied.

"You want to tell me you were a virgin?" he shook his head afterwards. He went to throw away the condom: he wrapped it in a paper napkin so his parents wouldn't find anything. But the strange thing was, as he walked around the room, all of a sudden he seemed to be almost translucent.

"I'm feeling a bit queasy," he complained, looking me over uncertainly. "I don't know when my parents are due back . . . ."

"It's okay, I'll leave," I burst out hurriedly. Now I would only feel bored with him anyway.

It seemed to me that he was also quite relieved when I said it. He escorted me to the door of the flat.

"Sorry I can't go with you to the tram," he apologized. "I still have to tidy up. To cover our traces and that kind of thing."

A quick peck goodbye on the cheek, and then the door shut behind me. But before I ran out, relieved, into the street, I heard the sound of vomiting from inside the flat. Doubt began to gnaw at me again. I hesitated, wondering whether I shouldn't go back to help him somehow, but then I headed off to catch the tram.

Two months later it was absolutely unambiguous. I had started to suffer from an upset stomach, and I felt an indefinable weight all over my body. Heaviest of all were my breasts, which from time to time even became quite painful. I wanted to sleep all the time. And of course my period was nowhere.

Jirka telephoned me twice. It wasn't that he wanted to get rid of me, he took it quite differently from myself—seriously and responsibly! It was just that he felt so very peculiar—he kept going from one doctor to another, he was on sick leave, but the diagnosis was somehow really strange—and he didn't want to meet me until it was sorted out. I asked him about the symptoms, but his replies were evasive—apparently there were a lot of them, they kept on changing and they were, as doctors like to say, non-specific. There was only one symptom he was willing to give away to me—he was losing weight and he had lost his appetite.

"That serves you right for wanting to fatten me up," I replied sarcastically. But shivers were running up and down my spine. It was a crazy situation because everything was starting to confirm my mother's theory. Of course, I didn't tell anyone about my pregnancy, neither Jirka, nor my mother. I kept it strictly to myself and spent my time thinking about it constantly.

Then Jirka called me from the hospital. His voice was odd. I became aware that he was leaving out a lot of words.

"Somehow I can't walk any more . . . Monika, the doctors—what could it be? And so I—I've stopped enjoying this . . . What if you came to visit me after all? Come—to see me! Come!!"

It occurred to me that he was in a proper mess, though maybe I was in one, too. But on the other hand, it's a fairly normal thing to have an illegitimate child during one's studies. I'd get over it. I almost fainted, though, when I imagined I would have to be like my mother . . . to spend my whole life avoiding men. Or maybe I could . . . but no, that wasn't possible. To pay for every sexual encounter with pregnancy and absorption . . . Good God, I jumped, did that mean I had truly come to believe it? Was it not that I had just gone as crazy as my mother?

I decided that I had to go and visit Jirka.

As a matter of fact, I probably never liked him very much, but the sight of him in the hospital would have shaken anybody—it wasn't important any longer who the patient was.

He looked like a skeleton, like one of those photos that one sometimes sees in the newspapers from countries where there is famine and war. He was covered only by pale, yellowish skin and a thin layer of atrophied muscles. Except he didn't have the same kind of over-size skull and protuberant joints that famine victims tend to have. And somehow that was especially horrifying. His skull and his long bones were growing smaller. I wondered whether the doctors had measured him and whether they were at least a little surprised. His head now looked as if it had been dried out by one of those tribes of cannibals who process human heads as trophies. His goggly eyes gleamed milky white and were barely able to recognize me. It was also evident that he was mentally absent for whole minutes at a time, uttering only monosyllabic cries, which made no sense.

"I . . . I am . . . inside you . . . and you . . . Mother . . . no, please, no . . . ."

For one insane moment it occurred to me that I had become his mother.

When I returned home, everything was visible on me at a single glance. I barely made it to the armchair in the living room and cov-ered my face with my palms in nervous exhaustion. My mother sat down opposite me and for a long time we were silent. I understood that, from this time on, I would no longer have any reason to doubt my mother's attempts to confide in me. Because now at last I be-lieved her.

After a while, my mother sighed. "Lord, those men . . . ."

"What should I do?" I cried. I was on the verge of a fit of hyster-ics, only I had never had one before, so I wasn't quite sure what to expect. But I felt like crying and breaking something brutally into little pieces, both at once.

My mother was stroking my hair, which was not her habit. "I knew it had to happen someday," she said. "I've never managed to find out what causes it. Perhaps some kind of terrible natural force, some kind of strange mutation which ensures that we women will never die out, no matter what the circumstances . . . ."

"So it's going to be . . . a girl?" I looked at her.

She nodded.

"But . . . that's illogical. Surely that means the total number of people in the world would keep getting smaller, if . . . ."

"Not people," my mother replied calmly. "Men!"

"Jesus Christ! And what if . . . what if I now went for an abortion?"

My mother stared at me, her eyes held wide in horror. "That's something which none of us has ever tried so far. Perhaps it would lead to something . . . terrible."

A picture occurred to me of Jirka coming to his senses in the operating theatre in the form of the strange phantasm, the zombie, the half-human creature that he now was, and living that way for several more decades. At the same time, though, something in my mother's outburst had brought me up short.

"Do you mean to say that . . . that you're not alone? That you know of other women who . . . ?"

My mother leaned towards me and whispered in my ear. "You know how every Friday I go out for an evening in the café with my women friends? Well . . . it isn't a café bar. Once you've had the baby, it'll be time for me to introduce you to our company."

Shivers were running up and down my spine again, but at the same time I realized that here was the explanation of my mother's sex life. And altogether of how she managed to live in a relatively balanced way among people who were biologically so utterly dissimilar.

I felt a sense of kinship for my sisters.

And it also occurred to me that their meetings—I already had an inkling that they were not so much a question of polite conversation over coffee, as of a bizarre, phantasmagorical orgy—might finally bring me the sharp, intense feeling of sexual ecstasy I could never hope to have with a man.

I understood that the man I had inside me—like the man inside my mother and the man inside my daughter—might yet bring me a great deal of pleasure.

Translated by Cyril Simsa

E = mc²

Alžběta Šerberová

LITTLE EUGENE ROLLED on to his left side and squinted enchantedly at the sun through the safety net of his cot. Each morning started exactly the same way; he looked forward to it already in his dreams so much he could hardly wait. Then he woke up and it was like that. Hey, it was like that!

From his dreams he proceeded straight into contemplation of light and day. Then a tall, warm, golden woman with azure eyes appeared from somewhere. The great thing about her was that you could yell at her or do the opposite: not speak at all. Today he decided for the latter, because he wanted to run through the evolution of the Sun in his mind once more, as he discovered it last night just before dozing off after his favorite bed-time story about the Little Honey Girl. He had been thinking about its future, but fell asleep half way through.

The woman parted the curtains. Stripes of light flooded the cot with the blue net and Eugene stuck his thumb in his mouth: if the core of the Sun is made of helium with an outer layer of hydrogen, the rate of energy generation inside the Sun will drop, the pressure of radiation will not be sufficient to lift the outer layer, the force of gravity will prevail and the Sun will shrink. That will make the temperature of the layer surrounding the helium core climb, causing a thermonuclear reaction and boosting solar energy. The pressure of radiation will inflate the outer layer of the Sun, its radius will grow and it will expand into a gigantic star. The Sun's luminosity will increase by approximately a hundredfold. Then, of course—

"Good morning," whispered the woman, pulling down the blue net. Little Eugene purred hypocritically and smiled at her. Long, silky arms embraced him and lifted him out of his cot. Then he was stood on a chair in his pajamas printed with teddy-bears and drums.

"We're going to dress our little boy. Dress him in blue and white for this lovely day," the woman was saying, and as she bent down to him he could smell the golden fragrance of her skin. He let her dress him, listening to her baby talk with detached interest. She went on about whether he would be allowed to play with his green car today. Smiling, she rummaged through the compartment with his sweaters. He peered over her shoulder, sucking his thumb. Today he wanted to wear a sweater brown like mud, a longitudinal one. The woman turned to him. "So, which one is it going to be?" She was still smiling.

"The sweata with oblong boat," he whispered.

"You have no sweater with a boat." As she pulled out a blue jumper with white dots on the front, he contemplated the difference between the sidereal and mean solar day. Then he was hoisted on to a chair in the bathroom to be able to reach the wash basin and brush his teeth. He zig-zagged over his teeth with the tooth brush, working his way through the intergalactic environment in his mind, just to keep himself occupied. He found it extremely exciting. His mouth covered with toothpaste foam was smiling as if he were secretly thinking about women.

After breakfast—he'd dealt with matter and anti-matter already on Monday—he had a ride on his toy tractor. Driving around the room and among the chairs with a pensive expression on his little face, he thought about nuclear power, occasionally switching to flying carpets. The glorious morning passed languidly.

"Aren't you hungry?" the woman peeked into his toy corner. To be on the safe side he always demanded lots of them. Most had been taken apart. Eugene smiled, shook his head and quickly hid the pencil behind his back. That was his only vice, he loved to draw on walls. "You're at it again!" said the woman sternly and took the pencil away from him. For a moment he put on a dejected expression, but he had another one stashed behind the large tiled stove. That was where the wall had more diagrams on it than anywhere else. Right next to the chimney was the spectral luminosity of black bodies (for the sake of order he drew a car and a house just above it). The transmissivity of earth's atmosphere to visible and infrared radiation crossed over into the exposed area next to the stove and Eugene was seriously worried about it. Just to make sure, he barricaded it in with a yellow teddy bear.

"Stay here, teddy," he ordered. The woman smiled.

His two older sisters with sandy hair were at school and he took the text books they'd left at home, and climbed up on the couch with them. The smell of fried onion wafted through the room. He quickly leafed through the books, skipping the black print, but closely examining the pictures. He knew that eventually scientists would move to a universal wordless language and so he wasted no time reading.

At eleven he toddled into the kitchen. For a long time he silently watched the gas flame, then the water running out of the tap. All is fire and water, he concluded, but then his thread of thought was interrupted by Kája, one of his sisters who had noisily returned from school.

"Where's dad?" she asked and tossed her red satchel on the chair.

"At work, of course," said the woman. Kája wrinkled her nose.

"What does he do there all day long?" She was in second grade. Eugene hitched up his pants and said into a towel: "Drinks coffee." Then he hid behind the towel. Both women laughed, the big and the small one, and sent him off to play in his room. He wandered into the bedroom where he had the curve of quasar brightness fluctuation. He was losing a lot of sleep over it. To keep it safe, he scribbled it behind a small beige cupboard which he had to shift a little. Then he squatted to look at it.

"What's that child doing there all the time?" the women wanted to know.

"Playing hide 'n' seek!" he shouted, got up and pushed the cupboard in its place. It wouldn't be worth the risk. He still remembered the racket he had to make when they rubbed out the Hertzsprung-Russel diagram with an eraser. That was before he graduated to a ball-point pen which could not be rubbed out from the wall with an eraser or bread. To punish them he refused to eat his dinner that night. Then he laboriously renewed the diagram, and that took several days of hard work, because all he was left with was a single curve (novas, planetary nebulae), and he had to use it to recalculate the temperatures and absolute magnitudes. That was when he felt his loneliness most acutely, the lack of contact with another scientist. Painstakingly, he had to detect his own errors weeks later, consulting with himself on all new discoveries, bringing every proof exclusively for the benefit of his own overworked brain. By noon he was always so exhausted that the big or the small woman had to lift him up on to the high chair at the dining table. He had no strength left. He ate little and longed to look at the newspaper while eating.

"Johanka is coming in the afternoon," announced the tall woman and wiped his mouth with a napkin. Johanka was his cousin and the only person he considered anywhere near to being a genius. Once, over a potted geranium, she whisperingly explained to him the theory of the "green hand" and the spiritual life of cells. She was fourteen then and smelled of licorice. Little Eugene smiled at the memory and peacefully allowed them to put him in bed to have his afternoon nap. And he needed it too. In his dream he saw a film about some woman called Lady Hamilton, in color, with Japanese subtitles.

He was awakened by irritatingly loud female laughter. There was too much noise here for him to be able to think in his cot. Grumpily he pulled the net, slipped down and ventured into the room where the noise was coming from.

"Look, there's Eugene!" said his cousin. He instantly felt unbearably embarrassed. She was much bigger than last time; her black hair was long, and the radiation around her was a hundred and fifty times stronger then he remembered it. She was daintily perched on a chair with crossed legs, drinking coffee and laughing all the time. She was beautiful and exciting and he was glad to be so small because he didn't have to court her. "Come closer," she breathed, scooped him up, sat him on her lap and ruffled his hair. He was disgusted and elated at the same time. He stuttered something. Johanka laughed and pressed him to her body. He felt his heart pound away like crazy. Ah, these women! Ugh!

He moved, stretched, slipped down, and in a state of extreme anxiety walked into the bedroom to calm his nerves by making a little calculation and drawing a curve. Then he drew the profile of pulsars, but still he was not satisfied. He added an active zone, but that woman next door kept laughing in such a disquieting way. With a feeling of bitterness, he threw his pencil down and paced the room, dressed in his pajamas. He felt quite put out.

Full of resentment he got dressed by himself and shuffled back to the room. He had already guessed that the disturbing, disquieting, rousing force had its source in that impossible cousin of his. To cover himself he was holding a broken trumpet in his hand.

"Can I borrow it?" said his cousin. As she aligned her legs next to one another he felt an impact of overwhelming warmth and something like an electric discharge which he had never experienced before. In his confusion he completely forgot the second law of thermodynamics. Standing there helplessly, he absorbed that indiscreet radiation with the whole surface of his little body. He felt faint.

His cousin took the trumpet, examined it and put it away on the table without interest. Resentfully he turned to go back to the bedroom; for one thing he couldn't reach the table, and then he was so terribly hurt by her indifference. He felt his head expanding. He took the ball-point pen, and in an arbitrary short-hand he added to one of his diagrams an old Indian word that described a missile in a range of positions. He went on scribbling, but after a while he developed a headache. He knew that he had come very close to understanding the essence of matter, but his thoughts became erratic, painfully slipping away.

In agony he poked at his afternoon snack. He could feel (but no longer calculate) that a minute on the electric clock was related to the sun beam shattered in a glass of soda water by refraction.

"You're not eating anything," said his cousin and reached for him. He ducked and nearly fell off his high chair. Mother took him down. The others were still eating, but he rushed round the room in a state—he'd give anything for a cigarette.

He stared as his cousin lit up and blew the smoke out. In an instant he understood that she was entirely different from his father who also smoked after meals. She was different even though she was doing the same thing, so fundamentally different, and he had no idea why. He sat in the corner with his toys, watching her and trembling.

"What are you doing there?" his mother asked. The cousin got up and peered behind the stove. He gave her a frightened, hurt look from under his long, child's eyelashes. For a moment, they stared at each other. He was afraid he might faint. Then he burst into tears.

"Come now, Eugene!" cried the cousin, gently pulled him out and pressed him to her body. Helpless and at the same time resisting, Eugene felt a bolt of electric current run through him. In shock, he grasped the polarization of living beings and nearly lost consciousness.

"Leave me alone!" he screamed, yanked himself from her hands, and staggered into the bathroom where he stood on his toes and turned the taps on.

"He probably didn't get enough sleep," said his mother, and Eugene stretched himself on the carpet in the bedroom. I did get enough sleep, he thought desperately, and the world was going up and down like a huge swing. The clear, magical realm of stars he projected on to the ceiling was suddenly blurred, cold and very distant. He kept closing and opening his eyes, then he felt he was crying, quietly, very quietly and humbly. My galaxies and calculations are going to disappear, it occurred to him suddenly, and the pain that followed was unbearable. Newton's law slipped into the darkness with a quiet, rustling sound.

He lay like that until dark. Nobody looked for him; the cousin was telling stories about Italy and he was forgotten. He lay there motionless, small and empty, aching from head to toe.

"Eugene, Eugene!"

He was afraid they might find him like that and he got up. His head was spinning, his hands were hot and his cheeks burned. Automatically he reached for his pen and approached the wall. I'll just jot down Gauss's differential equation, he consoled himself, Gauss's equation, he pleaded with the hand, but the words meant nothing, just as the scribbles on the wall meant nothing, nothing made any sense at all, and Eugene, prompted by a sudden brilliant inspiration, made a quick drawing of something hot and closed. The room spun and the universe cracked with a bang. Then there was darkness.

"Eugene! Good God, what happened to him?"

They bent over him, lifted him, shook him and patted him.

"He's feverish," he heard as if from an awful distance. It was the voice of his cousin. "And here he drew a heart!"

He felt his consciousness leave him, slowly and irrevocably, forever. Johanka, he thought in the last moment of clarity, and then he fainted again. This time it was dark and sweet like a huge pot of honey.

The forty-five year old Eugene Kraus stopped in Ječná Street. A drawing on the wall caught his attention. Just a few basic curves—but where had he seen them before? He stood there deep in thought. He had an inkling that if he remembered where he knew them from, it would help him solve the problem that had been keeping him awake for nights on end. If he could only remember . . . His thoughts were interrupted by a girl's laughter. "Professor Kraus!" a voice called. He turned round.

Zuzana Skálová. A girl with a huge, reckless mouth and hair like wheat. Confused, he glanced at the wall, touched his tie and automatically straightened his back under his jacket. It was summer and all the girls had golden legs like sun beams. And Skálová . . . Skálová . . . .

Translated by Alexandra Büchler

Talibe

excerpts from the novel Gimme the Money

Iva Pekárková

"Y OU MY WIFE, *MAIS* . . . ."

"Well, that's what I am—"

"You my wife but you no want to live with me. I miss. You. At night. *Mais* . . ."

"Talibe, don't you understand—"

"This I want? You think? I marry you? For this?"

With a gesture of contempt (a bit too theatrical) Talibe held up a wad of twenties, Gin's earnings as a night cab driver. She had ironed the notes so neatly with the palm of her hand only an expert would know that every one of them had been once hidden in her sock. Then Talibe let the notes flutter down from his fingers to the table, one by one, giving an angry snort over each one in turn. Seventeen times in all.

"I your husband. I. I want to live with you. *Mais* you—"

Gin sighed. During their year together she had come to understand that there was no point in arguing with Talibe about anything. A year ago she believed that by some astonishing miracle—just as she hit the rock bottom of misery—she got lucky and met a nice, quiet, pleasant guy she could talk to. Guys like that are described as "agreeable." Problem was that Talibe was agreeable only as long as she agreed with him on everything. And Gin was really in a hurry to get married. She managed to squeeze the getting-to-know-each-other-and-cooing-into-each-other's-ear stage of courtship into as little as two weeks. Two weeks of the mating dance were enough for them to make it all the way to the Justice of Peace, across the black-and-white marble tile pavement in front of City Hall, and seal that union which, after all, somewhat resembled the black-and-white pattern of the tiles. At least that was how Gin felt about it, but it wasn't a topic they would discuss together. Talibe himself bore no grudge against Gin's whiteness, none at all; he came from a country black enough not to know anything about color and not wanting to know. He simply didn't think in terms of black and white, and Gin used to like that. But the night they met he grabbed her paw over the drinks they were having in a bar (she a screwdriver and he orange juice with ice with one straw sticking out of it while Gin's had two, so that Talibe wouldn't mix them up and take a sip from her glass by mistake, because although he wanted her to think they were having a drink together, he really had to be careful. As a Moslem he was not allowed to touch alcohol, or tobacco, or women, although, as far as women were concerned . . .) and interlaced his fingers with hers, saying: "Beautiful, *non?*"—and at that moment she felt an urgent twitch of desire that made all her insides constrict with the anticipation of . . . something. That was the moment when over their two yellow drinks Talibe entered her being so dazzlingly, sweetly and fully that she nearly blacked out and the chess-board of their fingers blurred into a warm brownish grey, into the color their children might be one day. For several weeks that beautiful (because only imaginary) bond with him made her see with new black-and-white eyes, and suddenly she recognized that black-and-white chessboard everywhere. In the pavement in front of the City Hall. In piano keys. In the play of the shadows of trees on sunlit sidewalks. In the fresh snow falling on dark tree branches. That winter Gin knitted two wool scarves: a snowy white one for Talibe and a black one for herself. And then she felt a little hurt when Talibe used his for a pillow instead of wearing it.

"I your husband," pronounced Talibe painstakingly in his broken rather than poor English which, after five years in the States, was still saturated with French grammar, French pronunciation, French idioms and West-African thinking.

"Wife. Should live with husband. Wife. Husband, he no have to live with wife. He can with other wife live. *Mais* wife—"

"And how many goddamn wives have you got?"

"*Mais chérie*! Don't you know you—"

As a matter of fact, counting husbands and wives wasn't exactly Gin's favorite pastime. Sometimes it seemed to her that Talibe showed her the pictures of his beautiful sister's children with a pride befitting a father rather than an uncle. She also thought that every month far too many bucks disappeared in the pockets of his relatives across the Atlantic. But all of Talibe's countrymen confirmed that yes, that was the situation — Talibe was a loving son and brother to his family. But as they were saying that, they would often give a little suspicious wink, at least so it seemed to her.

The dialogue between Talibe and his wife had been notoriously lagging for months. Perhaps it never existed at all, but they hadn't noticed it until now. Gin moved out of Talibe's apartment on 116th Street and Powell Boulevard the moment she found out about the duties of a wife: she was expected to sit at home, not go anywhere, but make as much money as possible at the same time — it wasn't entirely clear how — change the bed sheets every day for the benefit of some tribal spirit who refused to live in soiled beds, clean, cook, take care of Talibe's well-being, spread her legs whenever he felt like it, and keep her mouth shut in case she happened to be unhappy about anything at all.

The truth was that she never cooked very much and when she did she managed to make a mess of it. More than once Talibe rightfully reproached her for not even knowing how to fry okra. All she knew was how to open a can of tuna. Their respective culinary tastes were diametrically opposed, and while Talibe kept saying that a single unopened can of tuna in the fridge was enough to attack all his food and spoil it, Gin's stomach was permanently inside out over the food Talibe cooked for himself and which she called his African inedibles. And so during the time they were trying to live together Talibe concocted his stinking African inedibles, and Gin ate outside, exiled to the fire escape in her winter coat, cap and gloves, her beautiful black scarf wrapped around her neck because it was a tough winter, devouring her tuna, salads, raw vegetables and wholewheat bread, washing it all down with grapefruit juice, and generally driving Talibe to despair.

"I not interested in here money at all, *chérie* . . . ."

(Gone were the times when she was willing to fall in love with Talibe just because of his French; when every word like *chérie*, mixed into English, turned her on with its exotic flavor and the romance of distant horizons! Now the fact that Talibe never called her by her name just pissed her off. Her real name, Jindřiška, would never pass his lips, and calling her Gin like everybody else — well, that would just remind him of a certain satanic beverage.)

But they had to wait for another year. Then the bureaucrats were going to invite them to the Immigration Department and interrogate them separately. They were going to want to know where Talibe and Gin lived together, what their apartment looked like, how many times a week they did it, and what brand of toothpaste the other spouse used. Gin was almost looking forward to it: at least to telling them about the kind of shit Talibe stuffs his face with and calls it food. And when it came to toothpaste — ha! Talibe wouldn't even dream of touching that devilish invention made in the USA. He cleaned his teeth by chewing the aromatic roots of some dreadful tropical plant for hours on end.

And when all this was over, then—then, HOPEFULLY!—there would be a permanent green card for Gin, a permanent work permit, no more living together, no three hundred and fifty dollars a month for her share of the rent in an apartment she didn't even live in. And all the husbands of the world, including Talibe, could ceremoniously kiss her ass.

"You must live with me," her husband sounded like a broken record. "*Mais* you—"

"But here in Harlem, it's kind of hard on me."

It was true. While Talibe, thanks to his blackness, had easily blended with West 116th Street, Gin hadn't. And even Talibe began to mind.

"I tell you. Many times. *Mais* you not want to hear."

"Talibe, please, don't start."

"When you drive with taxi. You need amulet. You not safe. Drive with taxi! Who hear of this! Woman with taxi! I not recommend this charm. To REAL women. They stop . . . have blood . . . every month. *Mais* you not real woman. It is not dangerous to you."

"Talibe . . . ."

"And charm works. Really! I hear many stories . . . ."

"Perhaps only in Mali?"

"In Mali? You think? In Mali people have not guns like here. In Mali policemen have not guns, let alone people! In Mali—"

"So what's the charm good for there?"

"In Mali you have charm for everything. For children! For love! For money! New tree. You bend it and hold branches by rope—"

"Okay, Talibe, so why are you working your ass off like a jerk in the US, when all you have to do in Mali is to bend a tree—"

"Not enough trees! This why people poor. And then you have to break rope. Else the charm bring you to the ground. Destroy. *Mais* this what I offer you, against bullets—"

"That one doesn't destroy you?"

"*Mais non!* You only wear amulet. Wear all the time. When you go out, wear. At home, wear. Because you hear stories: they shoot woman through her door. Accident. Accident bullet. If she wear amulet—"

"The bullet would bounce off her, make its way through the door the second time and hit the shooter right in his heart."

"Yes! So powerful! I worry for you, *chérie, mais* for me I don't have to."

"But you take it off before you go to bed, don't you?"

"Before I MAKE LOVE. When you wear it and you touch woman, the charm—"

"So you can't touch me now, can you? That's how it is?"

Talibe, with panic in his eyes, backed up against the wall. "Only touch, give hand, okay. *Mais embrasser, faire l'amour, non, non, non!* It lose all power." Talibe pushed Gin away with his left hand as he tugged with his right at the amulet, trying to take it off. He reverently placed it on top of a chest of drawers. The good luck charm was a worn leather strap with three tiny leather pouches. They contained quotations from the Koran, as well as secret animist inscriptions, known only to the tribal shaman. Talibe made sure it never touched metal or any other text. Then he threw himself at Gin.

On his bed the scarf she had made for him still served as a pillow, the white wool decorated with the minuscule black rings of Talibe's hairs.

His persistent thrusts had pushed Gin into the corner of the bed, until her head was all but trapped between his love and the sloppily plastered brick wall through which Harlem penetrated her skull, taking her thoughts away.

But the center of her body belonged to Talibe.

And to his velvety, ebony pencil dressed in a badly fitting, smelly, lubricated, disturbingly light-blue Trojan brand rubber.

Talibe kept thrusting and thrusting, mumbling "*Chérie, chérie, chérie!*" while Gin, who already knew that this was one of the few situations when Talibe was actually listening to her—at least a bit— said: "We gotta pay the phone bill."

"*Chérie, je t'a*— "

"$378.26. And almost all the long-distance calls are yours. I'll zip out and pay it, that's no problem, but you gotta give me the money."

"*Oui, oui, oui,*" said Talibe whose English worked only when he was sitting or standing, and then he began to mutter something in Mandinge.

The harmony of sounds and movements made Gin come pretty big time; a tropical ocean washed over her and a school of tiny neon-blue fish nibbled at her feet until they tingled. "Oh man, do I love him!" the words shot through her head and she tried to make that moment last forever, to imprint Talibe's face on her palms, to let the Mandinge language penetrate her more completely than all the police sirens wailing outside, the screams of kids in the street, the dirty snow, the thought of the phone bill—but as soon as the neon fish swam away, that gentle and hoarse language began to sound suspicious—perhaps Talibe was calling her names now, what did she know; sometimes she called him names too, tenderly, in Czech.

She stroked Talibe's panther shoulders. "I don't want to hassle you, but . . . we owe $378.26 for the phone and it's all for calls to Mali!"

"*Oui, oui, oui!*" Talibe pushed her further and further into the corner, closer to Harlem, that fragrant exotic neighborhood, "*Oui, oui, oui, oui, oui!*"

"So you'll give me the money right away? 378 dollars and 26 cents."

"*Oui, oui.*"

"And tomorrow I'll go and pay it."

"*Oui, oui, oui!*" Talibe moaned. Then he fell down on her like a freshly cut bamboo, repeating: "*Chérie, je t'aime, je t'aime, je t'aime!* Today I make you baby, baby, BABY!"

And his fatherly pride wasn't a bit hampered by the negligible fact that he'd just wasted his life juice into a badly fitting, light-blue condom of the most common brand.

"*Chérie,*" Talibe said one morning — that is, around one fifteen in the afternoon, guzzling down his cold palm soup, "I marry you, yes?"

"Well, yeah," his African wife replied cheerfully with a heavy Slavic accent, "It was very nice of you, I know."

"*Mais* I have one cousin—"

Gin didn't freak out. She didn't know what was coming. She was just a bit surprised that Talibe should be talking about some cousin at all, so early in the morning. ONE COUSIN certainly didn't belong among Talibe's relatives. Even the word brother meant nothing more than that they were—probably—of the same tribe. But even that wasn't for sure. Gin had already met several dozen of Talibe's brothers: they flicked in front of her, then disappeared—and when Gin dared to ask about the well-being of this brother or that, at first Talibe had no idea who she was talking about and then he waved his hand: "Oh, this one? *Mais* he move long ago to Michigan!" As a matter of fact, all you had to do in Harlem was come out in the street and you'd discover that everyone was a brother of sorts. Limamou, who'd been driving a gypsy cab in Harlem for some time now, told her about a customer who pulled a shiny gun on him, pressed it to the nape of his neck until the smell of steel shot through him as if he was an electric wire, and said, "Black brother, I kill yuh dead, gimme all your motherfuckin' money!"

One cousin, that must be somebody who came more or less from Africa, and whom Talibe drove last night in his taxi to Flushing in Queens.

"One cousin," Talibe continued. "More handsome than me. Very, very handsome. I ugly. He most very handsome taxi driver. *Mais* in Brooklyn. He make forty a day, most. And he need send money to Africa. He no work permit, illegal, you know."

Gin took a spoon out of a used Folgers Coffee can (which now held their cutlery) and stuck it determinedly into Talibe's breakfast. The soup tasted like re-fried orange termites, parboiled in turpentine. Until the end of her days she was going to eat on the fire escape. She went to the bedroom to get a sweater.

"*Chérie!*" Talibe yelled after her. This was unusual, he almost never raised his voice. "I your husband, *non? Mais* you no listen! I talk, you listen what I talk, *tu as compri?* You to my cousin get married. You this make for me!"

Gin dropped her sweater on the floor and then followed it, slowly sliding down the side of the fridge. She sat down on the tiles and hung her head between her knees. No, she wasn't fashionably fainting like a fair heroine in a romantic novel. She only kind of lost her balance, thinking about all the B.S. she'd have to discuss with Talibe in the hour to come. In the City of New York a culture shock lay in wait beyond every street corner — those little Park Avenue ladies who screamed bloody murder every time the taxi hit a pothole; "tough" Wall Street businessmen who used silver tubes to stuff cocaine up their noses in the back seat; Chinatown where she struggled with chopsticks and a bowl of chow-fun noodle soup, and where all the waiters retched every time a Westerner touched his face with his left hand; the laws of the Harlem ghetto where the residents decked-out in the latest fashions were begging for attention but at the same time a curious glance was a crime punishable by instant shooting.

By now Gin should have been used to culture shocks.

But she simply refused to believe that this sort of thing would happen on a more or less daily basis in her own kitchen.

"But Talibe! I am already married! To YOU!"

"He no have money, you know? Forty dollars a day, never more. And his family he has in Upper Volta, I want to say Burkina Faso. Problem, in Burkina Faso, you know?"

Gin had never heard about a single country in Africa which didn't have a permanent "problem," but she kept the observation to herself.

"But I can't have TWO husbands! Jesus Christ! Don't you understand?"

Talibe gave her a look of chilly appraisal. Personally he was convinced that Gin could have a dozen husbands, should the need arise. He could easily imagine her in bed with Limamou, with Traore— pretty much with any of his friends and acquaintances. The thought didn't even bother him any more. And Gin was not going to sleep with her second husband anyway, that wasn't part of the plan. Now he tried to concentrate on this deal, a deal a friend of his had set up. It wasn't going to happen overnight, but in the end Talibe might make as much as seven thousand dollars.

"Here we are in America, Talibe!" his wife was screaming. "I can't get married two times, or three times, or eight hundred and twenty times. I'd get DEPORTED, don't you understand? Everything's on fucking COMPUTERS, don't you fucking understand? If we were in Upper Volta or in West Sahara or in Crocodile-on-the-Nile-land, I'd marry all your cousins, male or female, you ever heard about. If it made you happy. But this is America. Can't you fucking understand?"

"*Mais* he very, very handsome," Talibe said.

Talibe's apartment stood in the middle of the ghetto (that is, if we ignore those experts who will tell you that 116th Street isn't quite Harlem yet, that the morgue begins on 125th, turning into a cemetery somewhere around 145th). In order to enter it one had to climb up a marble staircase smelling of gallons and gallons of dried piss, decorated in the corners with the green bile of junkies and orange bile of junkies-cum-methadone addicts, littered with cigarette butts and empty pot bags—and syringes so used that not even the most desperate of junkies were willing to use them one more time, and old condoms, and crack vials, empty of course, but complete with their orange, purple or pink caps, all that in various stages of brokenness. On the second mezzanine, several bullets were embedded in the plaster, forming a cute little semi-circle. Gin had no idea about their reason, target or success rate, but they sure looked dramatic in the soft, sickly light coming in through the cracked frosted window pane. The peeling paint on the walls was made more lively by the colorful curlicues of graffiti. Sure, they all looked a bit unfinished and awkward: the spray-paint artists didn't pay quite as much attention to them as to the murals on the more exposed outer walls.

(Graffiti in New York, by the way, seemed to be born straight from the plaster; it grew out of the gray concrete of highway overpasses like some strange decorative mold . . . it sprang up within days on any fresh surface; even in places where the artists couldn't get any other way except by hanging down from a rope you could soon spot huge, round, fat, silver-rimmed letters. Gin, who spent her nights sailing down rivers of concrete never once saw anyone actually spraying graffiti. But the designs on every corner, every street, every highway, kept changing all the time, like growing colonies of sparkling bacteria, like the sand dunes in the Sahara desert, shaped by the wind into everchanging shapes which, of course, were always the same for thousands of years. Perhaps this desert theory had a meaning of its own on 116th Street: in Harlem there thrived certain adaptable life forms: plants with amazingly deep roots capable of reaching down for the water of the Earth, thorny cacti storing moisture inside them, fast-legged ants who have half an hour to find food on the hot surface of the sand before they die of dehydration.)

Gin knew she was no desert flower, even though she would have liked to be one. And Talibe was terrified of Harlem.

So he turned his place into an oasis. A sweet-smelling, life-giving oasis.

The door leading to apt. 5C had peeling paint on the outside, and the silverish curlicues on it read PUSSY and KILL—but Talibe painted its inner side a celestial blue, and decorated it with pictures of his whole family: about thirty-five people who Talibe hadn't seen for at least four years. His grandfather, grandmother, father, mother, brothers, aunts and uncles, and also his beautiful sister with four children like little steps—the children Talibe missed so much he could cry.

Talibe's apartment had a spiffy wall-to-wall carpet, always spotless, and its windows were gleaming clean but covered with heavy curtains because, after all, they only looked out at the reality he didn't want to live in.

Talibe's apartment smelled sweet. Day in day out Talibe burned three scented sticks he bought in a botanica on 116th and Park Avenue owned by a certain Rasta. The sticks were supposed to purify the air, get rid of lousy smells and witches—and so Talibe would wave their little flames around the whole apartment day after day, spreading their cleansing smell into every corner.

In the bathroom, right above the spic-and-span tub, was a whole pile of fluffy towels and the metal faucets were all sparkly. By polishing the faucets, Talibe defended himself from the dusty, dangerous reality of Harlem, a neighborhood filled with unknown smells and littered with colorful garbage, papers, plastic cups, wrappers, bags—things children in Africa could play with but that here rotted by the sewers.

Talibe swept his apartment daily.

He swept away the wailing of the police sirens and took it out in a black plastic bag, all the way to the garbage can squeezed in between two blue Grecian columns in front of the building. From behind the dresser he swept out the never-ending fights of his upstairs neighbors. He collected Gin's dumb ideas on a large dustpan, and flushed his unfulfilled dreams down the toilet in the form of used rubbers.

Talibe's cleaning binges suspiciously resembled the exorcism of evil spirits.

All around Talibe's living room, on the clean, sweet-smelling wall-to-wall carpet, several Africans—about fifteen of them—were sitting with their legs crossed. Dressed in richly embroidered long shirts called *boubou* they drank green tea, which was served, as tradition prescribed, three times into the same plastic cup, and they chewed cola nuts which reminded Gin—both in look and taste—of horse chestnuts soaked in turpentine.

The light of a tall lamp reflected on their noses, cheeks, temples and foreheads in so many different ways that even Gin's untrained eye could clearly see that they weren't from the same tribe.

They talked—real loud—in African creole, of which she understood only a couple of words here and there.

As the only woman around she was appointed to serve tea and pile up (with her RIGHT HAND!) more and more cola nuts on a little tabouret in the middle of the room. In her spare time she was supposed to pretend she was cooking dinner in the kitchen. Talibe had decided to splurge on food delivered from a recently opened Senegalese restaurant on 117th Street.

Gin was not supposed to join in the conversation. Which was easy because nobody paid any attention to her anyway.

They were discussing her second wedding.

"You kiss him very, too much, *chérie*." Talibe waived his hands disapprovingly, angrily casting the last bits of a magic powder called Universal Track Sweeper—guaranteed to keep Immigration off their backs—around the subway station.

"We have to kiss at our own wedding, don't you think? That's normal."

"*Mais*, you kiss him. Very—real! With ton . . . tongue!" Talibe blurted out, and although you couldn't see it, Gin was sure he turned crimson. He wasn't used to talking like that.

"Maybe I liked it," his half-wife said brazenly. She grabbed her puzzled husband number two called Ouagadougou by the hand and intertwined her fingers with his, forming a black-and-white chess-board. Talibe began to stutter.

"*Mais . . . mais . . .* you must not be to me so . . . unfaithful, *chérie*, it . . . I Muslim. I not tolerate you . . . I not allow. I—I—I—"

The very same evening Gin followed Ouagadougou to his Brooklyn apartment where — while his three room-mates smoked in the kitchen — they lay down on their wedding bed.

It was a mattress, thrown on the worn parquet floor.

So far, Ouagadougou didn't wear a good-luck charm to protect himself from bullets. But it took him about fifteen minutes to re-move some other kind of magical contraption, made of shrunken snake skin, from his ankle.

They turned off the overhead light to cancel the contrast of their skin color which might disturb their wedding night.

They didn't say much.

Even if Ouagadougou could speak English, he wouldn't have a clue what to tell her.

He took off his pants. He'd only started wearing jeans a short time ago, one of his few concessions to this continent. They got on his nerves.

With a hand he wished belonged to a practiced lover he checked between Gin's thighs.

Gin gave a deep sigh.

Ouagadougou got up, pulled those damn pants back on (so as to hide his confusion) and stumbled to the switch.

Electric light had its uses, after all.

In its yellowish glow he saw an image he'd never seen before.

Wedged between the labia of Gin's private parts, was a protrud-ing wet pink bump. He'd heard about this thing before. But he'd never seen one. The girls of his tribe were initiated at the age of thir-teen: the older women sliced off what they called their "male part" with a stone knife, as tradition prescribed. The genitals of the women of his tribe consisted of a sewn-up wholeness, of devoted meekness, of a opening into which their husband sowed his sperm—and from where, after some time, his son would emerge.

The girls of his tribe were beautiful, dark, smiling and inaccessible. The ritual surgery removed from their bodies that little lump, that tiny bit of flesh, that control switch which would otherwise turn them on and make them unable to say NO.

In the yellowish glow of the American electric lamp Ouagadougou examined the pink genitals of his new wife. They seemed overgrown and untidy. They didn't look anything like the neat scar on the dark skin of the women he'd known so far.

The beautiful maidens of his tribe wanted nothing but a son. But Gin could be manipulated, switched on.

It was enough to touch the pink protrusion between the thighs of his white wife, and she began to moan and writhe, almost as if he was hurting her, but a little differently. She mumbled something in English. Ouagadougou didn't understand very well, but he was sure it was an invitation into the unknown depths of her loins.

In an experienced way, Gin pulled a light-blue condom on Ouag with two worldly fingers.

It wasn't easy to dream of sons.

Gin was climbing up the pukey stairs towards apt. 5C, a huge bunch of keys to all the security locks on Talibe's door in her hand, an arid desert in her heart. She hadn't seen Talibe's taxi in front of the door, and that made her feel a little better, but after a while she concluded that he must have parked a few blocks away. Talibe didn't trust 116th Street one bit, he was afraid the locals might know him, and he refused to park here ever since his taxi was decorated with silver-and-blue graffiti during the short period between four-thirty in the morning and half-past-eight.

My husband will be home, Gin thought, he sure will be home —
and she was already numb with terror. So far, Talibe hadn't really
shown any interest in his wife's sex life (even though, once in a
while, he would complain that a few whacks over his head with a
club would be better than having a wife like his *chérie*) — but he'd
have never believed that she would make a fool of him in front of
the whole African community.

Just as she was passing apt. 4C, the phone started ringing one floor
up. On the mezzanine, she quickened her pace because after the first
two rings Talibe still hadn't picked it up.

When she turned the fourth key in the fourth lock (the lowest
one, the one slightly sprayed over with the second L of the word
KILL), the phone rang for the sixth time.

Gin kicked the door open.

"Is this Miss Gin?"

"Yes."

"How are you?"

"Fine. Who's calling?"

"Good. Good. That's good. This is Limamou. How was the
night?"

Here we go, it's already starting, a thought flashed through Gin's
mind. And from now on, it's gonna be like that for months, what
am I saying—or YEARS. Until I'm dead and buried none of Talibe's
friends is ever gonna look at me without sneering. Why the hell did
I do it?

"I'm fine," Gin managed to say, "but if you want to talk to Talibe, I must tell you Talibe's not home right now, I don't really know
where he is, I myself have just—"

"Good, that's good that you are fine. What was the business like?"

"Business?"

"In the taxi . . . ."

"Well, yesterday I didn't—"

"Good. Yes, that's good," Limamou repeated absent-mindedly. "How about your health? Are you all right? Strong? Healthy? Nothing wrong?"

(Is he trying to hint that I caught something from Ouag? Or what?)

"Well, yeah . . . Why do you . . . Wanna leave a message for Talibe?"

"And you had a quiet night, I hope," Limamou continued, undistracted, his small-talk interrogation. "Nobody gave you a hard time in the taxi, nothing bad happened, the car didn't break down on you, everybody paid the fare . . . How much did you make, by the way? Was it all right?"

"Well, I didn't—"

The rest of Gin's sentence was drowned in a beep and the synthetic voice of a lady said: "PLEASE-DEPOSIT-FIVE-CENTS-FOR-THE-NEXT-FIVE-MINUTES-OR-YOUR-CALL-WILL-BE-TERMINATED. PLEASE-DEPOSIT—"

"*Merde!*" Limamou whispered, then something clicked and the pay phone at the other end of the line gave a contented gurgle.

"Limamou . . . hello . . . where are you calling from?"

"Harlem Hospital. Talibe is here. At night somebody shot him."

Gin was never good at cross-country running, let alone city-street running, but she made the one-point-something mile to 135th and Lenox Avenue in under seven minutes. Meanwhile, she managed to trip over a baby carriage, take down some guy who blocked her way asking for a cig, and get called a "fuckin' white bitch" by a gypsy cab driver who used up quite a bit of his brake pads on her account, at least judging from the screeching.

At the main entrance she jumped a whole line of visitors at the information booth and made her way to the window marked A-M.

"Wait a minute!" a woman behind her back said. "There's a—"

"FOFANA!" Gin screamed into the hole in the plexiglass.

"—line here!" The lady finished, sinking her two-inch long, red-and-gold striped fingernails into Gin's sweater.

The girl behind the window didn't hear her well. "Es like Sylvia?" she asked and turned her ear in the direction Gin's voice. "That's the other desk!" She made a gesture towards the hole named N-Z.

Gin, who was now being dragged backwards from the window by the woman with vamp nails, couldn't come up with a single nice word beginning with an F. Not even formaldehyde. "Eff for . . . FUCK!"

The hands of the black beauty behind the plexiglass began to dance on the keyboard. "Ef-oh-ef-ay-en-ay? I can't find him here. When was he admitted?"

"I . . . I don't know. At night. In the morning."

"He's not registered yet then. What's wrong with him?"

"He got shot."

The line behind Gin emitted a collective sigh. The angry lady carefully extracted her nails from the fabric of her sweater.

"Look at that! White folks dying of lead poisoning too, not just us niggers," a legless old man in a wheelchair commented quietly but clearly.

And that hoarse whisper followed Gin on her way to the elevators, bouncing off the cream-colored walls, invading the creases of her brain in tens of thousands of little echoes.

Talibe was lying on a bed, half hidden behind a plastic curtain, pale as death. For the first time in her life Gin could see little odd-shaped dots on his skin, amoeba-like, connected with limbs and thorns. For the first time in her life Gin felt that there were messages in an unknown language written all over his skin.

Suddenly—and painfully—Gin felt the need to read the hieroglyphs on her husband's body. She deeply regretted all the bad stuff she ever did to him. Within half a second she promised herself that she'd never ever make fun of Talibe again because of the tribal spirit on whose account she had to take a crisp new sheet out of the dresser every day. That she'd never again tap her forehead in exasperation, asking how anyone at least half sane can chew something as foul as cola nuts. That she would learn—

"Hello, *chérie!*" Talibe said and flashed a moronic smile.

He was covered with a thin hospital blanket with little holes through which she could see the bandage around his whole stomach and chest. His wrists were fastened to metal bars on the sides of the bed—and plastic tubes were sticking out of every possible place on his body, with variously-colored liquids dripping in and out. Around Talibe's head, a bunch of machines on little pulleys were beeping loudly.

And at his feet, half a yard away from his long, thin, beautifully shaped big toes, were standing some twelve brothers, cousins and friends, eyeing Gin with reproachful contempt.

"Mrs. . . . Fofana?" the doctor said, having read the name three times on Talibe's chart. Even this guy, though obviously smart, had a hard time putting Gin and Talibe together. "Your . . . husband . . . after getting shot . . . made it to the hospital in his . . . automobile and then walked by himself all the way to the Emergency Room. Pretty amazing. The very fact that he didn't lose consciousness shows he has a strong will to live." He patted Talibe on the mesh-blanket and Talibe gave a dazed grin. "Do you know anything about medical science?"

"Not much."

"Your husband, Mrs. . . . Fofana, lost an amazing amount of blood through internal bleeding. In similar cases it's very common for the lungs to collapse—they quickly fill up with blood, ceasing to supply oxygen to the body, not to mention the fact that the pressure of blood from the abdominal cavity on the pericardium often causes cardiac arrest. On the other hand, a quick lowering of blood pressure in the brain—MRS. FOFANA! Your husband is OUT OF DANGER now! I operated on him myself—I mean, with my colleague Dr. Weissbaum, who's our best GSW specialist. Your husband couldn't have chosen a better hospital, believe me! Here we have three, four cases a day, and people with much, much worse shot wounds go home perfectly healthy. Here in our hospita—"

The doctor looked at his watch, then at Talibe, then at her. "Now, it's twelve fifteen. Your husband is on morphine. He's stable. Can I invite you for lunch? MRS. FOFANA! Are you interested in medical science?"

"Man, that's funny, Gin, that's really funny!" Dr. Whitehead said, sinking his front teeth into a third fried chicken leg. "You mean that whole marriage of yours—"

"The marriage isn't fake at all!" Gin frowned. For the last hour at least, she'd been assuring herself that Talibe was the love of her life. "Talibe married me because—"

(She wasn't at all sure why in God's name Talibe married her but the physician helped her get over her embarrassment.)

"When your husband was coming to after the operation," he said, pulling—with surgical precision—the crusty skin off a chicken leg, "he started shouting something. In French. I'm not boasting, far from it, but, you know, I thought, why not dust off the few lousy idioms I learned in high school, so we began to talk. Do you speak French, Gin? Well, I don't really understand how you two communicated but . . . never mind. Anyway, your husband kept talking about some children or something. MES ENFANTS, that means my children, doesn't it? Who, he kept repeating, is gonna take care of my children? How many children do you have?"

"These are his sister's children. In Mali. In Africa. Talibe used to send them money because—because—I guess you know about families like that."

"I see. I almost thought . . ."

Dr. Whitehead was eyeing Gin—in all decency, of course, only from the neck up—but it was plain that he was trying to figure out how she was equipped between her legs. Gin had noticed a long time ago that her marriage to Talibe often made people do that. In front of Dr. Whitehead's inner eye Gin—spread out like a frog—was lying on a delivery table, a child's head, then shoulders, then belly, emerging from her loins. And the child (white? black? brown? striped? polka-dotted?) welcomed the sunlight of the halogen lamp with screams in some unknown African tongue.

"And you know what was the first thing your husband asked me, Gin?" Dr. Whitehead went on. "He asked me: Did you give me blood? Well, I had to tell him, what can one do, after all, he soaked up at least five liters, otherwise he'd have died on us right there on the operating table; I don't like to tell patients, you know, everybody's afraid of AIDS—but this wasn't your husband's worry, Gin. He says: And did you give me BLACK blood? *Le sang noir.* We were talking French. Do you mean Black man's blood? I say, and I can't believe my own ears, so I tell him: Well, I just don't know, we've got no tests for Black blood so far, we test blood for HIV and hepatitis and—well, you'd have to ask my colleagues the hematologists, they'd lecture you about it for an hour, but for BLACK blood, if you please, we ain't got no tests, I can guarantee that, even though I'm a surgeon, not a hematologist!" Dr. Whitehead said, spitting a thin, angry thread of saliva into Gin's face. "And if you're really so TERRIBLY concerned about getting BLACK blood, you should've told me right there, while I was elbow-deep in your guts. I'd have taken my claws out of your stomach and I'd have made sure that they dyed that goddamn blood black for you!"

"He's from Africa, you know?" Gin chipped in apologetically. "And in Africa blood is—you can imagine: ancestor worship, magic, animal sacrifice, tribal bonds and—"

"And me? I'm not from Africa?" Dr. Whitehead demanded indignantly. "Just look at me, look at the flattened nose on my nigger face. I'm BLACK which means I'm from AFRICA. Exactly which tribe am I from—well, that I don't know, I'm no Alex Haley so I suppose I'll never find out where the toubab caught my great-great-granddad but I'm an AFRICAN, just like your husband. And some full-blooded new arrival with his Black blood shit can kiss my— Jeezus, excuse me, Gin, I just—"

Dr. Whitehead's beeper went off for the third time, he made an apologetic gesture and got up to go. "Oh, don't let me forget, I got something for you." He fished out something from the pocket of his sickly green surgeon's frock. "I mean, it's against the rules but what isn't . . . this is what your husband had around his neck. You know it, don't you? What is it? Some African trinket?"

The object she hadn't been allowed to take a close look at rested in Gin's palm. The three little scrolls of goat skin inscribed with stuff known only to the tribal shaman. It was Talibe's good luck charm which made him bullet-proof. Its sweat-stained string had been severed with surgical scissors and the old leather was covered with Talibe's blood.

"Oh, shit!" Gin whispered.

Standing in front of the mirror in the flat which now belonged to her and Ouag, she tied the ends of the leather strap of Talibe's good luck charm together with a square knot. It seemed to her that the charm was burning her fingers, as though it were the only thing that still retained the warmth of Talibe's body.

With a wet piece of toilet paper she removed the caked blood. She dried it in her palms.

Then she hesitated.

She felt her femininity. Her womb that bled every month. What did Talibe tell her? "I not recommend this charm. For REAL women. They stop . . . have blood . . . every month. *Mais* you not real woman. It is not dangerous to you." Gin shuddered and turned her head. Those words were imprinted so deeply in her mind, it seemed to her that Talibe had just pronounced them behind her back.

Then she put the good luck charm around her neck. The dark smell of goat skin washed over her. She took a deep breath and shivered. The heat of Talibe's good luck charm shot through her body like an electric jolt.

At that moment Ouag peeked into the bathroom. Gin hoped he didn't see anything.

"The sheets need changing," she said dryly.

"*Mais* why, *chérie?*"

"Because sheets need changing every day. Otherwise the spirit of the bed wouldn't like living in them. What kind of an African are you if you don't know a basic thing like that?"

Ouag tilted his head to the side, listening to her English. He still spoke very little but Gin was convinced that he could understand her now. "The sheets need changing. Do you hear me?"

"*Oui, chérie,*" sighed Ouagadougou and went over to the chest of drawers to get new sheets.

She didn't see much of Ouagadougou lately. It was part of the strategy she adopted after Ouagadougou pushed his way into her apartment the very first night after Talibe's death.

Something clicked in Gin's skull and all of a sudden it wasn't hard for her to explain to Ouag—the very next morning—that she didn't live in this apartment for free. That the apartment cost almost seven hundred dollars, which means that Ouag will have to pay. "*Mais, chérie* . . ." Ouag objected.

"No meh-eh-eh meh-eh-eh," Gin said resolutely, "that's what goats do, bleat like that. Seven hundred dollars. Every month! And,

by the way," she added. "Was he your cousin? Talibe, I mean. Was
he or wasn't he?"

"Talibe? *Mon cousin? Mais non . . .*"

"Well, I could've figured that out," Gin said. "In any case, I suspected that I was probably not marrying his cousin. You're probably
not even from the same tribe, but I'll never know these details. Anyway," she continued, "Talibe left his second wife behind. I mean, his
original wife, and four children, I guess you know that. *Un, deux,
trois*, how the fuck do you say four, *les enfants*. Do you understand,
Ouag?"

"*Oui . . . .*"

"And every month Talibe sent them at least six to eight hundred
dollars. So we gotta continue doing that. At least for some time. At
least for a couple months. Until everything settles down a bit after
his death. Do you understand, Ouag?"

Gin grabbed Ouag's paw, entwined her fingers with his and curled
them into a fist as far as it would go. The pressure made her fingers
turn pink, but Ouag's stayed the same.

"*Mais* it hurt me, *chérie!*"

"So you should take care of that, Ouag! Because if you don't send
them money, Talibe's children will go hungry."

It was amazingly easy, forcing Ouag to sit behind the wheel of his
gypsy cab for at least sixteen hours a day. He moved his clunker to
Harlem and was beginning to understand its streets. The business
wasn't exactly great, but Ouagadougou had to make money for Talibe's children. And for the rent for apartment 5C. And for food. And
for phone bills.

Something clicked in Gin's skull and—

Every day she went downtown, to Forty-Seventh Street, and then
she drove around in Alex's brand new, never-never-land Yellow
Cabs, which sailed in gracefully from the street lights on Eleventh
Avenue at five o'clock p.m. sharp.

Every morning, when she got home, she shook out twenty-dollar bills from her sweaty socks, ironed them with her palm on the kitchen table and inhaled their pervasive green money smell. She caressed them. She put them into little hundred-dollar stacks and stuck the fragrant wads in brown paper bags which she then hid— when nobody was looking—into the seven stolen milk crates in the corner of the living room, that still stood there holding the essence of her life.

Translated by the author and Alexandra Büchler

The Martyr of Love

Eda Kriseová

W HEN I LEFT PRAGUE in the morning, the temperature was nineteen below zero, and this time the bus didn't have an accident. I walked through the valley and up the hillside; feeling hotter and hotter I took off my cap and gloves, and at the altitude of eleven hundred meters above sea level the thermometer on the porch showed twenty-four degrees. I brought out a deck-chair, stood it in a snow drift, and it kept sinking because the snow was melting, and I dropped into the chair and waited to see what the difference of forty-three degrees in temperature and nine hundred meters in altitude would do to my body. I lay there squinting at the mountain-scape, which is rugged in places and then again rounded like a woman's body, and the warm air shimmered above the snow. They say that last time there was this much snow was twenty-five years ago. The sun beat down on the snow as if it were the sands of the Sahara, the northern slopes of the mountains were steeped in blue shadows, and my own shadow grew longer and deeper. The sun ripened like an apricot and the frost was coming back from the valley where the glorious day had diminished it, reduced it to almost nothing. Presently it was creeping up, freezing the footprints that had thawed during the day, just as a person who has been briefly softened up by love freezes mercilessly in position when love is over. The day is deceptive, but the night is as truthful as death. Instead of freezing, one could of course do the opposite, mellow, open oneself to death and accept it as joyfully as we accept love.

The temperature drops back again by forty degrees, now it simply must affect me in some way. But I can't wait around doing nothing, because I would soon freeze to death. And so I go into the woodshed, find a heavy cast-iron wedge, get a thick log, so heavy I can't lift it up on the trestle and must work on the ground. It's a peeled spruce trunk; the bark was probably devoured by bugs and the rest finished off by the stink that grabbed the trees by the throat and choked them to death. I hammer the wedge into the log with the head of the axe and the wedge sinks in, and the more I hammer the less angry and the more pleased I become. I feel like Hercules, who is depicted in the Great Tarot Arcana with a club in his hands and the symbol of infinity above his head. The log resists my strength, but then I am aware that knowledge arises not only from the strength of the body but also from the power of the soul, hence infinity. In the Great Arcana the Devil is seated on a throne with serpent force burning upwards through his body, blazing like a flame on the top of his head. He is pointing with two fingers of one hand downward at the Earth and with the other hand up at Heaven; there is a black moon below, and a white one above. Balance is not in certainty but in accepted uncertainty, and knowledge is not in denial but in the act of burning out. Then it doesn't matter whether it is above or below. The worst happens when something up there that only poets and philosophers may occasionally touch in moments of grace, is dragged down to earth to be explained away, and some seem to think that they need nothing but reason to deal with it. People with whom everything begins and ends, and who can therefore change everything. Man as mortal matter, superman as ideology. God forbid! The Devil is in those who make an effort thinking that they can name and explain even the Devil himself, in those who are capable of thinking anew and differently several times within a single lifetime. I hammer them into the wedge with my axe, send them off with a spell into the tree stumps, making them stay there, materialized for ever. Let this world not be theirs, not even for the brief moment when they may be dreaming of it.

The cold has entered the woodshed; in a while my hand will freeze to the wedge and the logs will be covered with ice. I swing the axe up to the ceiling and with one last great blow cut the log in two, pry the two halves apart with my hands until they moan, and so I overcome the tree which grew massive over a longer time than I myself have been in this world, and it would have continued to grow, while my mass is ever diminishing and thinning. As long as the tree was healthy and alive, it exuded Herculean strength that will now be turned into heat, and later in spring, the charcoal ashes will be returned to the woods. When I am unwell, I go and draw strength from trees. Each one is good for something, but oak is probably good for everything.

The saw gets stuck in the spruce log. I need somebody to help me hold the other end, but the only one here with any strength is the frost. And so I suddenly long for the company of other people; I leave the log for tomorrow and set out for the big chalet to have a hot toddy. The manager is there, chopping chop chop on a board. Translucent bits of onion fly up, and he, strong as Hercules, occasionally wipes away a tear with his sleeve. He has to do the cooking himself, because the cook is lying upstairs bleeding: the janitor from the upper chalet had made her pregnant and she had to get rid of it. She has three children already and no man; her husband has left her, and ever since she came up here from the lowlands she has been in love with the manager. One day, the manager went with her to visit her husband, who had not paid her maintenance for months. They found him in bed in a single men's hostel with empty grog bottles everywhere, and when Mrs Halíková started reproaching him tearfully, with her head hunched between her shoulders, looking like a betrayed little blue-eyed girl, he didn't even let her finish, but got up, grabbed her by the neck and the bottom, and threw her out into the courtyard, where she fell on her knees. The manager, who would never hurt a woman, gave him a good hiding. They came back, and since then Mrs Halíková worships her champion with a devastating love. He is the first knight she has known in her life, her Prince and God the Father in one. It seems to her that the manager knows everything she doesn't know and can do all the things she can't. She mops the kitchen floor three times a day and takes a bath twice a week to wash off the greasy steam and the smells of the food she cooks. She dries her oily skin with toilet water until it is white and pink and smooth, but the manager doesn't want her, even though he doesn't have another woman. He can't become involved with her, because, for one thing, he is twice her age, and he knows full well that old stags are shot so as not to spoil the herd, and secondly, maybe because all the love has fallen onto one side, there is nothing to share and there can be no balance.

The manager would know how to fight a lion, yet he doesn't know how to handle women, because he doesn't know how to destroy them. He knows he has a sin on his conscience because he's not sleeping with Mrs Halíková, he knows he is responsible even for her pregnancy. He knows it well and that's why he looks after her children, now, when the poor woman is lying upstairs in terrible pain, deadly pale, with little blood left in her. It is possible that the manager wants to stay with his sorrow, because he is used to it and if he suddenly had to face joy he would feel ambushed and would probably back off, just as he backed off from Mrs Halíková, whose pupils dilate after a couple of drinks and whose eyes become covered with an opal-colored membrane like the eyes of a tomcat who's had a taste and wants some more. How often she ran up to the manager's bed and lay down crying so hard that he couldn't throw her out. In the end he had to call the maintenance man, who was in the middle of working on one of the female guests in his room, and the maintenance man had to get up and throw Mrs Halíková out, but she wrenched herself free and ran up past the trail-marker poles to the janitor, with her face red from crying and her hair wild. She would wrap a woollen scarf around her head and brave the northern wind, blood rattling in her veins; she is only twenty-two years old, and with every step she sinks deeper into the snow the same way she sinks into her own life. After a night like that she comes to the kitchen at six in the morning, her eyes bloodshot with dark circles underneath, her hands coarse from hard work, but her body is warm, silky and peaceful. She works as if she wanted to earn herself sainthood, as if she were doing penance for the sin of her life.

I sit at the bedside of this martyr of love, who tearfully confesses that she couldn't keep a fourth child, and that everybody thinks it was the manager's anyway, because no one believes that she could live with him under one roof in utter chastity and decency, and that she herself feels as if the manager was the baby's father and not the janitor, who merely substitutes for him in the dark. No one knows about her night-time trips along the trail-marker poles. She herself doesn't know where she's spent the night when the morning comes; her head is empty and she avoids the manager. He shouldn't have given her a slice of bread with butter when she was ill, he shouldn't have looked after her children. She wasn't used to crying when she was mistreated, but she cried when he was kind to her.

And when I return from Mrs Halíková's room where, yet again, I couldn't see the manager's love in her Tarot cards and therefore couldn't promise it to her, there is a party sitting round the table in the hall, talking about burglaries. I listen as they tell about all the things they had in their cottages: stereos and old books and paintings and record collections and fridges and lawn mowers. Next to me a woman's voice whispers persistently: "Go on, invite him, and when he comes, ask him openly what he has against you. Problems of this kind need to be aired. Is it your problem? No, it isn't. You're frank with him, but his behavior towards you has been quite unacceptable for the whole week."

"Shall I ask him directly?" the lady engineer asks the expert in human relationships. Earlier, she was putting on make-up in the ladies' room and told me, all excited, that she was going to invite the manager to join them at the table. I knew what he was going to say, and I waited, worried that he was going to tell her the very thing she never wanted to hear all her life, and I longed to escape to my freezing cottage, build a fire, get into bed and watch the reflection of flames on the ceiling as I defrost.

She's getting ready, I can see her blushing, the manager is just talking about his father, and the lady engineer interrupts him at the wrong moment, the manager is running full speed and when he comes up against an obstacle, he wants to swerve and avoid it, but she stands in his way once more, and that really gets to him and he is now convinced that she's a cow and always has been, and an old bag on top of that, who may have been good-looking thirty years ago, but now she's a frustrated fifty-year-old mutton pretending to be a young lamb.

The lady engineer puckers her face like a child, bursts into tears and rushes off, followed by the psychologist, who has pulled her upper lip over her teeth, which look as if they've been pried inward, and narrowed her eyes into two triangles. Her bangs bounce bellicosely; she's in her element. They go upstairs into a little room where the psychologist explains to the old bag that she is no old bag at all; on the contrary, it's the manager who is asocial, unbalanced and a psychopath, who speaks like a child, not like a parent or an adult. He's dissatisfied with himself, hence all his aggression. He was jilted once and now he takes it out on all of us women. A man like that should get himself treated, not work with people he can hurt.

Mrs Halíková is lying in the next room with blood clots falling out of her, transparent tears and white drops of milk she sheds for the unborn one running down her white nightdress. Nobody can explain to her why, at the age of twenty-two, she has three children and an alcoholic husband who used to beat them all up. Why she is stuck in that cauldron in which for generations nothing turns into the philosopher's stone or into gold, but remains ordinary rock, hard and heavy. What did I do to deserve this? she is asking, and while the psychologist would describe the question as childish, no one will ever give her an answer. Life is one continuous pain, Mrs Halíková says to herself, and she has no idea that she might write this somewhere, because she is convinced that the experience is hers alone and she wouldn't want to spread misery, not even in thought. As she grows old, she will protest less and less, and she will no longer find it easy to run astray on bleak, snow-covered slopes.

"I hear you're a writer?" says the psychologist the next day as we're queueing on the ski run. Up close she has the thinnest of eyebrows, plucked so that they look like antennae, a waspish face on which she is wearing a smile: we're on holiday, aren't we, and, after all, queueing is a common human situation.

"I have so many stories I could tell you," she smiles, revealing her pried-in teeth. "I could tell you reams. All juicy morsels for literature."

And while we wait, she tells me the story of a young girl who was afraid to go outdoors. She had undergone psychoanalysis, not symptom therapy, because that solves nothing. "We have to get to the root of the problem, find the cause, and we keep working, plunging deep, until we find it. And what a joy it is to see a complete person in front of you, a person you can understand; everything becomes suddenly clear because we've discovered the cause. Take this girl, for example. After several years we found out that she was afraid of her mother. Every time she got ready to go out, her mother would tell her that she wasn't pretty. And the girl would leave her house with a sense of not being liked by her mother, and subconsciously wanted to pay her back. She had nothing but her own virginal body, and, quite unconsciously, she wished to become a prostitute. But her wish clashed with fear and with general morals, and the patient was unable to resolve the ensuing conflict. And that was why she became afraid of going out in the street. Once a problem is solved, it appears to be very simple, doesn't it? We devote all our time to the patients, take them to therapy camps, and you wouldn't believe how they open up to us there."

It's not her fault, I tell myself. One has to blame science. She's simply the so-called technical type. Science flattens the world, evens out mountains and valleys, smudges all colors into one perfect gray. Science does not create the world, it analyzes it, and has given this woman power over desperate people, just as it gives power to everyone who asks for it.

"And does the girl go out now?" I ask like a sly fox from a Chinese fairy-tale. The lady doctor rises to my bait. She would have swallowed an empty hook, because she insists that human life has to be described truthfully; one mustn't make things up, but write down only what's been scientifically proven. Art should show people what's right and wrong, and what they should be like.

I ask again and she admits that the girl does go out, but reluctantly. She has learned to overcome her fear, she even goes out to work, just around the corner from her home. The wonderful thing about it is that it isn't taken for granted as with others.

And she goes on about cold-hearted mothers, how they're capable of abusing their children and what damaging effects this can have. At that moment she remembers that she is neglecting her husband, who is also standing in the queue, and she turns to him, bares her pried-in teeth and takes him by the hand, so that he knows and feels that they are on holiday together. With me she spreads enlightenment, with him love. And she tells me that on weekends they get up at ten, and have a long breakfast and that those are the most beautiful moments of their married life.

Her husband, also a doctor, gives a grateful, desiccated smile and says: "We would even look forward to our retirement if we weren't worried about not having enough money."

"We love our work," says his wife. "I may not want to get out of bed in the morning, but once I'm at work with my morning cup of coffee, I am happy. Coffee is the most innocent of all drugs and the only one I indulge in — I don't smoke or drink. We don't smoke and we don't drink because it would give us a headache, isn't that right?"

Her doctor husband repeats his smile. Was he ever sexy when he was young, before he became so flaccidly kind? A man has to be a bit naughty, not a crafty bastard but an open one, I say to myself, and look around to see whether I'm going to get a chair-lift seat together with that handsome young Slovak, with whom I have already gone up three times and who waited for me twice on his way down the slope. I like the way he draws a wavy line in front of me on the ground and in the air, like a demiurge, controlling his body from knitted cap to snow boots, as if it were one with his skis, gliding down beautifully, while I follow him much less skillfully, but more so than usual, as if he had shown me the way or at least smoothed it down for me. I hang on to his suppleness and lightness, skirting the bumps just as gently, the ground undulating under me, and the faster I go, the lighter I am, until I feel that I could take off and float above the blue valley.

"You'd find so much interesting material in our work," says the psychologist. "There are reams of people's life stories and nobody is ever going to use them. And these are resolved lives, mind, that's why they should be evaluated in art."

"I don't need any stories," I say. "I hardly have time to write them. In fact I have less and less time for writing, because I need more time to live. I'm wilder, more amorous, freer. And at the same time I know that as my life diminishes, my writing will diminish as well, but I don't care. It probably has to be both at the same time, or nothing at all."

"That's an interesting problem," say the psychologist, but I'm no longer listening, because I have just noticed that I am going to go up with the young Slovak again. He is the odd one out and so am I, and I hold on to my gloves and ski-sticks, so as not to lose them, because if I dropped something, the next wonderful ride would be lost.

Translated by Alexandra Büchler

The Good New Times

Lenka Procházková

Bruncvík has no sword.[1] Maybe it just broke. Material fatigue. Or maybe they're changing it, making a new one for him with a gilded tip. What do you think?" she asked. But he didn't answer. Absently stirring the spoon round and round in his cup, he was staring at the sketch of that stupid bed. Before, they used to talk at breakfast. "It's going to be a nice day," she said, trying to bring back the good old times. "I'll put the washing in to soak and then I'll do the shopping. I'm going to make potato fritters for lunch, what do you say?" He didn't say anything, because he wasn't listening to her. He was drawing in his pad. "In the afternoon I'll hang the washing out on the balcony," she went on with her pointless monologue, gazing out at the sunny courtyard below their window with unfocused eyes. "I'm sure it's going to dry before the end of the day," she added in a tired voice. As tired as if the end of the day had already arrived, as if she'd already done the ironing as well. The man opposite her looked up at the clock. It was eight. He gave a surprised whistle, finished his coffee and got up. "What are you going to do today?" he said quietly as he passed by her chair. She clenched her teeth, kept her mouth shut. "Just don't do the washing, it's going to rain," he said, and left the room. While she rinsed the dishes, she could hear through the closed door and through the sound of running water that he'd already started planing the wood.

When he first came up with the idea, she thought it was great. She watched him the whole day, his deliberate, unhurried movements, and inhaled the scent of sawn forest. Later, her enthusiasm evaporated, she no longer felt as if she had been chosen to participate in a ceremony. His persistent hammering and sawing drove her out into the streets. She would prolong her shopping and errands, queue for hours to buy bread and vegetables, taking in the trivial conversations of strangers. She even began to like the sound of honking cars. But then she would shut the outside door and the squealing of the electric saw replaced the supportive sounds of the city.

She began letting herself into the apartment ever since the second time he hadn't heard the doorbell, and she would go straight into the kitchen, feeling hurt. There, on the wobbly kitchen table, she prepared a cheap and therefore labor-intensive lunch. Around one o'clock she had the table set; that was the time when he would be driven in by hunger. Sitting at the table, she realized that he didn't care what was on his plate, whereas before . . . .

Before when? Only three weeks ago, she realized to her astonishment. It was only three weeks ago that he brought those planks in a van. The driver helped him stack them up on the mezzanine floor, and from there he carried them up on his own, while she, the expectant mother, sat on the stairs keeping an eye on the remaining ones, pleased that their nights on the makeshift foam mattress were at an end, that she had a man who could make a bed with his own hands. That was the first night when she could smell the forest on his palms, and in the morning he showed her a sketch of the bed. She was in awe at its complex design and dimensions, and she thought it was wonderful, also because he got his second wind after a long period of apathy. It wasn't exactly a solution to their situation (more than a new bed they needed a new bank account or any kind of gainful work) but it was an excellent activity for a convalescent. It took a few days before she understood that he didn't take the making of the bed as one would take a course of vitamins, that it was more like a drug, all consuming, one he couldn't do without, not a means to an end but an end in itself. She became certain of it when he started working into the night, clandestinely and almost soundlessly. The first time she caught him at it he was drilling holes to put in the pegs. Until then the skeleton of the bed had been nailed together and she thought that was final. The pegs meant that he was trying to prolong his work, that his aim was no longer to make but to keep making. He was working in his pajamas with sawdust falling on his bare feet. "Nobody in the whole city is going to have such a huge well-made bed," she said quietly then. "Nobody but the three of us." He glanced down at her round belly, and then led her to the foam mattress. "Go to sleep, you two. I'll be with you soon," he promised, but he didn't come, and she could hear the muffled pounding as he drove the pegs in with a hammer wrapped up in a rag.

But he will have to finish one day. The latest deadline is a given: she pressed her palm on her belly. But what are we going to live on until then? And after? She hung the wet kitchen towel on a hook and went to check their stocks.

The upper two shelves were empty, on the lower one huddled a lonely Proust, but they'd already rejected him the last time, and so she decided to cull Remarque. She applied a strict elimination method, convinced that Remarque would understand, and in the end, there were two books left on the shelf. *Three Comrades* and *Arc de Triomphe*. The victims condemned to being sold were placed in a bag, carefully, as if they were gold bullion. Once more she looked up at the thinning fourth shelf and then hastily backed to the door. If nothing happens within three days, it will be Heinrich Böll's turn, then Steinbeck's. (Except for *East of Eden*, which was safely ensconced among their emergency reserves, right at the bottom where she could reach from her mattress when she couldn't sleep at night, and listened as the hammer wrapped in a rag marked time instead of the tower clock.

There was a queue at the counter marked "Purchase" in the second-hand bookshop. She joined the end of the queue, put the heavy bag down and took out the gold bullion lying on top—*The Night in Lisbon*. At first she just turned the pages, read a paragraph here and there, but in the end she had to be reminded that it was her turn. "So now you got to Remarque," the buyer shook his head and started writing down the titles and the prices. He twice underlined the total and pushed the receipt towards her for a signature. "Only eighty-six?" She was astonished. The young man shrugged. "What can I say? These days nobody's interested in fiction. Bring me some dictionaries—English, German, or a recent road atlas—and I'll sell them like hot cakes. You see," he confided in a low voice, "people are being practical. Who's got the time to read?" he tapped the cover of the book lying on top. "*The Road Back?* Get away!" he concluded, agitated.

She was still thinking about what he said outside in the square and forgot to avoid the statue of the resentful Karolína whose books she sold and cooked through last winter.[2] "Forgive me, will you?" she now said repentantly, but Karolína just stared across the road with a frown on her face. "You see, these days people no longer have diamond brooches in their drawers to sell when the bad times come!" she blurted out indignantly, wanting to go on to say something more specific, when she heard some shouting nearby. It was an angry male voice. She couldn't make out the words, but from the monotonous intonation it seemed to her that he was repeating the same sentence over and over again. People stopped and turned around, looking for the source of the racket which was now joined by rhythmical banging of metal against metal.

It's coming from the traffic island, she thought, from the tram lines. Some sort of alarm? She held her breath and lifted her face to the sky. It had an even blue color, no white jet traces. With determination she started walking towards the tram stop. The road was deserted and so was the traffic island. A small crowd of gawkers stood obediently on the sidewalk, and she could clearly see the man who was madly banging a metal bar against the tracks. At first she was surprised that such a strong voice could emerge from such a slight body, until she finally understood what he was saying. "Number eighteen, come to me!" the white-haired old man shouted, no, screamed at the top of his voice. Standing with his feet wide apart, he held the bar with both hands, creating fireworks of sparks every time he brought it down. "Number eighteen, approach!" he commanded and people watched him with quiet fascination. Nobody was laughing, because the spectacle was in no way funny. "Number eighteen, approach!" he shouted one last time, before he straightened his back and clambered onto the traffic island to meet the tram he had just conjured up. His face was creased and so were the seams of his overcoat; he was leaning on the metal bar as if it were a walking stick, greeting the driver with a wave of the other arm. But before the tram stopped, a police car screeched to a halt. People stepped back into doorways and arcades, the metal bar clanged on the cobblestones.

"They'll let him go again," said the greengrocer, "poor guy, he's a certified nutter. He's the only one who can shout whatever he likes. I should keep the bar for him," he remembered and went out in the street to fetch it. On his way back he noticed her loose dress. "Take some oranges with those potatoes. They're not really worth much," he said, shaking the box with the shrivelled brownish-green fruit inside, "but there must be some vitamins in them. C'mon, be a good mother, I'll give you a kilo, what do you say?"

She returned with her shopping to the park. It was deserted now, shortly before noon, and she sat down on a bench by the pond. She took out an orange from the bag, wiped it with a handkerchief and started peeling it with her teeth and nails. The fruit was hard and dry inside and tasted like sweet sawdust. An old woman stopped by the cement edge of the fountain. Looking around cautiously, she pulled out a large enamelled container with a lid from her bag and two aluminum pipes. She deftly fitted them together, tying a wide net at the end.

The second orange was juicier, although it tasted slightly rotten, but she ate it anyway. Meanwhile, the woman caught three goldfish, slipped them into her container and went home to cook her lunch. Two large drops splashed on the path. She looked up, surprised. The sky turned dark, the sun had disappeared. How did he know? She tossed the orange peel into the litter bin and headed home, giving Karolína a wide berth.

The rain got heavier and colder. A covered truck came from the intersection, pulling up by the sidewalk in front of the butcher's. The people who had been hanging around the shop window quickly formed a long queue, others came running from the tram stop. The driver lowered the side of the truck, climbed up, drew back the cover, then tossed out two rolled-up flags. The crowd sighed with disappointment, a police car immediately raced down the square and a resonant voice called out: "Citizens, disperse! Your gathering is illegal!" The brakes screeched and four policemen jumped out, their white truncheons at the ready.

She ran through an arcade into a side street and there she stopped under a scaffolding, breathing fast. "*Prosze, panià*," a muffled voice said behind her in Polish. Excuse me. She jumped and turned round. The man had a stubble, but his grey suit looked nice, except now it was a little wet from the rain. In a handkerchief spread on a narrow palm she saw two gold wedding bands. "*Prosze, panià?*"—"No," she shook her head apologetically, and he bowed slightly like a rejected dancer at a ball. Before he backed into the semi-darkness of the arcade, she noticed that he had shoes on, but no socks.

She hurried down the steep street, whipped by gusts of cold rain. The door of the building wouldn't open until she leaned on the handle with all her might and managed to get the lock unstuck. It shut behind her with a loud bang, and then there was silence. When she reached the landing, she still couldn't hear the usual persistent noise coming out of their flat and before she could get her keys from the bag, he opened the door himself.

"Thank God!" he blurted out with relief, dragged her into the hall and embraced her tightly. "You were so long, I was beginning to worry." "Worry?" she was amazed. "You're soaking wet. Take it off quickly, while I run a bath for you. You mustn't get ill now!" he rushed into the bathroom, turned the taps for a while, then swore loudly. There had been no hot water for a week, but he probably never noticed it until now. "You know what, lie down and wrap up well, I'll make some tea right away." He brought it before she managed to put on her flannel night shirt, and she quickly slipped onto the foam-rubber mattress and pulled the blanket up to her chin. He knelt down next to her on the parquet floor and touched her hair with a searching hand. "Where's your hair dryer?" "In the second-hand shop!" she said cheerfully, and lifted the blanket invitingly. He shook his head, covered her up again and handed her the tea. She took a sip and blinked with surprise. "Where did you get the rum?" "Bought it. That and a few other essentials." "Like what? And what did you pay with? Has somebody sent us money?" "I had an emergency reserve. Drink your tea now."

She passed him the empty mug and lifted the blanket again. "No. You must go to sleep now." He covered her, got up and turned to look at the window whipped by rain. "And you?" she whispered. "What are you going to do?" "I still have some work to do on the bed." "I see," she yawned. "The bed. I'd forgotten all about it."

The humming of the rain went on, accompanying her into her dreams, but not even the sound of thunder and the wailing of the police car sirens outside could bring her back to consciousness. She dreamt that she was in a forest, she could hear somebody logging trees nearby, she could clearly hear the sound of the axe. There was the sound of shattered glass and a cold draught over her head, but soon she felt better when a pair of strong arms lifted her protectively, carried her to safety and tucked her under a duvet. She finally opened her eyes. She was looking straight into the blue sky against which circled powerful flocks of birds. Two seagulls were sitting on the high railing of their bed which was slowly rocking on the waves.

"Good morning," said the man next to her and unscrewed the lid of a thermos flask. "Coffee?" She sat up and stared around at the endless confusion of muddy water all around her. The horizon ceased to exist and the way back became a legend. She gulped down the hot coffee and rinsed the cup. "There is a pair of binoculars in the drawer. Can you find them for me, please," he asked.

Translated by Alexandra Büchler

1. Bruncvík: legendary knight connected with the Roland epic, whose invincible sword is said to be walled up in the Charles Bridge to be unearthed at a time of the nation's greatest need by St. Wenceslas who will arrive on a white horse and defeat the enemy.

2. Karolína Světlá: 19th century novelist, one of the founders of modern Czech fiction.

Dear Jirka . . .

excerpts from the novel Manure of the Earth

Zdena Salivarová

IMMIGRANTS ARE THE *manure of the earth, and for more than two centuries they have transformed this land into a blossoming grove.*

After many, many rewrites, I finally turned to the epistolary form. To me, it seems appropriate for an emigré novel—in exile, a letter is the best form of communication among people scattered to the four winds in this world of ours. Neither the telephone nor an audiotape can evoke in me the kind of joy I feel when I see the postman bringing an envelope with a message for me in his mail bag.

Dear Jirka,

You probably don't know that we're in Canada, David and I. But I know that you're in Frankfurt, and what's more, I know you brought the manuscript of your latest novel with you, the one they axed. No, nobody told me, but I am absolutely certain, because I can imagine what you packed when you ran. *Omnia mea mecum porto*[1] isn't that the way it is? As for your address, I got it as part of an extensive research project I've undertaken. I'm not the only one to have taken up this new sport—how else in this wide world would we ever find one another? One person knows a few others, each of those knows some more people, one and one are two, two and two are four, four and four are eight and so on. So far, I've collected some 300 addresses, including yours. And because I still entertain my idealistic faith in the old saying "A Czech has a brother everywhere," I shall continue to contact all our brothers and sisters and expand my list. What for, you ask? Remember what I wanted to do and actually started to do, back home? Now do you get it? What I want to launch here is not too different. A publishing company. Except this time I won't just be editor, I'll have to be bookkeeper, receptionist, secretary, typist, shipping clerk, and anything else that I fortunately can't imagine right now.

Do you know how many suitcases with axed manuscripts like yours have spilled out into the world? And have you any idea how many more could still be written, and this time not for axing, since the arm of the censors/axers isn't that long.

Thanks to my new hobby, I've already made contact with Otto Wagner (where else but in Israel), Bouza (washing shop windows for a living in Winterthur—an interim solution on this side of the world, but back home it would have been his lifetime career), Hulánek (Sweden), Matyáš (New Zealand), Pachát (USA), Zajda (Tasmania), Horník (England), Dušan Klásko (Vancouver), Koubková (in Italy, but she's ticked off at everything and told me outright that she doesn't want anything at all to do with that quagmire back home, so she's quit writing, and if she ever starts writing again, it'll be in Italian. I believe it. She's so smart that, if she set her mind to it, in a year she could be writing in colloquial Sanskrit. All I dare hope is that, in time, she'll get over being ticked off at our nation).

Actually, I don't think we can turn our backs on that quagmire. On the contrary, I think that, now that we're on the outside, we need to poke and prod to let the fresh air in. And I also believe that manuscripts tucked away in desk drawers could be lost or burned or could simply disintegrate, and ought to be published, printed, even if we can't publish them on the scale that Czechoslovakia's Readers Club used to. David worries and predicts disaster, while our good friend Mr. Karlík shakes his head and says that while it's a good idea, it's not all that original, because ever since the middle of the last century, as long as there have been Czech refugees, people have been trying to get something like that off the ground with little or no success, except for a free-thinker called Geringer in Chicago, who lasted a little longer than the others. And as a deterrent example, he cites the case of a certain unappreciated Mr. Vlach, an idealist in exile who literally worked himself into an early grave in the effort, not all that long ago and not all that far from Toronto.

And yet, after the Communist putsch in '48, huge numbers of Czechs scattered all over the world, and then, in '68, after the occupation, our wave of emigrants spilled out, and I can't help thinking that both waves included a lot of us who wouldn't be caught dead on a streetcar without a book, not to mention going to bed without one. And the doctors! Tell me, Jirka, have you ever gone to see a Czech doctor who doesn't start a conversation about literature as soon as he hears that's what you do, instead of asking where it hurts and when did it first start bothering you? Mr. Karlík replies that I may well be right, that his generation wasn't much into reading books, because they'd never experienced censorship or book-banning. Mr. Karlík is one of the people here who don't hold it against us that our beginnings have been easier than theirs. Ultimately, he agreed that it wouldn't hurt to give it a try, but advised me to proceed slowly and carefully, so as not to drown in it like poor Mr. Vlach. And he signed up then and there as our first subscriber. David vacillates: sometimes it seems that he actually likes the idea, sometimes his main concern is that we don't go bust, because if we do our enemies in Prague would be delighted. We do have some money saved up, we'll invest it in the project, our teeth can wait. Something tells me it will work, don't ask me to explain it rationally. The bastards in Prague maintain that those who left Czechoslovakia will perish intellectually in exile. Well, as I see it, it's much more likely that we'd have perished back there, where literature is in the hands of various Skálas, Kozáks, Pludeks, Pilařs and the like.

Jirka, do send me your manuscript. Or are you one of those who only want to write in German, French, English? If you are, well, you can go ahead. And then you can just keep right on going, because you won't be a friend of mine any more.

And I'll close with a motto: "There's no actor without an audience, no scribbler without a readership."
Your
Věra (still) Šimek
(Evil tongues back in Prague are spreading the tale that I made David defect to the West on account of mink coats, and now they say that he walked out on me, because he can't afford them.)
P.S. Could you drop by the nearest telephone booth and liberate a Frankfurt telephone book for me?

Dear Věra,
Enclosed is a handful of addresses, but each of them is a sure thing. They all think it's a fantastic idea, and are anxious to hear when the first book will be published. Bráňa is here too, he hung up his writing up on a hook and took a job with IBM in computer technology, back to his old metier. When I told him of your plan, he looked dubious but I know I put a bug in his ear. Never in all my life have I met a writer who wouldn't want to be published. Bráňa will come around, don't worry, and you'll be sure of at least one good title for starters.

I've never even considered writing in German, although as a foreign language I don't find it all that difficult. I read, I speak, I understand, now and then I can even put together a piece for the newspaper, or, more often, a letter to the editor (there's always something going on that cries out for commentary from our point of view) but prose, well, that would take more gall than I possess. I can't imagine myself writing a German dialogue that wouldn't sound like a conversation straight out of a German phrase book. Besides, you know how I love to play with words, puns, verbal imagery, street talk and pub talk, and if I were to try that in the language of our traditional enemies—who have actually turned out to be quite good to us these days—well, it's just beyond me.

I'm sending you the manuscript of *Life Among the Thorns*. Of course I brought it along, in fact, it's so thick that I hardly had any room in my suitcase for anything else. I left when the rumor started that they were going to deport bothersome authors to Siberia. Actually, it was Vydra who gave me the kick I needed. He came up with an invitation for some fictitious study trip to Germany, and shoved me on the train, at least, he said, for the worst of it. Everything would calm down in a year and we'd all be back home, at our old desks. True, he didn't sound particularly convincing. Or convinced. He didn't look all that well either. Skin and bone, wan and weary, and trembling all over. I wasn't the only one he helped get out, there was a bunch of us, and I don't want to think about the risks he took to do it. Especially since his dear departed mother can't protect him any more, now. She must have been spinning in her grave when the Prague Spring came and cast the light of day on all the "errors" the Party had made. Vydra certainly is no chip off the old block, and turned out to be a solid character. And to think we mistrusted him all those years. In fact, I was doubtful myself until the last minute, afraid that I might be falling for some kind of a ploy. But by then, both Bráňa and Vobruba had left the same way, so I risked it. It goes without saying that it wasn't long afterwards that Vydra got booted out of the Foreign Section of the Writers' Union, but I got word here that he isn't washing windows, not yet at least. He stayed with the Union, and is working in Technical.

The word is that Comrade Director is on a rampage, he purged all the dangerous (i.e. intelligent) editors and hired stupid ones who are "reliably on our side" (i.e. loyal to the Party). He is still more or less protecting Vydra, he probably isn't quite sure whether the old lady (who ostensibly was on a first name basis with both Gottwald and Zápotocký[2]) doesn't have pull from beyond the grave.

Dear, dear Věra, do you have any idea what you're letting yourself in for? You're laying yourself wide open, and there is no hope that you can please everyone. And how are you going to set type for books in Czech if you don't have the Czech accents? How are you going to market the books? Where will you get the money? And what about David?

I'm sending you the telephone book you wanted. I didn't have to steal it, it's my own, I have two copies because I have two telephones. There are plenty of Czech names there, but don't forget that they could be Germans too, just like lots of Czechs have pure German names. How are you going to sort them out? I think you'd probably be better off sending me a package of your brochures and I'll drop them off at various Czech restaurants and taverns and events here, so you wouldn't have to pay all that postage. For that matter, Věra, if you ever need any kind of help, you know how to find me. I can't spare any money, but I'm willing to lend a hand wherever I can.

Good thing your letter arrived on Thursday, because on Friday I had an interesting visitor, and if the two events had happened in the reverse order, the destiny of my novel might have been very different. A certain Mr Meyer paid me a call, a gentleman of elegance and refinement, and I could tell from the outset that he is someone who knows his way around literature. He told me that he had read *Life Among the Thorns* in manuscript, and when I wondered out loud how he had come to see it, he replied without so much as a blush that he had good friends at the Press Surveillance Administration[3], where all manuscripts slated for publication are submitted for a final OK from those who watch over the innocuousness of anything that reaches the socialist reader. He told me he immediately contacted some authorities to give my book the not inconsiderable weight of his support (he used to be a very respected Comrade) but unsuccessfully. Now, however, it will most certainly succeed, he said. He and several com . . . er, friends had founded a company to publish banned literature abroad. They have, he said, enough funds to begin with, and the assurance of continued support from German friends of Dubček's vision of Czechoslovakia.

He insisted that my book would be an excellent launch for them. I have a good name among the post-August emigrés as a writer who was constantly attacked and banned back home, and the few things of mine that did get past the censors and were published were among the few treasures, he said, that many people brought with them into exile. In short, he was buttering me up. When he had me well buttered, he reached inside his attaché case and placed on the table a printed dust jacket for my novel, pretty nice, and he had a smug look on his face, as if he expected nothing less than my immediate whoop of delight and my rush to sign on the dotted line in the contract that he just happened to have with him as well. The conditions in the contract—i.e. edition size, advance and royalties—were all very generous, from the point of view of an author in exile. I won't tell you how generous, so you don't think I'm implying how magnanimous I am to be giving the manuscript to you for nothing. (If you should happen to make a bit of money with it, just invest it in the next book.)

When he finished talking, I returned the dust jacket and the contract into the file folder, snapped it shut and passed it back to him, saying that he was unfortunately just a little too late. I told him about your project in Toronto, and he just raised an eyebrow and voiced his doubts as to your prospects for success, since they already had the names of 5,000 confirmed readers, and he reiterated that money would be no problem for them.

So, my girl, I don't know. You only have 300 addresses and you probably can't count on the financial support of the friends of

Dubček's vision of Czechoslovakia. They can. They're all one big happy family, and there is something enviable about that. They hang together because, unlike unorganized people like us, they are accustomed to discipline and "comradeship." Where they get their funds is no mystery, leftists in the West are tripping over each other in their eagerness to help, but of course, only to help their brothers and not any critics of Dubček, or any skeptics about socialism. Something else suddenly dawned on me too. Something I had never paid much attention to, so it never really struck me. Almost all of them got good jobs as soon as they arrived here in West Germany, jobs in universities or in various institutes. That fellow Meyer also mentioned that they weren't going to limit themselves to fiction, that they just wanted to introduce themselves with it, and my book would be ideal for the purpose. But they see their mission mainly in the publication of political literature critical of the current Party Line according to Brezhnev. The rest of it I figured out for myself: first a few attractive (saleable) titles by authors who have been banned and remain politically uncompromised, because obviously the Czech reader in exile isn't going to be anxious to be put on a waiting list for Taradash's *Critique of the Historical Approach to Marx-Leninism.*

Věra, my dear, they will be competitors for you, but I wouldn't be afraid of them if I were you. I believe in our people's healthy instinct, and when they see your editorial plan, with names in it like Wagner, Bráňa, Smiřický, they will surely make the right choice, unless of course they are ex-Marxist scholars.

Hold on to your hat, kiddo, so it won't blow away once you get rolling.

Your

Jirka

. . . I also want to mention a certain company called Libra Publishers and its proprietors, who arrived in our city of Toronto on the coattails of a

wave of emigrants fleeing the yoke of Communism, and weaseled their way into our midst. Feigning the laudable activity of a publisher-in-exile, they are intent upon infiltrating our Czech community by means of the publication of dubious books which border on the pornographic, thus poisoning the thinking of Czechs and patriots in exile. Thus also stealing our subscribers. Out of taxpayers' money, they have already published a book full of the language of the gutter, a book that no decent citizen of the world could read over dinner.

Their "company," however, is thriving. It started out with the most modern of equipment, state-of-the-art printing presses, extravagant furniture and Persian carpets, and an immense number of innocent employees who have no idea what cause they are serving. But people will do anything for money.

The husband of the woman who claims to be a Czech publisher is demonstrably a Jew, and she even has a Jewish past. According to reliable reports, she used to be called a white Jewess and the name she was called is Sára, whereas here she claims to have been christened Věra. The word is that she was also a Party trusty and used to inform on what people in the Karlín district used to say among themselves at the butcher's. A certain friend of mine—I have no qualms about making his name public, as he stands behind his opinions— called Milovan Strakatý of the University of Minnoglapahoe in the state of America was heard to say about the said woman, "She was a Party trusty who infiltrated the Communist folk music ensemble called Sedmikrása where I was a singer, and she made no bones about her intimate relations with everyone at the Police Ministry from the doorman to the minister."

Let every sensible Czech and patriot decide whether or not to purchase the books that this white Jewess has taken upon herself to publish. They are getting richer and richer, their property swelling to proportions unimagined by mere mortals and honest working folks like us. They not only have a hypermodern print shop with all kinds of wonderful equipment and technology, but also a car, and their luxury residence contains a washing machine, a dryer, a dishwasher, a central vacuum cleaner and an au-

tomatic garage. She goes around dressed in modest clothes, to draw attention away from her covert extravagances. She entices innocent people with the promise of so-called Czech literature, which she maintains is dying of neglect. Do we not have enough of it here? Do we not have sufficient patriotic essays, memoirs, anthologies about our true heroes and icons? What could she possibly contribute? What drives her, Jewess that she is, is nothing but the lust for profit. There isn't a single honest Czech in our environs who would fail to agree with my opinions.

The government here is no help in stopping her, since the system here gives everyone an opportunity and asks no questions. A grievously dangerous policy.

In order that we survive as a nation in these times, the gravest since the Fall of White Mountain, let us stick with our own devoted patriots, Professor Milovan Strakatý, Mr. Vlastimil Morrow-Moravec and others. One day, Professor Strakatý will mount a white horse and ride victorious to the Royal Castle in Prague, for it is inevitable.
Jan Preclík
Žižkovo palcát (Žižka's Mace)[4]
Toronto, Canada

Dear Jirka,
I'm sending you an article from the local press about me. I wonder when I'll read someplace that I wear see-through undies like a proper streetwalker, and that instead of bread I eat matzohs made with the blood of virgins. Have you any idea what a central vacuum cleaner is? I have a kind of sweeper, with two cylindrical brushes that turn inside it, for picking up crumbs and peanut shells, but that's manual, powered by my own hand. It does have a centrally placed handle, though.

Nonetheless, it is true that we're coming up in the world. We are still running the business from our apartment, and of course we don't hide the fact that we could really use an office, furnished not with

Persian carpets but with shelves and a decent packing table. I also dream of a printing press, only secretly, though, because David needs to be approached gradually. But it is true that we bought ourselves a decent car. Mr Karlík took two days to drive me around until we found a vehicle that is supposed to last us a while. The main thing it had to have was a fair-sized trunk.

We also found a company that manufactures photographic type-setting equipment, and they have various alphabets and accents to put on letters, all different languages mixed up together and none of them complete. And as for the type face, I don't even want to discuss that. Gothic is modern in comparison. The fellow did offer to adapt a machine to my specifications, so I spent a few days with their programmer, teaching him the Czech alphabet and its accents. The set-up has a keyboard that is hooked up to a kind of hole-punching device. When I type on it, I can't see what I'm typing, but a tape with holes in it feeds out of it, and I've learned how to read the holes. Then you feed the tape into another device called a reader (it weighs about twice as much as me), which reads it and translates the holes into normal letters on photographic paper which then gets put through another machine with chemicals that develops it. I cut it up into pages, paste them onto large sheets of paper, and read proof. They leased it to me for a decent price, but for all of three years. When they delivered the equipment, David (Ram that he is) nearly fainted. In order to get it to fit in the bedroom, we had to move our bed into the living room, which only leaves us a small corner to live in. Our tomcat hurried to mark it, as if to establish his own superior status.

Mr. Karlík suggested to the company that they should compensate us for the time I had spent with the programmer, since in fact I helped them create a proper Czech alphabet which they could now sell to other customers, and so they sent me two little rolls of photographic paper with an expired "use before" date. Still, the monster works, it clacks and rumbles and any day now I expect someone in the apartment building to complain about the noise.

That's also why I can't work at night. During the day, my noise gets lost in the even louder racket of radios and televisions.

The first thing I set on the machine was Bráňa's manuscript. I really sweated over it, Bráňa likes to do fiddly things and he is convinced that his already interesting short stories will be even more interesting if he improves on them graphically, and so he has some paragraphs shaped like a circle, others like a pyramid and one was even shaped like a woman's breasts (which plays right into the hand holding Žižka's Mace). But it is going to be a nice book.

I'm just starting on the Wagner, and he presents a different problem. He scribbles his lines tight up against each other, and makes corrections up and down the margins in his tiny spidery handwriting. He's saving paper, it's as if he never unlearned the habits he picked up in the concentration camp. Good thing he didn't send me the whole manuscript scribbled on cigarette papers. Even so I had to buy myself a magnifying glass, and when I'm working on the Wagner manuscript, I look like an eye, ear, nose and throat doctor with the magnifying glass tied to my forehead. Still, it's a lovely novel, well, what else can you expect from Wagner—Jews and more Jews, he'll never get over that trauma. And so I suppose we'll be playing into the hand holding Žižka's Mace after all, in keeping with the saying "Birds of a feather flock together", even if I am not a real Jew, just a white Sarah. But Preclík wouldn't need any more than that.

So, Jirka, be happy, and you can fall asleep every night with the satisfaction of knowing you helped us get off the ground. Interest is accumulating on your royalties, in Heaven.
Your
Věra

Dear Jirka,
There's a deadline hanging over my head that feels like the gallows. Every night I dream in Ukrainian. I've been typesetting the

Ukrainian textbook for almost as long as it took the professors to write it. Grammar examples echo in my brain: *Vin dovoditsya meni dovelosya poikhaty.* In fact, I think I could even converse in Ukrainian by now if I had to. The manuscript is 800 pages long, every line a different type face, a different layout. As I sit here working with the Cyrillic alphabet, it strikes me how many unpublished books in Ukrainian must be out there, lying around in desk drawers. And how many writers behind bars. And how many writers who've knuckled under. Here in Toronto, the Ukrainians have a 100-member choir, one voice better than the next, with a fabulous orchestra, a fabulous conductor—and their repertoire? Over and over again, round and round, the same old songs: "*Oy u luzi chervona kalina. Oy na hori vohon horit a v dolini kozak lezhit . . .*"[5] Maybe it inspires them the way we're fired up by our "Strength of lion, flight of falcon,"[6] or "The Fiddle Fair."[7]

When they arrested Moroz,[8] I attended a protest meeting at the Ukrainian Cultural Centre, a beautiful building with immense rooms, clubs and a restaurant. The protest was held in the largest assembly hall, tables groaning under the weight of food, and women in colorful costumes serving cabbage rolls, chicken and roasts with the proverbial Slavic hospitality, and desserts, vodka, wine. One huge dinner party—while Moroz was sitting in solitary, 30 days into his hunger strike. And here, feeding their faces in protest were 300 of his compatriots and one Canadian poo-bah, there to make a speech, since it was just before the elections and Ukrainian votes are not to be sneezed at. After all, there are a million of them here.

Well, maybe it's a national tradition, like the Irish hold a wake and feast to honor the dead. Besides, you can get financial support for something like this from the government, the ministry that deals with ethnic affairs, for a "culturally specific" spread like this.

It reminded me of the time a few years ago when I wanted to help the publishing house to some capital by taking advantage of the notion of "culturally specific" and "promoting national traditions".

Someone had advised us to apply to the Royal Committee for Book Publication, which, they said, supports projects such as ours. So that was the beginning of an extended correspondence, carried on, thanks to David, in superlative English. So we wouldn't look like a bunch of dilettantes, we had the letters typed professionally on a high-class typewriter on high class paper. It cost a lot, but we were counting on its paying off. After a lot of letters back and forth over a considerable time, they finally invited us over for a hearing on our application, at the Ontario Institute for Studies in Education, something on the order of our Pedagogical Faculty. The auditorium was so big, you could have produced *Boris Godunov* in it, live horses and all, and in the front row sat the jury panel, four civil servant types behind four microphones. They told David and me to take a seat on the stage, turned spotlights on us, and asked us to describe our plan in detail, and state what we would require. So David reiterated what we had written in all those expensive letters. I kept my mouth shut, so as not to do our cause more harm than good with my English. David outdid himself, he has practice from lecturing in English. He explained to them how back home, some 40 writers have been blacklisted, and how in exile, we also have many writers who have something to say, and how we had already published a number of books and expedited them to readers all over the world, but that we need capital. And then David was apparently kissed by the Muse of MBAs, and he added that we export over half of our products, supporting Canadian foreign trade and bringing work to Canadian printers. True, he said, it is only on a small scale, but it is common knowledge that the economy rests on small businesses rather than on the large multinationals. And if our publishing firm is given the chance to grow, it will employ people who may now be trying in vain to find work, given the high levels of unemployment today. In my opinion, he described it all perfectly clearly, but the jury was apparently too culturally inclined to pick up on the commercial rationale. When David finished, nobody said anything for a while, and then one of the panel members asked if we would export books to Czechoslovakia, too, since they're written in the Czechoslovakian language. David was so flummoxed by the question, at this stage of the game, that he simply replied "No." "Why not?" asked another member of the panel. By then David had recovered his presence of mind, and once again launched into what he had already told them and what we had explained to them several times over in our letters: the intellectual wasteland in Czechoslovakia these days, etcetera, etcetera. When he finished, a third panel member suggested that this is the very reason that our books should be in high demand there, if the blacklisted authors aren't allowed to be published there. Afterwards, David told me that he'd been on the verge of explaining the situation for a third time, but then it occurred to him that, although the members of the panel were well-versed in culture, they weren't all that well-versed in Communist cultural policy, so he would do well to pursue another tack. He told them that Czechoslovakia can't pay in dollars. That apparently made sense to them, because right after that, they concluded the hearing by telling us that we would be receiving their decision soon. And sure enough, not long afterwards we got a letter, sweet as honey, politely denying our request. The Royal Committee unfortunately does not support commercial activities. Which brought home to me the sobering conclusion that all we can truly rely on, now or ever, is our Czech readers, and their checkbooks.

Meanwhile, authors send us manuscripts from all the ends of the earth, usually accompanied by problems. Some of them are promising, but for the most part, they need editing. Where to find an editor? Here in Toronto, or for that matter, anywhere in all of North America. I don't know a single one who is a professional. The only one who knows where to put a comma is apparently Smiřický, because in his youth, he used to be an editor at the Belles Lettres Publishing House. So I hinted and cajoled and finally got him to agree to reading a manuscript for us every so often. He even offered to typeset his own books on our machine (we really do like his stuff!) and so I re-structured my own schedule around his free time. That way, when he's setting type, I'm doing other work. There's always plenty to do that should have been done yesterday. I'd say that he is a man of excellent breeding, even if the gossips out there maintain he has a dirty mind and a roving eye. That's what the Czechs say, the British would call him a "ladies' man." He enjoys having pretty young women around him, and if one of them turns out to be willing, well, that's her affair. He does have one flaw, though: he loves to eat. Well, he won't get much of that at our place.

Remember the woman at the Sova party who kept buttering me up with how fabulous I am and how fabulous it is that we publish books, and almost bored me to death with her big blue eyes, remember her? Well, as soon as we moved the office to Richmond Street, she showed up with her manuscript. It is a thousand pages single-spaced, typed on a manual typewriter with no Czech accents, and it's all the harder to read for the quality of the paper, a translucent onionskin, with every period and comma a hole punched through the sheet. The first 30 pages bear traces of having been read several times over. They are dog-eared, with illegible notes scribbled in the margins by at least five different hands. Apparently none of them could work their way past page 30, because that's where all marginal comments cease and the pages that follow are as pristine as if they had just emerged from the typewriter. Nevertheless, I am conscientiously making the effort to decipher it, in hopes of uncovering something worthwhile. I even take it to bed with me, driven by the absurd principle instilled in me by David, that once you start something, you have to finish it; if you are into a book, you have to read it through to the end; if you take a bite of bread, you have to finish the slice; and with the book, I keep hoping that at some point it will take off. I'm afraid it is a vain hope, but still I keep on reading, driven perhaps by some perverse momentum or inertia.

The 700 pages I have slogged through to date contain three erotic scenes—if you can call a kiss on a bare shoulder in an evening gown an erotic scene in this day and age. The rest are covered with forests, rivers, hillsides, pine trees, firs, birches, and dandelions and forget-me-nots. In those 700 pages, there are at the very least 25 descriptions of rich black soil. And the rural sections are meticulously counterbalanced by urban ones: factory chimneys, soirées, theaters, concert halls, Gothic and Baroque landmarks in Prague, Brno, Olomouc, and Bratislava.

Unfortunately, though, the heroine of the novel weaves her way through the narrative, from the Šumava region to the Tatra Mountains, like the thread in a darning needle. She is Ellen, a fabulous woman from the best of families, who moves through the metropolitan environment "with an innate natural elegance and charm," and with the same elegance, she lifts the train of her skirt as she steps over the tree stumps in the Boubín forest wilderness.

The author has taken as her pen name Jaromila Tatranská-Šumavská,[9] apparently to call attention to her love for both Czech and Slovak homelands, to capture the hearts and cash of both Czech and Slovak readers. Her real name is Božena Nováková, and I've heard that she is referred to in the local Czech community as the Terror of the Continent. She latches on to anyone she can find to read her masterpiece and demands praise. And she gets it, too. To get rid of her and to avoid personal contact, they send it to her in writing, which ends up putting me in repeated personal contact with her, since she keeps bringing the letters to me in my office, black on white. I am gradually trying to prepare her for a major disappointment, but I'm as much of a coward as the ones who got rid of her by writing laudatory letters, so I keep putting off the moment. I do feel sorry for those blue eyes of hers. Maybe I'll weasel out of it by saying that the manuscript is too long and would cost me too much to produce. But they tell me she's rich. She inherited from her brother, who was a broker.

Your

Věra

P.S. We just had a power blackout. Outside, it's storming, more like a typhoon, I can't do much of anything except sleep, and I don't feel like sleeping. Good thing we have enough candles. That's one thing I haven't gotten over, I still love burning them.

In the morning, when I was about to get down to finishing this letter, the blue-eyed Božena arrived unannounced, and this time she was on her high horse: I'm a fraud. I've had her manuscript for a whole week already and what are my intentions with her novel? It took quite an effort to calm her down. I sat her down in an armchair across from me, so we could talk about her book, and I intended to prepare her for the inevitable.

All of a sudden, her high horse vanished and she was transformed into a little girl listening to her teacher. Her wide blue eyes were on me as I went to begin with the novel's good points, but I couldn't for the life of me think of any, and she burst out with, "If you publish it for me, I'll give you—" She paused.

I waited, expecting her to offer to pay the production costs out of the money she inherited from her brother the broker, and if she did, I'd be up the creek. She was apparently fighting an inner struggle, deciding whether her work of art was important enough for her to overcome her innate frugality, and then she decided. "I could give you half my royalties." She took my breath away. "And don't worry about its selling, either. I gave it to Dr. Havránek to read, and you saw what he wrote about it, he said it's an excellent piece of work. He would surely buy a copy. And so would Dr. Souček and Mrs. Hellerová. You'll have no trouble selling it. I have about ten people lined up, and you, you have connections too."

"Actually," I said, "I'm not interested in half the royalties. You have to understand . . ."

"Oh, my," she interrupted, "that's such a noble gesture, you are so fabulous, no wonder they talk about what an idealist you are."

"Well, I'm not. I mean, what I want to tell you is that your novel—"

"Oh, so you love it too, don't you? Like Dr Havránek, he couldn't put it down. I'll be so grateful to you for publishing it. You're so courageous and I'll be so happy."

Not that I have anything against making somebody happy, but . . . I just didn't know what to say, and besides, my nerves were beginning to affect my thinking. The desk was piled high with correspondence, bills, book orders, page proofs, and by then it was nearly 11 o'clock. She'd been there half an hour already. "You know, Mrs Nováková, that manuscript of yours needs a bit of polishing, a few deletions . . ."

"Do you really think so?" she asked doubtfully. "What exactly do you mean by 'polishing'?"

"Some passages," I said, "call for—how should I put it—some creative editing to arouse in the reader enough curiosity to read on."

"But I did, it's all in there. For instance, look here," she moistened a finger and flipped pages in the manuscript. "Here, for instance, the portrayal of the scenery, the way I've captured the mountains and the little farm fields, the perfumes of our countryside, of course our people just love reading about it. And here—" she leafed through some more pages, "—I think it's on page 630 . . . that's such a cute scene, our people like that kind of fun, the way Ellen meets her sweetheart, not the first one, the third one, the one she met in Luhačovice, when she drops her umbrella and bends down to pick it up and so does he, and they bump heads and fall in love, isn't that a cute way for new lovers to meet?"

"You know," I say, "publishing a book, especially one as long as this one, costs a lot of money."

"I offered you half, didn't I?"

"Half of the production costs? That would cost you a pretty penny."

"Who's talking about production costs? Here I was generous enough to offer you half of what you sold!"

"What if it doesn't sell?"

"They call you an idealist, so why do you keep on talking about it not selling?" It was 11:30 by then. I pushed the manuscript aside and started sorting letters, hoping she'd take the hint. "For God's sake," she shouted shrilly and rose to her feet, "You've got a publishing house, haven't you? You've got everything. Printing machines, connections, why, if I had printing machines I'd publish it myself. What are you good for, then?"

I still had myself under control, but you can imagine that I was seeing red. "It's not enough just to publish. I also have to sell, Mrs Nováková. Your book is so specific that, in today's market—"

"See? You said yourself how specific it is. That's what people are interested in. All my friends will buy it. And you can send some to the old country to sell, can't you? Those poor dears over there, I bet they hardly have anything to read any more. They wouldn't publish it for me over there—well, of course, they wouldn't."

"Do you mean to say you offered it to a publisher in Czechoslovakia?"

She was a little taken aback by my question. "Well, yes, I did. I didn't realize that it was politically a little too much for them. I even wrote them that I wouldn't insist on getting my royalties in hard currency, that I'd be willing to come over there to spend it. But isn't that typical of them, they didn't have the courtesy to reply, they didn't even return the manuscript. Do you know how much it cost me to xerox the whole thousand pages? Not to mention the postage!"

I was on the verge of sweeping her masterpiece off the desk, but I got a grip on myself in time. I picked up the folder, snapped it shut, and said, "It needs to be shortened."

"Do you think so?" she asked, sitting back down in the armchair. I thought that I might have to throw her out bodily. "Shortened? But how?"

"By cutting it down to a hundred, a hundred and fifty pages. Throw out unnecessary adjectives, repetitive descriptions of landscapes and nature scenes . . ."

"Cut the nature scenes?" She was aghast. "Do you know how

much time I put into them? How many hours I sacrificed to get the descriptions of the countryside just right? I studied photographs. I even had them send me a whole collection of pictures from the Tatras and the Krkonoše Mountains, and now you're telling me to scrap it?"

"Exactly," I said, in what felt like a firm tone. "That's what writers do."

"But how do they do it? How can I shorten it if I don't know how? I mean you need to tell me how and where, don't you?"

"Unfortunately, Mrs Nováková, I can't spare the time."

"I'd give you—" —another pause while she battled her frugal instincts— "I'd give you all my royalties, if only you'd shorten it for me. Please?" Tears welled up in her big blue eyes.

"When?" I asked, wearily.

"I'll cook for you, I'll bake coffee cake for you, I have a recipe made with egg-whites, it's totally non-fattening, please, say you'll do it for me."

My work wasn't getting done, this woman wasn't getting up, and it was getting on towards noon. I rose, handed her the manuscript and strode deliberately towards the door. The novelist remained seated, opened the folder and turned some more pages. "So, if I do shorten it, then you'll publish it?" A spark of hope flashed through my mind. By then it was clear that I wouldn't get rid of her, but at least I might get a reprieve. "It all depends on how the final version reads. You'd have to take care and not rush through it. A task like that can take several years . . . For example, Tolstoy . . ."

"I'll have it done in a week, I'll sit right down and a week from today, you'll get the shortened version. I'm a hard worker, don't you worry."

"A week isn't enough. You'll have to clean up the text, polish it, and . . ."

"But how? How can I fix it so you'll publish it for me?"

So I sat back down, actually, toppled back into my chair in sheer exhaustion, and opened the manuscript. "Like here: 'Softly, elegantly, and gently, Ellen seated herself on the gilt-trimmed, dark green and red upholstered, luxurious chaise longue standing in a nearby shady corner, and gracefully turned her noble profile towards the Baroque fourteenth century painting that . . .' Where did you get that Baroque painting from the fourteenth century?"

"D'you think it isn't old enough? You're probably right. Let's make it twelfth century."

I decided to try another approach. "Why don't you say that Ellen sat down on the chesterfield and turned to the picture on the wall? And what do you mean by saying that Ellen 'turned her profile'? Where was she actually looking?"

"At the painting, of course!"

"How could she look at a picture with her profile?"

"Don't you see that I was describing it poetically? How beautiful and elegant Ellen is, and how graciously she moves?"

"Mrs. Nováková, when I want to look at something, I don't look at it sideways, no matter how poetic or elegant or gracious I am. When something captures our attention, we turn to look at it with both eyes. We turn to face it, straight on, don't we?"

"I don't know why you're picking at words," she pouted, "but here, give me a pencil and I'll fix it." She struck "profile", scribbled in "face" and turned her baby blues back to me. "You're the editor, I'll do anything you say, you're so fabulous, I'll correct everything just the way you want me to, all you have to do is tell me how, see how willing I am?"

(Right here, my candle burned out. I went to find another one in the dark, fortunately a flash of lightning helped me out, along with a thunderclap right overhead, so loud it sounded as if the world were being ripped open at the seams. It even woke David, who bawled me out for not being asleep at three in the morning. Now I have a fresh candle, David is back in the sack and the storm seems to be retreating. Water is pouring out of the sky, God is cross and I need a shot of something strong. There, and now I'll finish my story, because I ought to finish what I start, and besides, I'm not going to turn your writer's imagination loose on an anecdote that doesn't need any imagination at all to make it interesting. I'm describing real life to you, the way it actually happens. You'd never think it up like that, no matter how hard you tried.)

I pointed to the piles of papers. "I don't have the time, Mrs Nováková." It was half past noon.

"But it wouldn't cost you a thing. You could do it in your spare time!"

"I don't have any spare time."

"You don't say! Just the other day you went to the charity bazaar, and the poetry soirée at that fellow Sova's. Then at least recommend someone to me. You know so many people, I'll give you all my royalties. You're such a fabulous person and that publishing company of yours is such a fabulously worthwhile cause, I'll help you, I'll cook for you, do your ironing, I'll even scrub your floors, do your shopping, if you'd only fix it for me."

Two hours, lost irretrievably. "I don't have the time," I said desperately. Maybe she heard me.

"Then at least tell me where I should go to get it published." She was offering me a straw I could grasp at. It wouldn't exactly be fair, but they deserve to have some of the fun too.

"Try one of the emigré newspapers. They might be willing to serialize it."

"I offered it to them already, all of them," she whimpered, with even more tears filling her eyes as she looked around the room. Then, in a voice like nothing so much as my cat giving birth, she wailed, "You've got such a beautiful office and yet you refuse to publish my book."

Then I was struck by an idea that would get me off the hook. Wicked, but brilliant. "There is another Czech publisher in Germany."

The wet blue marbles almost fell out of their sockets. "Why didn't you say so?"

True, that's not a nice thing to do, even to your competition, but, rather than having to deal with . . . I started back towards the door, but she just sat there like a rock in a ditch.

"Give me their address, I'll send it to them. They're bound to be interested. But maybe I ought to get a copyright, what do you think? How do you get a copyright?"

One o'clock. "Nobody is going to steal it from you, Mrs. Nováková."

"You never know. The things I've heard . . . One Russian made millions and a Nobel Prize to boot for stealing someone else's novel. How much do you think it would be?"

"For a copyright? Not a lot."

"You mean I have to pay for a copyright? Well, I guess it's a sacrifice I'll have to make. No, what I was asking was how much a writer gets paid for a novel."

"We don't pay anything."

"You don't?" I've never seen a more stupefied expression on anyone's face, not even in a movie. "You mean authors let you publish their work without getting paid for it? You have to pay them, don't you? You must make so much money, then. Don't say you don't make a profit when you sell the books for so much money. And when you can afford such a beautiful office."

Jirka, when I get mad, the blood rises to my head and throbs and throbs there, and that's what it was doing, throbbing so much I thought my brain would burst, and I'd bleed to death right there in front of the Terror of the Continent, and the stream of blood would flow onto the manuscript and obscure it to total illegibility. I raised my hands to my temples and dropped into the creaky second-hand straight-back chair from Goodwill, rested my patched elbows in their sweater sleeves on the surface of the nineteenth century desk which I had personally sanded and repainted, rested my unkempt, badly-trimmed, desperately weary, not very round, though proportionate to my gaunt though once shapely body, little head in my hands, dug my broken, hangnail-rimmed, half-polished fingernails in my hair, stretched out my legs in their ill-fitting, badly pressed, partly pleated pants, threadbare and ragged and stained with winter ice-melting salt, legs at the end of which were feet in run-down tennis shoes, without any laces, and a hole in the toe of one that showed a yellow sock, I turned my profile to the lady novelist and with a vacant un-focused gaze stared at the stack of correspondence which could have been answered already, and I think I was out of my body for a while. My soul slipped away and I watched what was transpiring glued like a fly to the ceiling. One thing I do know, it was in black and white.

Mrs Jaromila Tatranská-Šumavská glanced at the chair where the inelegant Ellen sat in a state of collapse, and shook her head. "So what do you live on if you're not making a profit? You have every-thing: machines, a car, you live in a fancy high-rise, with central vacuum and a washer and dryer and dishwasher. You really ought to be doing something else. There are so many people here who wish they could do what you're doing and you won't let them at it. Why don't you let them and go do something else?"

Mr Záturecký, gentle angel, I saw black and I saw fuchsia, I saw magenta, I saw crimson, I heard the falls at Niagara roaring darkly in my ears and all the blacksmiths in the world united to pound on their anvils in my breast.

When I floated down from the ceiling, the door was wide open and a merciful draft was gently carrying one page of the great nov-elist's masterpiece after another out the window.

My dear Jirka, there you have it: my first literary effort. I'm sure you'll just love it terribly. Please refrain from making any changes or deletions. It is a perfect and fabulously precise, unvarnished and imaginatively unembellished true-to-life description of reality. If you want to use it somewhere, first I have to know how much you'll pay. Yours,

Věra

P.P.S. The storm is over but the power is still out. I think I'll go pour myself another shot in the dark and go to sleep.

1. *Omnia mea mecum porto*: Latin saying "All that is mine, I carry with me."

2. Czechoslovakia's first two Communist presidents: Klement Gottwald (in office 1948–53), Antonín Zápotocký (in office 1953–57).

3. Main Press Surveillance Administration: The euphemistic name of the official censorship authority mandated to rule on all written materials submitted for publication. In Czech: HSTD, Hlavní správa tiskového dohledu.

4. Žižkovo palcát (Žižka's Mace): Named after Jan Žižka, a charismatic and innovative Bohemian military leader during the Hussite Wars in the 15th century.

5. "*Oy u luzi chervona kalina. Oy na hori vogon horit a v dolini kozak lezhit . . .*" Ukrainian folk song, roughly translated: A snowball tree in the meadow blooms, a fire wild on the mountain burns, and a Cossack lies there in the vale.

6. The anthem of the Sokol (Falcon), a Czech patriotic gymnastics organization which was driven underground under Nazi and Communist totalitarianism, but was very active in exile.

7. *Fidlovačka*: (The Fiddle Fair) A 19th century musical comedy in the patriotic enlightenment vein, with all the bathos of its era; revived under the Communists. It contains the song that would become the Czech national anthem, "Kde domov můj" ("Where Is My Home").

8. Valentin Moroz, a Ukrainian writer, arrested in the USSR during the early 70s; ultimately, the protests against his arrest were successful, resulting in his leaving the USSR and settling in Canada.

9. Literally translated, the surname Tatranská-Šumavská indicates a woman from the (Slovak) Tatra Mountains at the eastern end of old Czechoslovakia, and from the (Czech) region of Šumava at the western end.

Joseph Stalin

excerpt from the novel Stalin's Shoe

Zdena Tomin

BETWEEN HER SEVENTH and twelfth years Linda Strízlík/Wren was in love with Joseph Stalin. She came to love him through the art of socialist realism, not so much poetry and sculpture as cinema and painting; and through the overwhelming knowledge that he, Joseph Stalin, loved her.

Her teacher, an emotional lady with bleached hair, had told her so, and her mother, when asked, confirmed it with a dark remark, eyeing her skinny child with the usual suspicion:

"I wouldn't put it past you!" This added a touch of mystery to the love affair.

Emily found no reason why she should love Joseph Stalin; she had come to distrust men in general and handsome men in particular. Apart, of course, from her son Jan; her love for the boy was excruciating. Jan often thought her rather abrupt; he did not know that when she cut him short and left him, it was to hide tears of overflowing emotion.

Emily was a practical woman and she knew that what Joseph Stalin once won, he would not give away, and there were enough rumors about the darker sides of his power to make him a rather undesirable Father for the Nation. On the other hand, for the same practical reasons, Emily had little to say against communism. It held no threat against her and her family and even though it promised no riches either, especially if one had such a weak gentle soul for a husband, it had two distinct advantages.

First, she no longer had to slave for her children's future. The state would pay to have them educated, almost bribe them with all kinds of grants; any school would be overjoyed to have them, even if they weren't all that brilliant. They were the children of the working class, the hitherto under-privileged, who from now on were to have their way up paved broad and smooth whether they wanted it or not. As far as Emily was concerned, there was an undeniable justice in it, whatever some people might say.

She wouldn't, however, rely on justice alone; she saw to it that her children had a bonus: their undoubtedly proletarian father was a communist too. Václav Strízlík/Wren, with his wife's strong encouragement, had become a member of the Communist party in 1945. He never made a career of it, it was pick and shovel for the rest of his life, but his children profited mildly.

Secondly, with all medical care free, she no longer had to pretend that she was merely tired. She was sent to what used to be a first-class, really quite posh, sanitorium, and even though it rapidly deteriorated to second-class and below, and was rather crowded, Emily still enjoyed her leisure. Doctors and nurses were very fond of this cheerful, smiling, uncomplaining woman, whose tuberculosis was badly advanced and painful.

Upon her return, and before she had to undergo another prolonged cure, Emily took on voluntary work for the local branch of the socialist Women's Union, gaining respect for bringing some decency into that quarrelsome body of over-excitable, flag-waving and anxious women. It was her idea, amongst others, to replace the portrait of Joseph Stalin looming over the meeting room-cum-office with that of La Passionaria, whose stern face had a decidedly calming effect.

Only after Emily's death had it become known that throughout the twenty-five years she lived in socialism, she had secretly kept all members of her family on the Evangelical church list, paying the annual contributions out of her meager savings. Whether out of kindness to the persecuted church or out of a desire to play it safe with her Maker is anybody's guess.

In the evenings, when the family gathered around the new kitchen table to dine on their potato goulash or dumplings with dill sauce or pancakes or sweet dumplings or carrot stew (meat remained a Sunday treat for which Emily had to queue four hours each Saturday), Emily would tolerate no politics.

She had a very good reason; Václav Strízlík/Wren, who had become a second gardener in the Tree Park, had developed a very peculiar political theory indeed. The older children would have either laughed at him or quarreled with him, neither of which was permissible in a good family; and there was always the danger that little Linda might repeat some of it in school, which wouldn't do at all. Only after Hela and Jan ran off to their evening classes or youth clubs and Linda was in bed in the other room would Emily, safely anchored by her knitting or darning or sewing, listen to Václav's querulous musings.

Václav enjoyed these evenings in the family's new two-room flat very much, although the flat itself was in fact another of his failures. During the first days after the war, he was dispatched by Emily to talk to the local National Liberation Committee and claim one of those empty apartments the Germans had left behind. Since his family's living conditions were about the worst in the whole neighborhood and he had a fresh communist party card in his pocket, Václav ought to have stood a good chance. Several times he went, and always came home empty-handed, while Mr. Beránek/Lamb, for example, secured a four-bedroom apartment full of mahogany furniture and silver cutlery. But, to Václav's surprise, Emily was not bitter. He could even tell that she was secretly pleased. Emily was ambitious but not greedy and certainly not immoral. She knew she could not have enjoyed living in one of those apartments which the Germans had most probably taken over from Jewish families, who had either fled when there was still time or had been herded into cattle wagons and never seen again.

Within a few months, she had found these two fourth-floor rooms full of light and with lots of sky behind their windows, only a few hundred yards from their basement, in Little Quick Street. There was no bathroom and no central heating, but there was the luxury of a completely private loo and a neat little larder into the bargain. So now they had a large kitchen-cum-living room with a couch for the boy to sleep on, and an even larger bedroom which they quickly got to call The Room. The parents, the child Linda and the grown-up girl Hela slept there. Come Christmas, the tree would be put up by the window, the ceiling-high, green-tiled stove would be lit for three days and nights, and the family would gather around. Otherwise only Jan would be permitted to use the Room during ordinary days, to practice his violin, and on Saturdays Hela would be allowed to serve coffee and cakes to her current fiancé there.

Linda went to bed willingly; she had waited for a proper bed of her own long enough, but she would never go straight to sleep, for that would be wasting a good thing. Before the great discovery of *Books*, Linda would sing quietly to herself, or listen to her father's voice coming only slightly muffled through the ill-fitting door.

Václav's politics were a pretty bad mishmash. Weak and soft as he was, the man had collected and cherished every cruel idiocy of his century. Rich and poor there always were, and always would be. A poor man never stands a chance against a Jew. Hitler was a dirty swine but one thing had to be said for him: He knew what he was doing when he killed the Jews. (Here Emily would hiss at him, but he would come up with what he thought was a trump.) Look at

Joseph Stalin, he hates them too. Whatever is wrong with the communist government is because the Jews have penetrated it. And because there are still too many monkish priests and ministers at large. Religion is the opium of the people and churches should be shut down, all of them. (Here, Emily would whisper something but Václav would not be shaken.) Poor people like him did not know any better, they had been poisoned by the opium fumes, until the party had opened their eyes. The party is doing a good job, the trouble is that a poor and honest man never really stands a chance. There are too many people getting rich again, on party jobs. Scoundrels, intellectuals and Jews. And too many women are taking men's places. Women should stay at home, take care of their children and husbands. The party should know better than to give them jobs, and far too many hopes. (Here, Emily would say something sharp, and Václav would retreat.) One thing is for certain; there is no greater man alive than Joseph Stalin, never was and never will be. The capitalist hyenas in the West may bare their teeth as much as they want, Joseph Stalin will defeat them with his little finger. The trouble is, a poor man never really gets to him, to tell him, as comrade to comrade, his problems . . . how the rich cheat the poor . . . always and always. (Here, Emily would hush him and soothe him and send him to bed, almost as if he were a child, and Linda would close her eyes and go to sleep, with Joseph Stalin in her heart. Only later, in her teens, would she remember the rest of her father's mumblings and cruelly, uncompromisingly hate him for them.)

There was a painting in the new wing of the National Gallery at the gate of Prague Castle, a monumental wonder in bright-colored oil, covering an entire wall.

Generalissimus, said a golden plate underneath, but Linda would not be deceived. The man on top of the splendid marble staircase, godlike in his shining white uniform with gold trimmings, and handsome with his graying hair and bushy mustache, his penetrating eyes softened by a few lovable wrinkles smiling down at her, was Joseph Stalin and no other.

The sky was painted a warm, summery blue with a few darkish clouds evidently disappearing into the past. The marble pillars on each side of the staircase were adorned with vine leaves and hung with ripe dewy grapes. And on each stair, kneeling, sitting, standing, their faces and their arms raised in adoration, towards the Generalissimus, were the lucky people painted to be with him forever: soldiers, workers, peasants, a man in a white coat who looked like a doctor, athletic young women and mellow-bodied mothers with children in their arms, a boy and a girl in Red Pioneer uniforms, an old man with a crutch. Flowers were scattered around and there was a large wreath made of golden wheat and barley with a few red poppies and blue cornflowers to make it merrier.

The gallery attendants soon got used to the skinny girl with two thin plaits of hair tied with white ribbons, who stood in front of the Stalin painting for long minutes at least twice a week; they thought she had probably been asked to study it for some school project, although, frankly, this was overdoing it a bit. Such an awful painting too; but this, of course, was not an opinion to be shared. Poor child.

Linda, her heart pounding, was imagining that she was the girl Pioneer in the painting, the one standing almost on the top of the staircase, holding out a bunch of red roses. Surely, in the next second beyond the painting's time, Joseph Stalin would take it from her and give her a kiss or maybe lift her in his arms, as he often did in the movies.

But dreams are dreams; in reality, Linda stood no chance of being painted or kissed, she knew it only too well. She was smart enough, there was no other Pioneer in the whole city who could recite poems as well as she could, and she was always chosen to do recitations in the Castle, on state anniversaries and party birthdays, even for the President. But she was always coupled with Danda, a boy from her school, who stood beside her while she was doing the talking. It was he who was holding the bunch of roses, his cheeks even rosier than usual and his dimples deepening, his dark eyes round and large, a picture of a child as governments and parents like them, healthy and innocent. Invariably it was Danda who got the kiss and the embrace, while Linda stepped back and was forgotten but for some secretary who took down her name and school for future reference.

She did not mind; there were only two people in the whole world for whom she passionately wished to be kissworthy, her mother and Joseph Stalin. But with her ugliness, it would have taken a miracle, and miracles, under communism, did not happen.

Even without Joseph Stalin, Linda would probably have liked Communism. It couldn't make her any prettier, nothing could, but it did give her dignity. There was no longer any shame in being poor, it had become—overnight, or so it seemed to her—an asset, a privilege, a pride. Maybe only for children, that was hard to tell; mother certainly treated Linda with more respect.

Linda knew all about indignity; she started school just a few months before Communism, in 1947; at that time, parcels from America were still distributed around the country for the needy victims of war. One rainy day, the teacher asked all such children in her class who were "socially weak"—well, in fact poor—to raise their hands. Linda did not, but the teacher put her name on the list nevertheless; in due time, the "socially weak" children from all of Prague's schools were escorted to the town hall and sat in their hundreds in row upon row of cold wooden seats. Speeches were made; and then, one by one, the children were called by name to the platform and received a large parcel each.

At home everybody was delighted; even proud Emily seemed to appreciate the tins of condensed milk and packets of cocoa and white flour. Sister Hela was beside herself about some silly faded jumpers and blouses, and brother Jan blushed with pleasure over a pair of old jeans.

The only piece of clothing which looked new was a bright red flannel dress with enormous green and yellow parrots printed on it, the most ridiculous thing anyone had ever seen. Linda howled with laughter, forgetting the indignities of the town hall; it was a joke, after all. Mother asked her to put it on, and Linda did, and danced a Red Indian war-dance in it, and laughed herself to hiccups . . . until she saw the look in her mother's eyes.

The skirt was shortened and the waist gathered in by mother's skillful fingers that very evening. Crying, pleading, choking with terror, Linda was made to wear the dress to school. The teacher sent a note, but Emily was not to be shaken; winter was coming and the dress was made of pure, warm, high-quality flannel. Only after brother Jan complained that his mates started calling him Parrot instead of Wren did Emily try to dye the parrots off. They proved totally resilient to such attempts and the dress was cut into leg-warming strips for father's gardening boots.

The episode took no more than two weeks; enough for the burning shame to leave scars in Linda's little soul forever—and to teach her about dignity.

Linda was twelve when Joseph Stalin died. She heard the news in town, where she was being X-rayed because of a suspected weak chest; traveling home on the open platform of tramway line number eight she cried her heart out. The clouds were white and swift on the winter sky and Linda's tear-flooded eyes transformed them into gigantic doves carrying Stalin's soul to Heaven and beyond . . .

Everything pointed to an era of grief. Sister Hela was married but soon back home again, sitting up at nights by the window in the kitchen, smoking cigarettes and yelling at father whenever he feebly protested that the smoke was seeping into The Room through the ill-fitting door.

Brother Jan was serving his two years in the army, and when he came home on leave mother threw everybody out of the kitchen, bathed his blistered feet in a camilla-bath and endlessly whispered to him. From time to time, above her whisper, Linda could hear that Jan was sobbing; there was such despair in it and hatred and humiliation that her heart turned cold.

One morning Linda woke up with a heavy head and blue circles under her eyes and there was a bloodstain on her sheet. Mother sighed heavily, and for a moment she was compassionate and gentle. Then she presented Linda with the horrifying arsenal which those times, at least in that part of the world, had for menstruating women: a couple of home-crocheted crotchpieces with ribbons on each end which one tied to one's suspender belt, and a supply of rags cut out from old sheets. These had to be soaked in cold water, boiled, washed and dried for further use. It was a messy, smelly business, bewilderingly private and yet, on the washing line, terribly public; nothing but ache, shame and sorrow.

Life was never the same after Joseph Stalin died.

A Barbarian Woman
in Captivity

Věra Linhartová

N O, YOU WILL NOT keep me from dreaming. Wherever you are,
you will always be the target of my thoughts, the one at
which the arrows of my presence choose to aim. I do not regret having come to this capital, which I loved and wondered about long before I arrived here. Meanwhile I am dreaming already of that other
city, which probably I will never know. For me, in reality, you inhabit that country: the Pure Land, immaculate, that we reach by
virtue of a primordial vow. I have taken that vow, and I renew it
daily.

It is my duty to put down here everything I did not say to you at
the right moments, note in advance at least the words I won't say
when the right moment comes again because, once more, I'll be too
weary, or too moved, too absorbed by other reveries, to swiftly give
you what is yours by rights. You have to be aware that I speak to you
constantly, even if, in your presence, words fail me.

In any case, don't worry: I'll not be a burden. You'll scarcely be
aware who I am or from where this voice comes to you. At the moment, I watch you move and breathe, and that alone already makes
me happy. And it has occurred to me whom you resemble: the statue
of a living god, such as one finds in this country we both love. Your
face, pale, often with beads of sweat on your forehead, around your

mouth. Your nose not very prominent, firmly set, your eyes half closed, lively though, and filled with eternal kindness. But will you not be offended if I say that you resemble anyone at all? Is it not an infringement of love's rule that demands the obvious: that the loved one must be seen as unique, unlike any other? It is neither your face, perhaps, nor your somewhat stooping figure, that brings to mind that immobile image, but rather your gestures, your bearing, the words and the way you choose to address me. It is my silence in reply which evokes the same radiance that struck me on seeing that magnificent work in stone.

Will it ever be possible, do you think, to step out of this role you never chose yourself? You were appointed my tutor without being asked for your opinion; you accepted without consulting me, never asking yourself if I might or might not want you in this capacity, if I wanted anyone to guide me in whatever field. Are you still able to throw over the order of things which you eventually enforced as if it had been your own idea? How could you take it seriously? You are in the best position to understand that I have nothing to learn from anyone, especially not those useless things you have been instructed to hammer into my head. Would you at all be able to abandon this fortuitous assignment that paralyses any real commerce between us? You know how my sudden flights, sporadic as they are, come up short against the glass you thought wise to erect between us? Will I break it some day? Or will I rather crack my skull in the attempt?

Here all is calm. No one is howling, getting dead drunk or leaping out of a window. It is all so perfect, so remote, it sometimes sends a chill down my spine. Today at noon, a ray of sunlight struck the shelves on which my books collect dust. I thought at first I had forgotten to turn off some lamp, then I realized that in fact spring is approaching, the sun rising again above the roofs of the neighboring houses, making its way into my room. How many years now has this good omen appeared to me?

What is the real power of my thoughts? Could I rely on bending your decision with the force of what takes shape in my imagination? Can my thought in its intensity be capable of touching you, can it reach you and imperceptibly permeate your own ideas? Of course, not for a moment do I doubt that my thought is a force, provided, however, that it does not aim wrongly. To act, to materialize, it must first of all turn away from you, it must not stare at you directly in wild obstinacy. As long as it is bound to you, it remains powerless, sickly. As soon as it abandons you, it can move freely, can change, can simply *be*. Even if you are its source, you could not be its object. My thought requires a space which is far wider than the one you have to offer, for it moves mountains, diverts oceans, to establish an unknown landscape, where you could one day, after the storm, come to live.

If you only knew how vast the expanse of indifference is, where everything I see, each and every one of my urgent pursuits and everything that seems to engage me has taken root. This is exile: this immense backdrop of indifference to my whole existence, so uprooted and yet so unaltered. It is what I wanted, what I sought. Some monks, some ascetics obviously strive to attain it in other ways and with the help of other means. Believe me, it is so simple. I apply myself with all my energy, with my whole heart to the smallest task that I have taken on, and yet, before I've brought it to an end, it slips back and dies away in this welcoming net where any appearance of variety alone would cause only a vague and indistinct shudder. In this diaphanous web, the color of ashes, you are the only breach.

Nevertheless, to mellow my ways one would have to be stronger than you. You teach me to read and write, which is no small thing, but it is not enough for a profounder change in my universe, wild beyond remedy. I will never be a good pupil. If I seize everything you hand me with evident voracity, it is only to confront that fragile knowledge, to confuse it with what I have always borne within me. In what depths, then, are your learned words lost? Oh, I welcome the whole world that you generously offer, not to make it mine, but to elevate what I know already, in other words, to kindle higher what I, for our lack of mutuality, can never disclose to you. Unless you were to come into exile yourself, were to join me on my wondrous isle. Have you the courage? Would this be too much to ask?

Yesterday, you did not come to give me my usual lesson. I did not miss you. I spent the time dreaming of battles where I followed my old companions, clinging to the manes of their horses. Merciless battles, I have seen endless numbers of them in my life, and I have always charged without regard for risk. Why do you want me now to stay sheltered, why dress me up in uncomfortable clothes, inappropriate to a campaign that might well last into the summer? Oh, you are niggardly! I have no use for your scraps of learning. Dress me a proper mount, I'll wait for you to open wide the gate of the fortress, and even if you yourself do not sally forth, I will not be surprised, I'll go alone. Don't ask me to proceed step by step, to compromise, to equivocate. I've heard the call of the wind.

I often fear that I may crush you, hurt you with a love that is not meant for you, that only passes through you to take me ever farther. That is why I ask nothing of you. Certainly not that you heal the wound you dealt me. I would rather lie open to love, confront life with this raw spot, this breach in my indolence. Since you've approached me, you've nothing more to give me. From afar, I spring at you to go past you, to break the hard shell of a complacency that would be my true prison. Can I blame you if you strain to avoid my glance, baleful no doubt for a being so frail, so vulnerable? If only your life could remain calm, serene, unruffled. But some unknown fate decided that you travel on my path and that I, in spite of myself, cannot swerve aside.

I have not even told you that you resemble, not only the living deity whose statue I showed you, but also a dead friend, a craftsman of other nameless deities of whom I don't remember any image, or imperfect imitation. I couldn't tell you all my successive lives, it would take too long, and be of no interest at all. Besides, while I always look towards what comes in the glory of innocence, I scrupulously observe, come what may, the prohibition on looking back. Behind is putrefaction, and death, there are monsters and spectres which rend and devour one another. Life is only what has not yet taken place. You live on the side of what will never take place, and I do not want you to cross the threshold of the real, of agony. I do not know what my fate will be in this city, becoming more foreign to me as I discover it. But I do know that I am only here in transit.

I gathered secretly some leaves, some herbs only I know of, collected some birds' feathers, to combine with other ingredients into a compound which, at a propitious moment, I stored in a safe place. Then I cut from a piece of birch bark two human silhouettes and slipped them among the text books, whose gratuitous beauty is the only bond between us. You handled them thoughtlessly, with no notion that you were exposing yourself to contact with the charm. One day you will inevitably take them with you, not suspecting how you have sealed your fate. Wherever you go, henceforward you can never untie this knot, which tightens as you pull away , especially as you must first discover its existence. What ill luck for you, to have been appointed to my service, although originally your services were meant as part of a strict supervision of my captivity. I have, however, a way of turning to my favor the most malevolent intentions, the most disastrous circumstances.

You are quite right to mistrust me, but you are not yet careful enough and take too many risks. No doubt you hope to maintain a just proportion, never to step out of a well-marked terrain, where we are pledged, on both sides, to follow the rules of the game. Do not forget that I come from regions far more uncouth, from a more violent climate. I would only need to allow invasion of this little well-ordered room where my books and papers submit to the quiet cadence prompted by the magical movement of your hands, and all this would fly in pieces, the precarious arrangement of this snug world turned topsy-turvy, your best intentions crushed, swept away by the storm you often feel coming but before which you close your eyes, stop your ears. Love me while love lasts, it is not an eternity, it is a passing moment. You stand bent above a well: is it fear that peers at you from the pit? Already your bouts of fever have betrayed you.

They are false prophets who appeal to the golden mean, unaware that the straight way is an edge honed fine by the strength of excess, by the incessant action of immoderation. If you never deviate, if you do not stray continually and as far as possible from your path, soon it will grow over with moss and you will be unable to trace it again. You must trample it furiously, you must leap about, turn somersaults when the mood strikes you, so that it will remain legible, negotiable, clear. Spare me the trial of comfort. I would rather reel on the edge of an abyss than be carried in a gilded palanquin over safe, well-tended roads. If your golden mean is not on the cutting edge, then you have lied to me, or else you do not understand a single word of what you are supposed to be teaching me.

Whose shadow are you looking for? Is it my silhouette that haunts your nights of feverish insomnia? Do you know that what we love grows larger in proportion to its distance from us and that, consequently, our only homeland lies beyond what we can imagine? But that, by an abrupt and unexpected reversal, here it is, now, always? That the unattainable love is the one closest to us, what we can touch with our fingers in the simplest, most unconsidered immediacy? At high noon, we've no shadow . . .

The chronicles of the time tell us that the young person who wrote these pages, whose candor will never cease to surprise us, disappeared one day without trace. Rumor has it that, some time after, people saw her in a distant land, but they were not certain whether it was really her or merely a person who resembled her. There were other rumors, but nothing could be said. with certainty. Her tutor, who was seriously reprimanded for having let his charge escape, was somewhat vexed by her disappearance, but then, as time obscured his memories, he reconciled himself to it.

Translated from the French original by Keith Waldrop

Fragments and Likenesses

excerpts from a novel

SYLVIE RICHTER

HERE SHE USED TO think I began. Here I used to think she began.

I don't love him. It is quite clear that I don't love him. She was preoccupied with the reasons why she didn't love him, and she found many, all trivial. Rushing to work she felt cold and sleepy, and the tram was important because it wasn't coming, and the weather because it was raining, if it really were raining. Her resentment stemmed from the fact that she had not prepared for work. She wanted to do some reading, to prepare, draft something, but she didn't read or prepare anything, and the draft she wrote she thought better to leave at home. It was meant to be on the sensitivity of plants, and she thought there was some connection with the fact that she didn't love him. A loose connection. Or none at all. The sentence 'I don't love him' was a discovery for her, and that was far more significant than whether it was true.

She went to do her shopping, then cooked a meal, thinking angrily that she could have done with just a piece of bread and salami. Change of stage set and the same room where they both sat in armchairs, where they needed to buy a wall radiator for the bathroom, where they went for holidays to the mountains. She didn't feel like looking at him and her gaze bored into his forehead. His face, of course, was certainly handsome. A residual sense of justice. That he was reading the paper in an armchair led her to the conclusion that in the end I would do exactly what I wanted. Would do in the end. But which end? She also didn't know what it was she would do. And why in the end? What's that got to do with him reading the paper? I no longer know, and then again I do.

She crossed over from the city that stands in the center into the city that converges and diverges. Yet never disappears. She wept, but she didn't wish for reasons any more than she wished for pain. Tenderly she cherished the name of Bear Street, via dell'Orso, in her memory. I deny her compassion. I caught myself feeling sorry over my attempt to park the car in the middle of the square three years ago, now brought absurdly into the present. Germinal and tear-inducing, then it was also inaugmentable. I have repeatedly recoiled from that time, sometimes with a feeling of revulsion.

An attempt to turn clearsighted, best on public transport. Knowing how to plant strawberries, a skill taught to me by my grandmother many years ago, comes in unexpectedly handy, even in Rome. I say in Rome, because if I had the opportunity to plant strawberries and didn't know how to do it, anybody could teach me in ten minutes.

Growing potatoes was vital, milking the goat, preserving fruit and vegetables for the winter, drying damsons and pears. Rows of glass jars with preserved fruit. A fragrant pantry with shelves lining the walls, made of rough-hewn planks which he cut when the harvest was over and all the grain was stored.

But it is late, it has been late for these things from the start; what does it matter under which roof the grain is stored? Even talking about it sounds preposterous. The only serviceable thing from that time I could still use was outdated syntax.

She washed the dishes, the tiles above the sink, then the stove and the tiles above the stove. I started crossing out whole sentences and paragraphs. But in the end some of them will have to stay. The apartment is her womb, fiercely, the greater her anxiety. After all, since I became aware of it, I have also read it in a review of a book by a French woman psychologist.

I looked around and repeated to myself for the hundredth time that, regrettably, none of that was a coincidence. And that's why I worked so hard to whitewash that lack of coincidence. White walls.

Is she different today? Once more, I speak differently, from a different position. But it is not going to be easy to leave this marital triangle consisting of one person. One person behind bars. I'm not forgetting, though, that there is only one place one can truly leave and return to. And only one person I can safely remove myself from, as I continue being stuck in her.

But the tiles are still cold to the touch and there's nothing I can do about that. Crossing out words without obliterating all traces, not fleeing, but genuinely gaining distance.

On to the tiles she was polishing she projected a film. As the grease slowly disappeared and the shine grew more intense, her own image, her face, emerged from the depths of the glaze, but hideous and grinning. She laughed ha ha at herself, the inside of the throat exposed, blackened teeth in the front plane. In the next tile, a distorted hand with hooked claws. In the third, naked buttocks, the hips moving as if she were shuffling on the spot. In the pan she had scrubbed with steel wool a train moved forth, a woman's body under the wheels. Here we have a reference to Anna Karenina—a little weak, but for a brief moment it pleased her. An enlarged detail of an iron being slowly driven into the lovely face of a young girl, the point opening the way, the weight flattening. A tender hand with a silver thimble stitched an ear on either side of the flat form. The idea born in ugliness suddenly appeared beautiful. But it was not.

And he sat there as if struck by lightning. Sat and exploded at regular intervals. Believing everything he said with volcanic inevitability.

When she returned home at noon, he wasn't there. She passed cautiously through all the rooms, but he really wasn't there. She fried up an egg and bacon, ate it straight from the pan while reading a newspaper, resting her head in the palm of her hand and her foot on the chair opposite, smacking her lips every now and then, although she hated it.

Having washed the pan, she started cleaning the whole flat, then sat down in the armchair with a book, put it down again and got up, telling herself that she was going to write her lecture notes tomorrow. She took a bath, mended a torn skirt, sewed a button on to a pair of trousers and fixed the loose buttons on her coat, prepared clothes for the cleaners, washed the dirty laundry, decided to buy a white carpet and to paint the room white. Buy books she wanted to read and read the ones she had bought a long time ago. Then she went to the florist's to get three tulips, arranged them in a vase and placed the vase in the bedroom. Finally, she wrote down a detailed schedule for the next day. The schedule, which she was going to follow to the letter, gave her a great sense of security. She wrote it on a sheet of square-ruled paper which she then placed on the empty top of her desk. She got into bed almost ceremoniously, as if she were being watched by an invisible person. She also promised herself that she would get up half an hour earlier than usual.

He returned—returned—he came, that is. When he came in, she didn't immediately realize that he had returned. She greeted him and only then did she feel a pang of anticipation, only then did she become alarmed. He collapsed into an armchair, without a word, he came in silently and collapsed into the armchair, as if he'd never

212

moved from there. He was there, he had always been there. And again he didn't move for weeks, only shouted every now and then, grabbed her by the hair, his kisses resuscitating and then again smothering, he found reasons, proof, evidence and examples; sometimes he cried.

So he came, he returned, he's there, there, never to leave again. She had not bought her freedom with the blows she received nor with the tears she cried. Not to mention the few drops of blood from her nose, but that's too ridiculous to bring up. Her suspicion that she'd had an easy escape was correct, wasn't out of place, out of this place, where several blows were waiting, several, many, few. Any sudden noise and she runs. Any mention of the word "blow" and she adds the word "fatal" in her mind. For a whole week she didn't look in the mirror.

I used to wish that this story be without mercy: she an egoist with no heart, he an egoist with no head. Or the other way round. I was impatient, my God, all I wanted was an end to it. And the end came indeed, only now I don't know what to do with her, where to send her. It happened on a Sunday morning, grayish and shivering with cold. It belongs elsewhere and it no longer matters which one of the two is going to find a new place to rent.

II

The lake is transparent only between the bottom and the surface. He kept holding on to boulders to prevent his excessively light body from rising back to the surface.

It was a truly awful poem; in the end my lungs forced me to take a breath of air after a long battle with willpower, and I never finished it. The preceding text, of which there is almost nothing left, was originally meant to complete the story of love which had or had not taken place earlier.

She moved house several times and I did several re-writes, but I cannot answer the question earlier than what? Than that? As it happened, the first thing to be written was a text about the end. Attempts to start from the end have no beginning and no ending.

There is also the love for the poet who was not at odds with his own time nor with ours. The place of meeting neither here nor there.

Passage of death and life. They departed from the same point, but since then they have been approaching one another, each moving in its own direction. Even our meeting was truly inevitable and perhaps fatal. Knowing the mouth of the river, can we reach its source? It seems that we cannot, but we know the entire watercourse. We could follow it again blindfolded. And were we to emerge suddenly and unexpectedly from a deep wood on its banks, we would be able to tell with certainty each of its bends by their unmistakable signs. For we know the river down to its smallest reeds, down to the tiniest wild duckling that has just hatched from its egg. Though I love rivers as tenderly as metaphors, we never reach their source with its spring of cool, fresh water. From memory and with the use of words we shall dig up that river bed again. And then, only then, shall we strike it.

Don't tell me you were afraid. Weren't those who were lost from our story only its dead characters?

I lack a solid form. The moment he comes close enough, my body takes on a form that corresponds to him, to the accidental. He says that's not accidental. He is right. I am also deeply convinced of it. Why is the one right and the other one opposed to me? Despite myself I am drawn to both, as if they were one.

That she never dealt a blow. That she never even raised her hand. Now she knows it with certainty, now she has it near herself, within herself. Those wounds still. She knew, after all, that they were not going to heal, but she did not want to say it. But why not? Perhaps to distance herself, for example, to soar. To live as far as possible from oneself. Dioeciously. That would be the best way to put it. She knows what it means, but to say it would be too many sentences forming a gauntlet one has to run. Bad luck sticking like resin, the tears of trees. The bark covered with amber tears. Shortly before sunset she rejoices in what the low rays of the sun create on the bark. The hardened drops of resin still have a liquid center under the solid surface. Testing cautiously with her finger. That she did not hit the hand pulling hair, did not bite with all her might the tongue not stealing kisses but robbing the soul. What else should she call it if not soul, since she could not escape? Once more I remember the little girl wandering through the forest in August, preparing herself for something. Preparing herself for something. Then again the city. The day, expanded by transparent blue air to high heaven. Sudden pink blossoms on fragile peach trees with slender black trunks. The pink in the crown of the trees against the sky decapitated all considerations of justice. Took away their breath and their words. The buses kept coming with the same approximate probability, all overcrowded. Going round a bend she had to hold on to the handle above her head; had she sown salvation by not striking? The thought like the pulp of an over-ripe orange difficult to peel, sticking to the zest, juices running.

Even if he had never existed, I have to find out whether he was black or white. And most importantly: to prove that he wasn't gray.

He also advised me to emphasize the geometry of bodies. Their bodies. He came to the logical conclusion that it might benefit the entire form. But I will no longer emphasize geometry. After all, I harbor a slight suspicion that he may have thought I did not like my own body. But the rest of his advice was valuable. In one chilly moment he gave me back speech, having understood that the stones and the cold also have a place here. I take from him what I find useful. I thank him and see him down the stairs. With a smile I return what I have no use for. Or perhaps turn it round. And a little bit against him. But, above all, I value his friendship.

III

Inevitably also the question what is jealousy? There was a time when she tried to convince herself that it did not exist at all. Now she is lying across the undisturbed marital bed. Covering the face with her hands, she slowly turns from a position on her back on to her stomach.

I could give more complete evidence if I were able to refrain from touching her body and her mind.

To look at oneself through the eyes of an angel, to look at oneself through the eyes of the devil. How many times. When the only thing she desired was for him to exist. As if the most urgent need could make him appear. At least as a witness. Eternal and omniscient, so that it would mean mercy and salvation. She wants to have a witness, being still able to articulate the word "solitude," having excluded it from speech but not yet included it in her soliloquies.

She slowly lifts her belly and pelvic bones which are glued to the bed. Seeing sharply. And not just seeing. Now even knowing that she is pink inside. Tender contractions, the life of tissue.

While he drank her face with his eyes, I raised my hand to test the smoothness of her velvety skin with a light touch. I came up closer to her, caught her breath on my face and so shaded even her eyes. Hiding them from his gaze when her pupils narrowed with excitement.

I inserted myself between them so adroitly to hide his lover from him and to show myself to her in his place, more beautiful, more seductive, stronger. She had to find me irresistible; only I could give her the tenderness she needed. Only I was able to fulfil her so that she could at last become whole. And I, only I, could also subjugate her like a shadow, only I can make her remote like a film projected on to a screen, or disperse her the way we disperse darkness by turning on the light switch. Only I can leave with her in this way. And she must leave with me.

He would hesitate before giving a kiss, even brush his teeth. He would undress her in his mind, then turn off the light. He would couple with her, but I penetrate her more completely, breathe her in and out through my mouth, her breast in my breast. My breasts, my body, the body on the undisturbed marital bed, across in pain.

I grow larger and stronger, my arms hold her tighter and tighter. She no longer knows about him and he keeps searching for her in vain. He cannot take her away from me. For a moment I release her breasts from my palms and give them back. A conflagration in the twilight. How conceited of him to think that he could come to know her.

My eyes were closed and I was worse than numb. At the same time I could not forget the pink.

I closed my eyes with the pressure and pain. For the last time I touch her silky hair and draw her breath. Will she still recognize him when I step back from her? The skin on the back of the right hand bitten through by female teeth. For a moment she tried to convince herself they were not her own.

Those minuscule letters in the book about death.

And hitting the target, the target that was in the margin. On the very edge. At last, after an incredibly long time, laughter like the ringing of little bells.

Marcel is deposited in his room. Albertine is lying on her day-bed in semi-darkness. And since today Marcel is compliant, obedient, submissive, Albertine hardly thinks of him; she is thinking about her next great work of literature, deciding firmly for the thousandth time that she will start writing tomorrow. She really finds Marcel's presence boring and troublesome.

But how to undo the fact that Albertine was killed in a horse-riding accident, instead of writing her literary work? What a stupid death.

I do not want to fight you in a duel. I am returning into my sex. Into my territory. The laughter suddenly stops. She wanted to shout, roar in a terrible voice, but she made no sound in the bedroom, apartment, building, in the city, in the whole world. My dear sister Medea.

The echo returns; which wall does it bounce off? That he returned transformed. It could have been expected, it was no surprise to her, none at all. But it scared her, it did.

Having survived her own death, she is returning by detour. On the way a couple of slaps across the face. The question is whether her doubt could divert her from what her self had been carrying for a long time.

IV

Her memory was mostly written. I don't know whether this has its advantages, or whether it carries particular inherent dangers. Yet, there was nothing she could do to change that, even if she were to lose or destroy everything she had ever written. She could not but find remembrance in other books.

I don't know whether she would ever achieve true maturity, she still needed much to really grow up.

But she wrote down her own childhood. It filled a hundred type-written pages; some things were left out and she changed almost everything, yet it was her childhood and nothing more was need-ed. It took her many years to write, and when she made the last full stop on page one hundred, she was finally certain that her childhood was at last complete, giving a sigh of relief like a mother whose son has been safely through all the childhood illness. She made a reso-lution to write down her adolescence as soon as possible, hoping that if she hurried, she would catch up with herself before she died. At the same time, she had no doubt that such a meeting might prove fatal. Yet, she hoped for the first alternative.

Later, whenever she felt like recounting her past life to her friends, she would repeat whole passages from the book, as if she were reading them, without the slightest alteration. Not only did she remember all the stories and events, but every single expression and sequence of words. Because, as her grandmother used to say, as she played patience in the early evenings in her room where nobody was allowed to disturb, see or hear: shuffled and drawn. Once changed, you cannot make amends.

Two years have passed since I wrote this page about her memory residing in books already written and as yet unwritten, and I found the issue a little frightening. But were she cross it out now, I would have to worry even more.

Fortunately, when re-typing the text, she was prudent enough to have left out the sentence: I want to write my way out of myself, to write myself into not being. But in her mind she tried to translate it into other languages. *Je veux m'ecrire hors de moi.* The meaning changes, not insignificantly. *Voglio iscrivermi fuori me stessa.* I fell pas-sionately in love with the Italian language when I discovered that the verb to keep balance, to hover or keep in the air by flying and also to fly is *librarsi*. Like *libro.* Book, *le livre, das buch.* As if books gave them wings.

She knew that it was necessary to proceed slowly, in agreement with herself and also with something else. She also knew that it was not entirely clear to her exactly what it was. But she was convinced she would find out only if she proceeded according to that insufficiently formulated and maybe as yet undiscovered law.

There are two more things she still has to mention, even though she would prefer not to invoke them. The first one was waiting. The second was the sound of the door being closed from outside. Of course, the sound of the door being closed and the echo of departing footsteps could come first and waiting second. The order did not matter, as they were two points marking out an unrelenting space. Marking out, not surrounding, but it was enclosed all the same. Wherever she went on foot, or on the train, drove a car, or flew by airplane, she could never reach its curved end.

At the same time she found that there was no point in climbing walls, burying her nails in plaster, because they break, but above all, because it is simply stupid. Like walking round a table pushed to the wall. She stared at the door with such intensity that it opened on its own. He had forgotten his cigarettes and lighter. She never heard the door close the second time. Alcohol. No point talking about alcohol. Cold sweat, why not also a desire to become ugly? To look like inexcusable pain?

The most important thing was to avoid touching any object. She is standing slightly bent forward, standing, forgetting she has hands. She doesn't know I can see her, she thinks that nobody can see her and she changes. Enchanted garden at the bottom of a deep well.

Fairytales. She'd give anything for a snowstorm. While one year passed in the enchanted garden, one day passed on earth. Or the other way round. Or the other way round. Can everything always be turned the other way round? She realized that she was standing, opened her fists, nail-marks in her palms. Why wasn't she the one to leave, why isn't it she who keeps him waiting, what is she really waiting for and why? If she can do anything else, that is. She couldn't. That was why she had to find something irreversible. Something that would be impossible to turn the opposite way. The furniture slowly shifted into the corners, disappearing within the walls. A crocheted doily slipped off the coffee table. An excuse to laugh. If at least it were hysterical laughter, she would have something to laugh about. But it wasn't, it was clear like the time that fulfils itself.

The sofa with a woollen blanket dawdled the longest in the middle of the room. As if it wanted to sit down, as if the sofa wanted to sit down for a while. It is unnecessary and unreasonable to blame the tower clock for striking one o'clock after midnight, simply because it had done it many times before. There are so many of them that she can only keep quiet about it. They quote themselves. They quote themselves. The clock, the hours.

She is turning the sharp edge against herself with unexpected energy. Even if it may not have been very clear to the eyes of a stranger. Still doesn't know she isn't invisible.

It was being born like a statue. At least I believe that is how statues come into being.

Walking on stone. Often with my bare feet. Lying down on stone. There is a black volcanic rock, sloping steeply into a blue sea. There is a white limestone rock, dropping vertically into a green sea. The place is at the very top, comfortable to sit in, as if the stone opened a spacious palm. Resting safely, dangling my feet over an abyss. Before me, nothing but the sky, below, the sea or the ground. Known to attract irresistibly. About a meter and a half under the stony throne a rock juts out, an inviting step. It would be enough to support myself on my hands and slowly shift down on to the step, stand up on it as if it were the prow of a ship raised towards the skies on the crest of a wave. That rock is a point of no return. Once you are on it, you cannot turn round, let alone go back, you would not be able to climb back, you would never return. *Il punto del non ritorno.*

I descended the rock in a roundabout way, along a path overgrown with green grass.

This is how I know stones. It took me a long time, though, to understand that it would be a statue.

I can stand on a stone, I know what it is like under snow and what it does when it rains on it, I know how its temperature rises around noon. And I gazed at it furtively, until it seemed to me that I knew what it looked like inside.

But there was a time when I was unable to make out anything, not with my eyes nor with my mind. Almost impenetrable, it surrounded me with oppressive urgency. I strove with superhuman effort, but I doubted whether I was moving at all. I was inside and it seemed to me that I myself was turning into a boulder, or at least that I was stuck like a prehistoric fern in a coal seam.

One day, however, cracks appeared and the boulder slowly began to separate itself from the rock. A year later I could comfortably walk round it.

But even then I still failed to understand that it would be a statue, and although I emerged whole from the hard, sharp vitals, it brought no relief. I had to concentrate uncompromisingly, with my whole being, on finding a balance for my boulder. Then I could not lift it; it was much larger than I. Nor could I lean it against something, as we were continually moving away from the rock. I cannot even tell the shape it was then, I was unable to take a single step back to look at it. It must have been very uneven, as I searched in vain for its center of gravity. Always threatening to crush something or someone, most often myself. To keep it at least relatively immobile, I had to run round it incessantly, support it from different sides, hold it up, push, roll, slowly turn it, support. In time I learned to keep it in balance with the least effort, my touches becoming lighter and lighter, gentler and more intimate. In the end I controlled it by means of my look rather than by physical force. Yet I could not part from it for a moment. We never left one another, not even when I regained regular sleep, not even when I started eating regularly, not even when I returned to my daily duties and occupations. Anything could stand between me and the boulder, yet our bond would never be severed.

It was only by touch that I first realized it was changing. As if I felt a smooth facet here and there, a caress. It delighted me and brought me relief.

I cannot even tell exactly when I saw a figure emerge from the boulder. When I saw it for the first time, it seemed that it was just my shadow or perhaps a dream I projected on to the stone surface. I put it down to the the exhaustion I felt and I told myself with irritation that one can comfortably project pictures on to a wall in one's room, instead of laboring Sisyphus-like with a chunk of rock.

But it turned out that the figure really was emerging and that was when I panicked. Something so clumsy, unattractive, massive, hard to take in at a glance. That was when I first thought of escape. Thought about it and longed for it. Escape might have been possible then, but futile, as he was closer to me than I was to myself. For so long we staggered together, until I smoothed out his face with my hands and mouth. Until I learned to look him in the eyes. And he really opened them. I know now what it is he resembles. And he no longer holds me.

Translated by Alexandra Büchler

Permissions

ABOUT THE AUTHORS

Alexandra Berková was born in Trenčín in 1949. She trained as glass-maker, then studied Czech and Art Education at Charles University in Prague, earning her PhD with a dissertation on Karel Čapek. She worked as a publishing editor before turning to writing prose and TV scripts full time. One of the most interesting writers to have recently emerged on the Czech literary scene, her experimental prose is a mixture of fairy tale, allegory, dada and satire. Her collection of short stories *Knížka s červeným obalem* [*Book with a Red Cover*] was published in 1986 and novellas *Magórie aneb Příběh velké lásky* [*Loonyland or the Story of a Great Love*] in 1991, and *Utrpení oddaného všiváka* [*Sufferings of Devoted Lousehead*] in 1994. In English, her work appeared in *Storm*, *Yazzyk*, in the Picador anthology of Eastern European prose, *Description of a Struggle*, 1994, in the Serpent's Tail anthology of Czech fiction *This Side of Reality*, 1996, and the Catbird Press anthology *Daylight in Nightclub Inferno*, 1997.

Tereza Boučková was born in Prague in 1957. Daughter of the writer Pavel Kohout, one of the prominent figures of the Prague Spring who was later forced to emigrate by the authorities, she was prevented from obtaining higher education. Her collection of four narratives *Indiánský běh* [*The Indian Run*], 1989, was awarded the Orten Prize for young writers. Her second book, *Křepelice* [*The Quail*], came out in 1993, her third *Když žena miluje muže* [*When a Woman Loves a Man*] in 1995. Her work has been translated into Dutch, German and English and published in the magazines *Yazzyk*, *Trafika* and in the Catbird Press anthology *Daylight in Nightclub Inferno*, 1997.

Zuzana Brabcová was born in Prague in 1959. After taking her matriculation examination, she worked as librarian and later as publishing editor. Her novel *Daleko od stromu* [*Far from the Tree*], first published in exile in 1987 and later in Prague in 1991, brought her immediate recognition as one of the most representative and original voices of the new literary generation which grew up in the repressive atmosphere of the 1970s. Her second novel *Zlodějina*, [*Thievery*] was published in 1996. Her first novel was translated into Dutch and an extract was included in the Serpent's Tail anthology of Czech fiction *This Side of Reality*, 1996.

Jana Červenková was born in Prague in 1939. She studied history and Czech at the Faculty of Pedagogy in Prague and worked as a teacher. Later she stayed at home to devote time to her children and to writing, and worked in several short-term jobs. Since 1990 she has been working as editor for literary and cultural journals. She has published stories, novels and books for children. Her novels *Semestr života* [*The Semester of Life*], 1981, and *Věno pro Yvettu Márovou* [*The Dowry for Yvetta Márová*], 1989, explore the emotional and moral problems of young women confronted with the reality and conformist hypocrisy of "socialist consumerism." Her latest novel is *Jak vypadá nic* [*What Nothing Looks Like*], 1994.

Daniela Fischerová was born in Prague in 1948 and studied dramaturgy and scriptwriting at the Prague Film School. She worked briefly as an editor in a publishing house and has been a freelance writer since 1974. She is known primarily for her plays, including *Hodina mezi psem a vlkem*, 1979 (Engl. *Dog and Wolf* in *Czech Plays*, 1994) *Princezna T.* [*Princess T.*], 1986, and *Báj* [*The Myth*], 1987, her radio plays and books for children. Her short fiction collection *Prst, který se nikdy nedotkne* [*The Finger That Will Never Touch*] was published in 1996. A story from this collection was included in the Catbird Press anthology *Daylight in Nightclub Inferno*, 1997.

Eva Hauser was born in Prague in 1954. She studied natural sciences at Charles University in Prague and worked for some time in genetics research before turning to science fiction and fantasy as writer, editor and translator. She has made a significant contribution to the so far very subdued debate on women's issues and to the introduction of feminist theories into the Czech environment as the author of the first Czech "feminist manual" *Na koštěti se dá i lítat* [*Broomsticks Are Also for Flying*], 1994. She edited the science fiction magazine *Ikarie* and her prose is informed by her science background and her feminist views. Her collection of short stories was published in 1991, her novel *Cvokyně* [*The Madwoman*] in 1992. Her stories have been included in a number of Czech and foreign anthologies.

Daniela Hodrová was born in Prague in 1946. She studied Russian and Czech at the Faculty of Philosophy of Charles University, then French and comparative literature, earning her PhD with a dissertation on the beginnnings of the novel in Old Russian literature. Theory of the novel remained her main interest when she became a research fellow at the

Institute of Czech Literature and she has translated Bakhtin's *The Dialogic Imagination* into Czech. Apart from her scholarly writings she has published a trilogy of novels *Trýznivé město* [*The Suffering City*], 1991, and a poetic homage to Prague *Město vidím . . . [I see a City . . .*], 1993. Her work has been translated into French, Italian and German. English translations of her prose have appeared in *The Prague Revue, Prairie Schooner* and in the Catbird Press anthology *Daylight in Nightclub Inferno,* 1997.

Eda Kriseová was born in Prague in 1940. She studied journalism at Charles University in Prague and worked as a reporter in the 1960s, publishing a number of articles on her extensive travels. Having been banned as a journalist in 1969, she worked at the Media Institute and later in the University Archive, staying at home to write prose between 1976 and 1990 when she became a presidential adviser. Author of short stories, novels, books for children and a biography of President Václav Havel, published in English by St. Martin's Press in 1993, her writings include *Křížová cesta kočárového kočího* [*The Coachman's Calvary*], 1977, *Klíční kůstka netopýra* [*The Clavicle of a Bat and Other Stories*], 1982, and *Arboretum,* 1987. Her novels include *Pompejanka* [*The Woman of Pompeii*], 1979, and her latest *Kočičí životy* [*Cat Lives*], 1997. Her idiosyncratic prose, often dealing with the inner, emotional reality of women's lives, combines reportage-style narrative with elements of fantasy. Her work has been translated into German and Dutch, and English translations were included in the anthology of Czech literature *The Writing on the Wall,* 1983, and in Picador's *Description of a Struggle,* 1994.

Věra Linhartová was born in Brno in 1938. She studied art history in Brno and aesthetics in Prague, and later gained her PhD in Oriental art in Paris where she has lived since 1968. She has written widely on art including books on Tápies, Šíma, Medek and on Japanese art, and she now works as curator of Oriental art at the Museé Guimet in Paris. In the 1960s she was a member of the Surrealist Group and her experimental prose published at the time immediately placed her among the most important postwar Czech writers. Her books are *Meziprůzkum nejblíž uplynulého* [*Intersurvey of the Nearest Past*], 1964, *Prostor k rozlišení* [*Space for Differentiation*], 1964, *Rozprava o zdviži* [*Discourse About an Elevator*], 1965, *Přestořeč* [*Despite-Talk*], 1966, and *Dům daleko* [*A House Too Far*], 1968. Since 1969 she has been writing in French and her published work includes *Twor,*1974, *In-*

tervalles, 1979 and *Portraits carnivores*, 1982. Her work has been translated into German, Italian and Japanese, and English translations have been included in Penguin's *Czech and Slovak Short Stories*, 1967, and the Serpent's Tail anthology of Czech fiction *This Side of Reality*, 1996.

Iva Pekárková was born in Prague in 1963. She studied microbiology at Charles University in Prague, but emigrated to the US in 1985 before taking her degree. She lived in In New York until 1996 and worked as social worker and night taxi driver. Her early writing was circulated in samizdat; her published novels are *Péra a perutě*, 1989, [Engl. *Truck Stop Rainbows*, FSG, 1992], *Kulatý svět*, 1993, [Engl. *The World is Round*, FSG, 1994] and *Dej mi ty prachy* [*Gimme the Money*], 1996. She now lives in Prague working as a freelance writer and literary translator.

Lenka Procházková was born in Prague in 1951, daughter of the writer Jan Procházka who was active in the 1960s liberalization process. She took a degree in journalism in 1975 but because of her father's activities could not work in her profession and made a living as a cleaner through the '70s and '80s. She is the author of prose, theater plays and song lyrics. Her writing, which revolves around the themes of woman's emotional life, single motherhood and erotic relationships, and was banned until 1989, includes *Tři povídky* [*Three Stories*], 1980, *Přijed' ochutnat* [*Come and Have a Taste*], 1981, *Oční kapky* [*The Eye-Drops*], 1982, *Hlídač holubů* [*The Pigeon Keeper*], 1984, *Smolná kniha* [*The Black Book*], 1989, and short stories *Zvrhlé dny* [*Perverse Days*], 1995.

Sylvie Richter was born in Brno in 1945. She studied French and Italian and earned her PhD from Charles University with a dissertation on the poetics of Jacques Prévert. She has lived in Italy since 1971 and was awarded her second doctoral degree for a thesis on Věra Linhartová. She has taught Czech literature at universities in Rome, Padua and is now Professor of Czech literature at the University of Viterbo. She has translated the work of a number of Czech writers into Italian and has published theoretical writings on Czech literature in Italy, France and the Czech Republic. Her critical essays were collected in the volumes *Slova a ticho* [*Words and Silence*], 1994 and *Ticho a smích* [*Silence and Laughter*], 1997. Her three collections of short texts, *Návraty a jiné ztráty* [*Returns and Other Losses*], *Místopis* [*Topography*] and *Slabikář otcovského jazyka* [*Primer of the Father*

Tongue], were first published in exile, then in Prague in 1991. Her latest books are the novels *Rozptýlené podoby* [*Fragments and Likenesses*], 1993, and *Druhé loučení* [*The Second Parting*], 1994, and poems *Neviditelné jistoty* [*Invisible Certainties*], 1994. Her work has been translated into Italian, French and German, and English translations have appeared in *Yazzyk* and the Serpent's Tail anthology of Czech fiction *This Side of Reality*, 1996.

Zdena Salivarová was born in Prague in 1933. She started as a singer in the state folklore ensemble, later acting and singing in the theatres Laterna Magica and Paravan which staged productions of a new wave of cabaret and so called "text-appeal" shows. She studied at the Prague Film School and acted in several films in the late 1960s. She and her husband, the novelist Josef Škvorecký, left Czechoslovakia in 1969 and settled in Toronto, where they established the Czech publishing house 68 Publishers which, together with the homebound samizdat activities, kept Czech "unofficial" literature alive through the seventies and eighties. Her first book, a tryptich of novellas *Pánská jízda* [*A Gentlemen's Party*], was published in Prague in 1968, her novels published in Canada were *Honzlová*, 1972 (Engl. *Summer in Prague*, Harvill Press, 1973) and *Nebe, peklo ráj*, 1976, [Engl. *Ashes, Ashes, All Fall Down*, 68 Publishers, 1987), which was made into a TV movie in 1991, and *Hnůj země* [*The Manure of the Earth*], 1994, which was written with assistance from the Canada Council. She was awarded an honorary doctorate by the University of Toronto and the Czech Order of the White Lion for her contribution to Czech culture and literature.

Alžběta Šerberová was born in Příbram in 1946. She trained as a mechanical and electrical engineer, and later earned a degree in philosophy and history at Charles University in Prague. She has worked as newspaper and magazine editor and freelance writer. She is the author of four novellas and novels, *Dívka a dívka* [*Girl and Girl*], 1970, *Manekýna* [*The Model*], 1974, *Ptáci na zemi a ryby ve vodách* [*Birds on Earth, Fish in Water*], 1979, *Sbohem, město M.* [*Farewell, Town M.*], 1991, and four collections of short stories, including *K mé kávě tvá dýmka* [*Your Pipe With My Coffee*], 1976, *Vítr v síti* [*The Wind in a Net*], 1982 and *Ta druhá* [*The Other Woman*], 1993.

Zdena Tomin was born in Prague in 1941. She earned a degree in philosophy and sociology from Charles University in Prague and worked as an interpreter until 1977 when she lost her job as a consequence of becoming involved in the democratic rights movement Charter 77. She became one of its three spokespersons in 1979. In 1980 she accompanied her husband, the philosopher Julius Tomin, to Oxford, and, having been deprived of Czech citizenship by the authorities, they decided to settle in Britain where she has lived since. She started her literary career as a surrealist poet and published articles, essays and short stories in the 1960s. She worked until recently for the Czech broadcasting of the BBC and has been writing in English. Her novels *Stalin's Shoe*, 1986, and *The Coast of Bohemia*, 1987, were published by Century. She lives in London.

About the Editor

Alexandra Büchler studied art and literature, and left her native Prague in 1978 to live in Greece, Australia and now Britain. She has translated novels, short stories, poetry and theatre plays from Czech, English and Greek, and books on art and architecture from Czech. She is the editor of *This Side of Reality: Modern Czech Writing*, Serpent's Tail, 1996, and of a collection of Australian short stories she has translated into Czech.

About the Translators

David Chirico was born in Britain, received his doctorate in late 19th century Czech literature from Cambridge and lives in Prague where he has taught Czech literature to foreign students and works with a Romany rights organization. He is currently working on the translation of poetry by the fin-de-siècle Czech poet Karel Hlaváček and on an anthology presenting the work of the Catholic priest and writer Jakub Deml, to be published by Twisted Spoon Press in Prague.

Tatiana Firkusny and Véronique Firkusny-Callegari are a mother and daughter team who have published translations of Daniela Hodrová's work in *The Prague Revue* and *The Prairie Schooner*. Tatiana Firkusny grew up in Czechoslovakia and lives in New York where she followed her husband, the concert pianist Rudolf Firkusny. She has a degree from New York University and has done translations from Czech for a number of publishers and institutions. Véronique Firkusny-Callegari grew up tri-lingual in Czech, French and English. She has a degree from Barnard College and apart from collaborating with her mother on translations from Czech she also translates from French, German and Italian, and works with opera singers as Czech language coach.

Káča Poláčková-Henley was born in Czechoslovakia, the daughter of an American journalist and Czech novelist. She lived in the USA, where she earned a degree in journalism and worked as a freelance feature writer. She spent the 1960s in Czechoslovakia, working as a translator and editor, and since 1975 has lived in Ontario. A veteran translator of Czech literature, among her best known works are Ludvík Vaculík's *The Guinea Pigs*, Pavel Kohout's *Hangwoman*, Josef Škvorecký's *Bass Saxophone, Talking Moscow Blues* and *The Mournful Demeanour of Lieutenant Boruvka*, and Antonín Liehm's books on Czech and Eastern European cinematography.

James Naughton was born and brought up in Edinburgh and teaches Czech and Slovak at Oxford. He is the author of textbooks *Colloquial Czech* and *Colloquial Slovak* and has published a number of translations of Czech and Slovak writers' work in magazines and anthologies including *Description of a Struggle, The Picador Book of Contemporary East European Prose* and *This Side of Reality, Modern Czech Writing*, as well as Miroslav Holub's *The Jingle Bell Principle* and Bohumil Hrabal's *The Little Town Where Time Stood Still* and a selection of Hrabal's lettres to Dubenka, forthcoming from Twisted Spoon Press.

Cyril Simsa is an Anglo-Czech translator and critic with a long-standing interest in the literature of the fantastic. His translations and articles have appeared in a wide variety of publications, including *The Encyclopaedia of Fantasy, Foundation, Locus, Science-Fiction Studies, Yazzyk, BBR* and *Fantasy Macabre*. He lives in Prague and in his day job works at the Faculty of Social Sciences, Charles University.

Keith Waldrop teaches at Brown University in Providence, Rhode Island, and, with Rosmarie Waldrop, is editor of the small press Burning Deck. His recent books include *The Silhouette of the Bridge* from Avec and *Light While There is Light: An American History*, Sun and Moon. He has translated, among others, Anne-Marie Albiach, Claude Royet-Journoud, Edmond Jabès, Paol Keineg, Dominique Fourcade and Jean Grosjean.

Welcome to the World of
International Women's Writing

Ask the Sun by He Dong. $12.95. ISBN: 1-879679-10-8. Short stories about the Cultural Revolution from the perspective of a child by a Chinese writer who now lives in Norway.

Wayfarer: New Fiction by Korean Women, edited and translated by Bruce and Ju-Chan Fulton. $14.95. ISBN: 1-879679-09-4. A fresh and powerful collection of short stories by eight of Korea's top women writers.

The Cockatoo's Lie by Marion Bloem. $11.95. ISBN: 1-879679-08-6. Family history and a steamy love triangle weave together in this modern novel of Dutch-Indonesian cultural identity.

The Four Winds by Gerd Brantenberg. $12.95. ISBN: 1-879679-05-1. Gerd Brantenberg is one of Norway's cultural treasures, and a lesbian author with a huge international following. This is her hilarious and moving novel of coming out in the sixties at the University of Oslo.

Unnatural Mothers by Renate Dorrestein. $11.95. ISBN: 1-879679-06-X. One of the most original novels to appear from Holland in years, this compelling story of an archeologist and his eleven-year-old daughter's attempts to build a family is by turns satiric and heartbreaking.

An Everyday Story: Norwegian Women's Fiction edited by Katherine Hanson. $14.95. ISBN: 1-879679-07-8. Norway's tradition of storytelling comes alive in this enthralling anthology. The new expanded edition includes stories by contemporary writers.

Unmapped Territories: New Women's Fiction from Japan edited by Yukiko Tanaka. $10.95. ISBN: 1-879679-00-0. These stunning new stories by well-known and emerging writers chart a world of vanishing social and physical landmarks in a Japan both strange and familiar. With an insightful introduction by Tanaka on the literature and culture of the "era of women" in Japan.

Two Women in One by Nawal el-Saadawi. $9.95. ISBN: 1-879679-01-9. One of this Egyptian feminist's most important novels, *Two Women in One* tells the story of Bahiah Shaheen, a well-behaved Cairo medical student—and her other side: rebellious, political and artistic.

Under Observation by Amalie Skram. With an introduction by Elaine Showalter. $15.95. ISBN: 1-879679-03-5. This riveting story of a woman painter confined against her will in a Copenhagen asylum is a classic of nineteenth century Norwegian literature by the author of *Constance Ring* and *Betrayed*.

How Many Miles to Babylon by Doris Gercke. $8.95. ISBN: 1-879679-02-7. Hamburg police detective Bella Block needs a vacation. She thinks she'll find some rest in the countryside, but after only a few hours in the remote village of Roosbach, she realizes she has stumbled onto one of the most troubling cases of her career. The first of this provocative German author's thrillers to be translated into English.

Wild Card by Assumpta Margenat. $8.95. ISBN: 1-879679-04-3. Translated from the Catalan, this lively mystery is set in Andorra, a tiny country in the Pyrenees. Rocio is a supermarket clerk bored with her job and her sexist boss. One day she devises a scheme to get ahead in the world . . . .

Women in Translation is a nonprofit publishing company, dedicated to making women's fiction from around the world available in English translation. The books above may be ordered from us at 523 N. 84th St, Seattle, WA 98103. (Please include $3.00 postage and handling for the first book and 50¢ for each additional book.) Write to us for a free catalog or visit us at our Website: http://www.drizzle.com/~wit/